CW00515639

Change

Maureen Duffy was educated at state schools and King's College, London. She is President of the Writer's Guild of Great Britain and is Chairman of the Author's Lending and Copyright Society. She has published many highly successful novels, as well as five collections of poems, and six of her plays have been performed. She has written a number of works of non-fiction, including *The Passionate Shepherdess*, her pioneering biography of Aphra Behn. She lives in London.

by the same author

That's How it Was
The Single Eye
The Microcosm
The Paradox Players
Wounds
Love Child
I Want to go to Moscow
Capital
Housespy
Lyrics for the Dog Hour
The Venus Touch
The Erotic World of Faery
Evensong
The Passionate Shepherdess
Memorials of the Quick and the Dead
Inherit the Earth
Rites
Solo
A Nightingale in Bloomsbury Square
Gor Saga
Londoners
Collected Poems

Maureen Duffy

CHANGE

A Methuen Paperback

A Methuen Paperback

CHANGE

British Library Cataloguing in Publication Data

Duffy, Maureen
   Change.
   I. Title
   823′.914[F]   PR6054.U4
   ISBN 0-413-57650-7

First published in Great Britain 1987
by Methuen London Ltd
This edition published 1988
by Methuen London Ltd
11 New Fetter Lane, London EC4P 4EE
Copyright © Maureen Duffy 1987

Printed and bound in Great Britain
by Richard Clay Ltd, Bungay, Suffolk

For M.W. and F.W.P.
who were there

Contents

And first, the Earth (great mother of us all)
That only seems unmov'd and permanent,
And unto Mutabilitie not thrall,
Yet is she chang'd in part, and eeke in generall:

For all that from her springs, and is ybredde,
However fair it flourish for a time,
Yet see we soon decay; and being dead,
To turne again unto their earthly slime:
Yet out of their decay and mortall crime,
We daily see new creatures to arize,
And of their Winter spring another Prime,
Unlike in forme and chang'd by strange disguise:
So turn they still about, and change in restlesse wise.

Edmund Spenser

I *Innocence*

It was one of ours; it was one of theirs. She lay on her back in a prickle of grass and heat with the sun dazzle pouring on to her near-closed lids and soaking through in a hot bloody flux that dazed and dissolved her as she followed the faint cross drawn high up on the stretched blue silk marquee of sky. The Broadway traffic slurred like washed shingle beyond the high black railings. Occasional high-pitched cries detached themselves from it and rose to join the soft whine and click of the trolleys.

The grass was sparse and brittle. It smelt of the thin dusty earth its roots tangled in. Here and there bus tickets blown from the street through the bars showed as oblongs of orange or putty, small marker flags the parkie would pick up later. The dry stems scratched the back of her calves and thighs. It was wrong to lie on the ground, even when it was baked as hard by weeks of sun as this. She would catch her death or at least get the screws. Damp with sweat after their game, she should put her blazer on but she was too sated to move.

'What's the time?' Sylvie's voice drifted up beside her.

She raised herself on one elbow and looked about, eyes bleary with sunlight. Two girls were playing on the other court, the ball swinging between them with a soft chock at the end of each arc.

'It must be nearly teatime. I'd better go.' The limes were lengthening their silhouettes across the bowling green and the privet hedge threw its own height blackly down the far side of the courts.

'Oh Hilly, not just yet. I'm whacked.' Sylvie lay full flat length with her long thin legs two smooth brown stems, end stopped neatly by white ankle socks and daps. Hilary never went brown. Her legs were blotched red from running, and the gritty dust when she brushed it from her elbow left pinhead red pockmarks on her soft white skin.

Suppose it had been one of theirs and had rained down its

black load on them as they lay there. She wouldn't admit it to a soul but sometimes alone in bed at night she imagined rape, the handsome blond-headed burglar climbing in through her window so that she had no choice but to submit and no one could say it was her fault. They said that parachutists might drop from the sky on their silk mushrooms and then too it wouldn't be a case of what you would do 'if' as they discussed endlessly in break, pacing the bubbling tarmac of the netball pitch, she and Sylvie together while the thirds and fourths jostled, skipped and hopscotched around them.

'I really must go. Dad gets home quarter of an hour early on Friday.' She picked up her racket, slung the bulging satchel of homework over one shoulder and pushed her blazer through the strap. Sylvie stood up too, smoothing down the green and white gingham skirt of their summer uniform and brushing the dots and dashes of dust and grass from her permanently silk-stockinged legs.

She hoisted a saddlebag of books on to her back. 'That English'll take me all weekend. I'm so slow at essays. I can't ever think of anything to write. Anyway I don't see why we should still be swotting now School Cert's over. We've earned a rest. It's bad enough having to wait for the results. History's only reading; that's okay. What else have we got?'

'I've got Latin.'

'Poor you.' Sylvie's sympathy was tempered by the fact, never discussed between them though it sometimes brought a coldness, that only the top group did Latin. Everyone understood that without it you couldn't get into college which meant you were marked down for a bank or nursing.

'What would you do if that was a German up there and it suddenly started dropping bombs?'

'My mum says it won't happen; there won't be a war.'

The smell and noise of the Broadway broke over them as they passed through the tall open gate, a din of coster cries from the market, the clop and rattle of carts, the growl of lorries. The sunlight was gauzy with fumes and the air thick with the reek of cars and the acid of horse droppings, over-painted as they passed the market by the hot whiff from orange and cabbage, and fish under its canvas shade, smelling of bladderwrack stranded at high tideline.

Her street when she turned into it lay empty and she quickened her pace until she could rat-tat with the black iron knocker that hung like a long nose between the eye panels of the brown door.

'What time do you call this? Daddy's been in ten minutes.'

'We couldn't see the clock.' She followed her mother down the dim narrow passage, past the coal cupboard into the back room. The far door was closed, meaning her father was washing in the scullery. When she was little the coal cupboard had frightened her. It seemed to wait quietly, a sleeping animal, at the heart of the house; its blackness stretched somehow much further than the length of the staircase that covered it, as if it went down into the earth and was the tamed entrance to the mine itself. Today the coal left over from last winter smelt as though it was fermenting in the heat, even through the oily tang of bloaters in the pan.

'Hallo sweetheart!' Her father pushed open the door and peered round. He had washed his face and hands and was drying himself on a towel. 'How are my eyes?'

'Not too bad Daddy.'

His eyelids were outlined in a mixture of soot and ash that, if he wasn't doing overtime in the morning, he would clean meticulously away after tea. Even so there was always a faint shadow dyed into the fine skin that gave a greasepaint touch to the slim Jack Buchanan features. Hilary heard him now humming to himself until the tune dissolved into the moist bronchitic cough, glottal stopped by the ball of phlegm he would spit into the sink and sluice away in a flush of washing water from the enamel bowl and its precipitate of grey curded lather. Sometimes fatigue made him less careful and she would find thin green strings of mucous tinged with soot stuck by one end to the biscuit-coloured porcelain and streaming towards the plug hole in the fierce rush from the tap as she soaped her hands with the piece of waxy Sunlight, and although she loved him her gut would knot and retch.

He came through into the kitchen and took his place at the table where newspaper was spread between his plate and the cloth.

'You washed your hands, Hilly?'

In the scullery the bloaters hissed quietly in the heavy iron pan over the gas ring. She washed quickly, drying her hands on the thin damp towel that hung on the back door.

'Sit down.' Her mother spooned the headless fish deftly on to the three plates: soft roe for her parents, hard for Hilary. She knew how carefully they would have been chosen, the fishmonger made to take down a rod of smoked herrings, their mouths spitted into a horny gasp, and squeeze the silvery bodies until a few sago grains or the milky male slime was forced out beside the ventral fin. Back home they were beheaded, the wet silver balloon of the whistle carefully removed and then the neat wedge of flesh and bone was dusted in flour before going in to the black pan her father had brought back from the trenches.

They began to dismantle the fish. 'Have a bit of bread. You can't eat all that without a bit of bread.' Her mother pushed the plate of buttered slices towards her. To avoid an argument she took one.

'You going in tomorrow, Wilf?'

'No. The foreman asked me but I give it to Gossy. He said he was skint. There you are Ducks.' He passed the buff pay packet unopened across the white tablecloth. Each corner was a field of embroidered daisies in pink, blue and mauve silk. Underneath spread the damson softness of chenille that hung fringed almost to the floor. When she was a child Hilary had sat on her own little stool beneath it, hidden from everyone, though she couldn't now remember what game she had played out of sight there alone.

The packet was opened, the slip studied and a pound passed back across the cloth for tobacco and beer money.

'Shall we have a ride out after tea?'

'Where do you fancy?'

'Take the bus up the Nightingale?'

'All that way?'

'Might not be able to do it much longer.'

Her mother halted the fork halfway to her mouth and looked at him. He went on systematically filletting his fish, inspecting every piece for the least hair-fine bone that might lodge in his gullet and choke him to death, and wiping it away from his fork on the newspaper under his plate so that when he was done the remains fanned out like a leaf skeleton with backbone and tail for the calcified stem.

'You think it's coming?'

'The capitalists are going to have their war.' He pronounced it with the emphasis falling on the second syllable so that they sounded 'the pitiless', top hatted and frockcoated, riding roughshod.

'Russia's joined sides with Germany.'

'D'you want my skin, Hilly?'

'Yes please.'

He passed over the sheath of salty crackling, delicately balanced on his knife blade while he cast around for ways to justify the Russian defection. 'They've got their reasons. Anyway, I've never said they was perfect.'

'No politics, no religion at the tea table,' her mother put in briskly. 'You coming out with us, Hilly?'

She considered. 'Can we go to the pictures tomorrow afternoon?'

'We might run to that, though it's a shame to be indoors in this weather. You want a piece of bread and jam, Wilf, to take the taste away?' Kippers and bloaters were always rounded off with something sweet.

'I think I'll stay in, wash me hair and do me homework so I don't have too much tomorrow and Sunday.'

Tonight was probably the last night she could wash it for nearly a week. Already she felt a heaviness in her limbs and a slight ache in her stomach. All that running about in the sun might have brought it on early. While her parents were out she must look for the sanitary towels washed and put away last month and the safety pins that always seemed to be missing when she needed them most.

She watched her parents going down the street towards the bus stop before she shut the door on the dark, cool passage and had the house to herself. She was proud of them dressed up: her father in an alpaca jacket handed on from an uncle and pressed grey flannels; her mother in a stone-coloured summer coat with white hat, lacy gloves and beige court shoes. Her hair was carefully moulded round a band of elastic into a plump French roll; her slim legs she put down to not having had umpteen children but instead concentrating on doing the one job, Hilary, well.

Hilary liked being alone in the house. Opening the scullery

door she went out into the back yard where the tobacco plants had lifted their rag trumpets into the evening sun and filled the dusty air with scent. The latch of the lavatory door almost burnt her hand as she pressed it. Inside smelt of hot distemper. Hilary pulled her knickers as far as her knees and inspected them for signs of blood before she sat down. Light filtered through the gaps at the top and bottom of the door in two broad blades. Above her head daddy-longlegs drowsed in the darker corners. Indistinct voices came to her: the even mechanized tones of a wireless and further away children calling in some summer game. Soon their mothers' voices would halloo through the street, hailing them in to bed. Hilary had never played out. Although her mother was always polite and friendly as a family they kept themselves to themselves. 'You don't want all and sundry knowing your business.'

Indoors again she tucked in the white collar of her dress, filled the bowl with hot water from the Sadia, dunked her head and smeared Amami over her hair. When the rinsing water in the bowl showed clear Hilary twisted the towel into a turban and went through to the living room where she could prop herself on the fender and lean forward until her nose was almost touching the glass of the mahogany overmantel to inspect her skin for blackheads. Squeezing out each pintop with its following worm of a body was immensely satisfying although she knew it would all have to be done again in a few days.

When she felt her hair was dry enough she got out the pairs of metal jaws, combed green slime of wave-set through the damp fronds, pinched it into shape and locked it fast in precise corrugations like a child's imaginary coastline. Her scalloped face looked out from the central panel of the mantel, framed into a portrait by the smaller pieces of glass and the ornaments on the narrow shelves supporting them. Behind her lay the reflected living-room, the focus of their winter life when the black grate was alive with burning coal. On the yellow oak sideboard at her back she could see the big wooden wireless looking over her shoulder. She remembered when electricity had first come to the street. Before that it had been gas lighting, and the heavy glass accumulators filled with dangerous acid she'd been forbidden to touch that had powered their set.

They had bought a new Ferranti when the house had been

wired. One of Wilf's workmates had made them the new speaker, with its tan cloth front behind the wooden sunrays cut out to let the sound through, which stood coupled to it by brown fabric-coated flex; the aerial ran in a loop along the picture rail like a circus high wire. Hilary never understood why with this web of filaments it was still called the wireless.

She switched it on now and waited for the set to warm up. The domed dark oak and chrome clock on the mantelpiece said five to nine. She should listen to the news. A burst of music poured into the room, a song from a flick they hadn't seen yet.

I'm as busy as a spider spinning daydreams. . . .

Sometimes when she had washed her hair Hilary screwed the turban tighter so that her eyes were drawn into an oriental slant, and sucked in her cheeks like Garbo. When she was sixteen, in a couple of weeks' time, she was going to be allowed to wear lipstick and powder. She might get some stud earrings too. Pierced ears were common, her mother thought, but a mother-of-pearl stud, for special occasions, might be allowed. Her mother of course didn't wear them. Married women, nice ones, wore brooches and sometimes a necklace, a single string of beads. Anything else was 'flash' or 'mutton tickled up lamb.'

'I've got a good complexion just like my mother,' her mother would say, 'because I never put a load of old muck on me face.'

She wouldn't be beautiful Hilary thought, but she might be interesting. Dutifully she switched from Luxembourg to National. Daddy might ask what the news had said when they came back. With half her mind she was already standing in the queue for the pictures, the sun beating down on their necks as they inched forward when the Rex, Regal or State opened tomorrow afternoon. She hoped there would be two good Hollywood flicks on, not some supporting British 'B' film of inept detectives in long dreary macs and trilbys.

'Poland,' the newsreader said in the dark cocoa voice used for serious happenings. Guiltily she brought herself back to listen. A blackbird called suddenly from his stance on a chimney pot above next door's ridgepole, then flung himself chattering urgently in a steep dive past the window. '. . . today signed a formal treaty of alliance between Poland and Great Britain. . . .'

What did it mean? Was it good or bad? Russia and Germany against England and Poland. Sylvie's mother believed it wouldn't come but her father seemed to think it would and men knew more about such things than women. That was why when you married, as Mummy always said, you took on your husband's views. Except that Lil didn't quite follow her own precepts. She was more practical; women had to be. The last war that had seared her father's lungs with mustard gas had left deep shrapnel splinters in his mind. The wounds had closed over with time, entombing his pain deep inside him, so he could never speak of it though they all knew it was there. Lil was the manager, who ordered their lives to run as smoothly as the trolleys, while he worked for the money that kept them decent. Hilary felt the house cocooning her against the disorders that brought down others.

The key turned in the front door lock.

'Put the kettle on Hilly,' Lil was calling.

Her father came in taking off his cap. 'Did you listen to the news Ducks?'

'Britain and Poland have signed a treaty,' she said proudly.

'Then they're really going to fight.'

'What are you two standing in the dark for?' Lil switched on the light, making them both blink. 'I asked you to put the kettle on Hilly. Never mind I've done it meself now.' She looked from one to the other. 'What's up?'

'There's going to be a war.'

'You won't have to go will you?'

'Not this time. I'm too old and worn out.'

Hilary looked at her father's thick black hair that showed no trace of grey except for an occasional coarse silver thread she would carefully pull out when she trimmed the fuzz from his neck. He was forty-one.

Circuits and bumps the instructor had said. Well he had done three and there was only one more to go. For the moment he let the little Moth almost drift while he enjoyed the solitude of the pale reaches of sky. The stunted houses and trees had dwindled to Hornby models beside the railway track on his bedroom floor. He seemed a hawk or gull hovering; the engine chirr, like a grasshopper in the sun, gave him no sensation of powered flight and the sky was too wide for him to make any measurable progress through it. He was exhausted from the rounds of the night before. His blood seemed clogged and his mouth was like the bottom of the proverbial parrot's cage. Totting up he realized he could remember the first fourteen pints but nothing after except the ride back in a canvas-covered truck that had flung them about like a wire basket of tossed chips until Smithson had threatened to spew his guts up over them all.

With a jolt he looked up into an acre of glittering sunlight that bounced back from his eyes, making them blink and water. Already they'd been warned about the Hun – out of the sun. He'd have been a goner by now and he'd let himself drift, the nose drop so that he was on the point of stalling. He gave a touch to the throttle and pulled back on the stick until the horizon fell and the plane rose against the surprisingly blue backdrop. Somehow he'd expected Scotland to be all grey, not this Indian summer tweed of viridian and ultramarine. He felt a reluctance to turn on to the heading for his last bump. Up here he was safe and free. 'The lonely impulse of delight,' W.B. Yeats had called it, but how could he have known? Had he ever been up in an aeroplane and if not how could he tell how a pilot, airman as he had called him, would feel? Yet wasn't that the poet's job: giving Shakespeare's aery nothings a local habitation? It wasn't the only way though. Owen and Sassoon had written in the mud and blood of the trenches. That was partly why he'd volunteered when he could have been going to university, kept out of it a bit longer. He was glad he'd done that. It gave him an edge on the types coming in now, conscripted anyway the day war was declared. Now he'd soloed he'd soon be going to his Operational Training Unit where his fate would be decided: fighters or bombers; pilot or navigator.

He knew what he hoped for and it was the same as all the rest, to be alone up there with the enemy, face to face in combat, something that had last been possible for the knights of the Middle Ages until the flyers of the last war had flung themselves at each other in a chivalry of doped canvas and wood. He hadn't seen a Spitfire yet. The Flying Training School had only the Tiger Moths and a couple of the new American Harvards. He hoped to get a crack at one of those before he passed out.

For he couldn't fail. He could fly, was flying and now it was a matter of the written exams that he had always been good at and logging as many hours as the sergeant instructor would let him. 'I can't say where I am of course but I can tell you I've gone solo pretty quickly in eight hours flying time. Some people take nearly twice as much,' he had written to his mother. He wouldn't tell her about the ones who didn't make it, especially Watkins who had dropped mysteriously into the loch upside down and been cut drowned from his harness with, it was said, a half smile on his face.

> Under the tungsten waters of the loch
> A boy's pale smile glimmers.
> The fish nudge at the transparent bowl
> He hangs in. . . .

This wouldn't do. A glance at the gauge showed his fuel was getting low. He'd been stooging about too long. Alan brought the Moth round in a slow turn into the wind, letting her glide down over the boundary hedge. At the last moment he realized he was a little too fast and too low and braced himself for the inevitable bounce as he lined her up and cut the engine. He felt the aircraft buck twice before he was down and rolling towards the hanger.

'What took you so bloody long? I've never seen such a constipated circuit. Give yourself a dose of salts before you go up again. And don't let me see another cocked up landing like that one or I'll let the bloody army have you.'

'You're trespassing. You shouldn't be here.'
'How's that then?'
'This is my school. These are our grounds.'
'It didn't say "Private" anywhere.'
'It doesn't have to. Everyone knows.'

'I didn't. Where's the school then?'

The girl turned and pointed. 'It's through the trees. You can't see it from here.'

'Show me,' the boy said. She could see he wasn't like the brothers of any of her friends, that he was common.

'I can't. I'd get into trouble because you're not supposed to be here.' He knew her way of talking was posh.

'I don't believe it's really there.'

'Oh all right. Follow me. I'll take you as near as I can.'

She led him along the sunken path, overhung with trees whose roots seemed to be trying to heave themselves out of the earth. The ground was buried deep under shaggy nutshells and crumbling leaf mould. It smelled of the mildewed boards in the kitchen when his mother had lifted the lino to look for her wedding ring after it had slipped down a crack. He could see it rolling away from her now as she'd tried to put it back on a soapy finger, and hear her little cry of anguish.

'It's all I've got left.'

They walked on under the bare branches. Suddenly she put a forefinger to her lips and shushed at him. Then she turned off the path, and beckoning with a small hand passed through the avenue of trees into a jungle of denser, shorter evergreen bushes. Together they parted the glossy leaves and peered through. Ahead was a large redbrick house with many windows full of little panes. A bell sounded inside. She drew back from the curtain of leaves signing to him to follow.

'That's not a proper school. It's just a big house,' he said when they were back in the lane.

'Yes it is proper. It's my school.'

'Why weren't you in there then having lessons?'

'I haven't been well. I've been in the san. Matron said I was to go for a walk this afternoon. Why aren't you in school?'

'I've done a bunk.'

'What's that?'

'Playing hookey,' and then as he saw she still didn't understand, 'playing truant.'

'You've cut lessons. Isn't that bad?' He shrugged. 'I know it all anyway. They're behind us here, the country bumpkins

I mean. In me old school I was already on to decimals. Here they're still doing long division. Do you go home after school? Where do you live?'

'I live in school. It's a boarding school. Except for the holidays; then I might go anywhere.'

'Don't you live with your mother?'

'Do you?'

'I did until the war came and we was evacuated. Then she left me here and went back to our old house. She was afraid someone might break into it and anyway she couldn't get on with the lady we was billeted with. Now I'm there on me own.'

'Do you get on with her?'

'She's alright if you don't give her any lip.'

'My mother's very beautiful.'

'Mine's beautiful too, well very nice.' He remembered that it was sissy to say things like that. Men didn't notice what ladies wore. His mother always said his father never noticed.

'She goes to lots of dinners and Ascot and parties.'

'She can't; there's a war on.'

'Well she does. Are you an evacuee?'

'That's right.'

'Where do you come from?'

'I come from London,' the boy said proudly. 'Where do you come from?'

'We don't come from anywhere. We're always moving. My father's a soldier.'

'So's mine.'

'My father's in France.'

'Mine too. Here, perhaps they know each other.'

'I'd better go in. Matron said I was to walk briskly and not dawdle.'

'You do look a bit blue and pinched. Shall I come another day?'

'If you like. We're allowed out for a walk on Saturday afternoon. I could creep away and meet you in the lane.'

'Not a weekday afternoon like this?'

'I told you it was special because I've been in the san. And anyway you shouldn't do a bunk. It doesn't help the war effort. Everyone has to work hard to beat the Germans.'

24

'Could you come to Saturday morning pictures?'
'I don't think so.'
'Why not?'
'Nobody does.'

And give him a good clout and then was sorry for it, of course, because it wasn't his fault: it was the war. Only he'd looked so like his father standing there, was growing more like him every day. She supposed he missed him, was bound to, growing up without a dad, but it wasn't her fault neither. She had to get on without a chap about and she didn't believe, whatever they said, it'd all be over in no time. 'By Christmas' they'd said at first and that had come and gone. You couldn't talk about it because you weren't supposed to get downhearted and spread the miseries but she couldn't see it being over for years. They hadn't even properly started yet in spite of what was going on abroad. When Hitler had finished with all the foreigners he'd turn his mind to us and then we were for it unless we give in. Some said them up the top was all for that, having a lot in common as they always did with them up the top all over the world, but she couldn't see ordinary people putting up with it though she supposed they'd have to as they always did if it really come about. You seen them before the war on the newsreels from Germany all laughing and singing and hiking about when they wasn't hail-Hitlering and sticking their arms and legs out in that daft goosestep. You had to be a bit different to go on like that without getting the giggles. No, she couldn't see ordinary people taking it seriously.

So tomorrow she'd take herself down to the Broadway where she'd seen a recruiting van from the Ministry of Labour for war work. She didn't have to of course. Lennie was only twelve, going on thirteen, but she couldn't stop in the house by herself all day, she'd go potty, and she couldn't stop down in the country with the pigs and the turnips and that old cow of a landlady who'd made her feel all the time what a privilege it was for her to be taken in and allowed to sleep with her son in a couple of bunks as if they was down the shelter.

He'd got on with her better, smarmed up to her, just like his father who was so even spoken she wanted to throw things at him sometimes. Where was he now? In some French village drinking wine and making up to the local mademoiselles while she was stuck here on her tod, short of fags and a drop to drink, trying to make do on her bit of his army pay and with eight shillings a week still to shell out for Lennie. Thank Christ they'd opened the pictures again. She'd see if she could rake up enough shekels for tomorrow afternoon. She didn't fancy going by herself in the blackout when you couldn't see a hand's turn in front of your face and with the nosy parkers upstairs listening for when she come in, whispering that she was being unfaithful already and him only gone a few months, else why had she come back from the quiet and safety of the country unless it was to some bloke, a column dodger in a reserved occupation, and all because she liked a drop of gin and a fag, to get herself up in her glad rags and see a bit of life instead of moping indoors.

So she'd go and help the war effort. They said you could earn three quid a week with overtime. She hadn't had a job since she was married but she remembered the laughs there'd been, all in together girls, nice fine weather girls, arm in arm along the front on the works outing. No doubt it'd be different now but there was the money even if it didn't turn out to be quite as she'd painted it. She eased on to her stomach in a valley in the flock mattress their bodies had kneaded to a stew of knobbly dumplings, buried her face in the pillow which smelled faintly of haircream, she always slept on his side now, and smothered herself to sleep.

Christ it was cold, a cold such as they'd none of them ever known and hadn't looked to see in April. Didn't spring never come up here, only the days lengthening until they ate up all the night and there was nothing but clear bright sky for the flaming Stukas to scream out of while you lay there picked out against the snow like a herd of walruses and about as mobile? 'Someone had blundered' alright, which was what you could expect in war and had been since time immemorial; sent us out with the wrong kit and training. We should have had white overalls like the Norgies you sometimes saw flying away through the trees on their skis, that was if you were silly enough to lift your bonce out of the snow and risk getting it shot off.

Even the ski patrols couldn't stop Jerry though. As soon as you thought you'd pinned him down you found he'd worked round and above you and was shooting you up the arse. The lads are full of rumours. They say the Guarda is holding on near Narvik and that they're bringing in the regulars and we're going to be evacuated.

I shan't be sorry to go but you had to be sick at the way things had turned out, disembarked with three kitbags apiece to hump and no transport. No artillery to speak of either and minus air cover. That was what broke us up, set some of the lads running. Jerry had big guns and planes and we just had to lay there, popping off with bloody rifles in reply. The sergeant was an old soldier but you could see he was browned off, though he never said nothing. You had to admire him and the other regulars. They knew their job and made the best of it while we got windy because it wasn't more than a matter of months since we'd been just ordinary blokes with ordinary jobs. 'Hold very tight please. Ting, ting. Three outside, two in.'

We're a weedy lot too: skinny arms and legs and sunk chests when we lined up for the medical. We're better now, filled out a bit with army grub and standing up straighter, but not much of a lot beside Jerry and the Norgies, though you daresn't say so. That'd be unpatriotic. But that dead Kraut we come across in the woods yesterday he was like an old-time hero, a young Viking, though without all the face fungus. When you saw them on the news cycling about, boys and girls together, in their leather shorts they looked like young bulls, strong and well fed. You could see their legs were all brown and plump, the kind film stars have in the pin-ups.

He was lying with his face in the snow when we turned him over to go through his pockets. Funny I'd never really thought about snow til we come here. Back home it soon gets piled up in the gutter, a filthy nuisance of grimed heaps, packed ice sooty with black frost, turning to brown melted water the wheels chuck up all over you. You know it'll be gone in a week or so at most. Here it's got a way of its own. The road's covered inches thick with a beaten white tarmac you skid and slither on and that strikes up gradual through the soles of your boots til your feet are frozen lead.

We took his watch and compass and a nice white hand-kerchief. Somebody, Dipper I think it was, was all for having the boots and socks off him as better than ourn but it didn't seem right to leave his poor feet sticking up in the cold, all defenceless. He had the usual stuff in his wallet we all have: snaps of the wife or girlfriend, some foreign money, letters. Big Ted had the wallet. He said it was a good bit of leather and he should know, being a knacker. The girl was quite a looker, curly hair and laughing. Someone said, 'She'll laugh on the other side of her face when she finds out.'

She put me in mind of Millie, how she used to be when I first met her, always laughing and singing til she had the boy. Then she changed. I suppose women do when they can't get out and the money's got to stretch further. Really I was too quiet and soft for her but I was never brought up to knock women about. Mum said I shouldn't marry a girl from the Bush, that she wasn't our type and she'd lead me a dance. But then that was how we met, at the Palais, so it must have been what I wanted, to be led a dance, deep inside.

I wonder what she's up to now? She was never one for writing much. If Mum was still alive she'd write and tell me quick enough. So maybe everything's for the best as the man said. That's where they'll come first of all, up the road the Norgies have fallen back from, what's left of them after the pasting they've took. And we're supposed to hold on. Tretten they call it. Outlandish names you can't pronounce half the time. Where was it we marched from yesterday? Lillehammer. No that was the day before. Some of them dropped their kit as they went, up to the knees in snow that stung like needles if it touched your bare skin and then soaked you through to the bone. I'm glad, though, I hung on to mine, enough for a brew up when we stopped.

Then there was Faaberg where they pounded the shit out of us with mortars, and the road back from there with their planes dropping on us out of this everlasting daylight so you lose count of time. I hope she's alright and the boy too. If I ever get out of this lot I'll give them both a good time. Here goes the guns again and we've nothing to answer them back. I suppose you'd say the mountains was lovely, iced rock cakes against the sky with Christmas trees for a frill, if you was here on holiday.

Something moving down there on the road. The guns have laid off for a bit. Something big and black, and another and another like great gun carriers. They must be tanks. . . .

She nosed the car carefully through the clotted main street of Camberley behind a convoy of trucks.

'I'm in Bridport. At the Greyhound. Come to dinner,' he'd said on the telephone. It would take the last of the petrol but it was rather exciting, setting off in the pale May evening with pink cherry and yellow forsythia decorating the Surrey gardens. Nature, even the tamed dame of suburbia, went on whatever people were up to. Even so she had got a whiff of excitement, of tension as she drove through to the A30 and on to Basingstoke. They were all elated of course. She'd been glued to the wireless for days like the rest of the country. Now it was all over she was half waiting for that feeling of let-down, like the morning after the Rose Ball when quite the right partners hadn't materialized. She shouldn't be thinking like that now of course as a wife and mother, and in wartime but there it was: breeding will out. She laughed to herself a little nervously. That world had gone, at least for the time being and possibly for ever. Symbolically the sun began going down ahead of her as she cleared Salisbury, past the great stone gate of Wilton and climbed up for the run down to Shaftesbury with the setting rays striking through the narrow windscreen of the little Morris to half blind her.

He hadn't said much on the telephone except that he was 'fine' but then she supposed he couldn't and in any case it wasn't his way. Once or twice as she'd listened to the news she'd felt her mind reel with the thought that he might already be dead. Then she'd reminded herself how clever he was, a survivor even in the confusion of the beaches that came through the studied calm of the newsreader. He must be all right, and she'd clenched her small hands until the blue veins were flattened under the white skin. She would have her hair done for when he came back. That was a piece of sympathetic magic she could invoke.

After the Great War there hadn't been enough men to go round. A lot of girls hadn't married at all. Some of them had become their teachers, and they had all pitied them at school even when they had crushes on them. It might be the same after this war, though it couldn't be quite as bad in terms of her own class and at least she had been married, was married. This time was different, she knew instinctively. We weren't bogged down in miles of trenches in France. We had got out. He had got out.

Daphne passed the turn off for Sherborne where he had been at school. It was such a pity Ailsa hadn't been a boy, so that she could follow him there. She must try to make time to get down and see the child, perhaps take her out to tea in Reading at half-term. She wrote such queer little passionate letters about how much she missed them. If only they didn't decide to evacuate the school to the middle of Wales or somewhere right off the beaten track. She was going through Yeovil now; such a dreary town, full of shabby people. The country poor in bleak little market towns always looked so beaten and shuffling. She would die in a place like this. Perhaps she should have taken the lower road through Dorchester: that had so much more charm.

The light was going fast. She pushed the accelerator harder. She didn't want to arrive in Bridport in the blackout. Only another ten miles, dropping down towards the sea, through new green hedgerows, still snow-showered here and there by May blossom and the last of the blackthorn. It was as well she knew the way for the signpost had gone and she was easing into the little port's outskirts almost before she realized. Now she had to find the Greyhound. Suddenly as she turned the corner she was forced to change down to bottom gear by the mass of men jamming the narrow streets and strolling in the roadway. She pressed the horn to break a wedge through the khaki ranks.

A group strung out in front of her wheeled to face the car bringing it to a standstill. She was half aware that those on the pavements were standing still too, that she was surrounded by weary men in what she now saw was torn and stained battledress, their chins stubbled and their eyes red in the sooty rings of fatigue over the drawn cheeks. She saw too that they weren't just tired but angry. The man in front of the bonnet with one stripe on his sleeve, opened his mouth in a soundless roar.

She had never seen a human being snarl, now there were faces all around her with the lips drawn back on tobacco-stained teeth. The soldier in front pounded on the bonnet. She saw him mouth 'Fucking cunt!' and realized she was trembling and, horrors, might even be about to wet herself. She knew the others were joining in, that the snarls were now half leers. She thought some of them were drunk. At any moment they might wrench the door open and drag her out. The squaddie beat his fist on the bonnet of the Morris again.

But one of his mates was pulling him off. The boy bowed a little towards her and waved the car on with an elaborate satirical gesture. She began to inch forward, hearing the catcalls and feeling the car rock as others thumped on the side panels while she crawled between them. Then she was through the press and out into a clearer stretch of road. 'East Street' he'd said and there it was. She drew up outside the pub but was shaking too much to leave the car. She leaned against the glass side panel and realized that she had begun to cry. When Harry opened the door she almost fell into the street.

'I saw you drive up from my window. Are you all right? Let's go and have a large drink.'

He helped her out and guided her into a bar where he left her in a dark corner to recover while he fetched the drinks. She hoped she didn't look too much of a mess. She had wanted to come upon him radiant, irresistible and now she felt stained and smudged by her encounter with the soldiers.

'It's so wonderful to see you,' she said when he came back with the drinks.

He lifted his glass. 'Make the most of it. They'll soon have drunk the town dry.'

She shuddered and took a gulp.

'What's up? Has anything happened?'

'I ought to be asking about you. . . . It's just that I ran into a group of soldiers coming through the town. I thought they might be going to drag me out of the car and rape me or lynch me or something.' She laughed. 'They seemed so . . . angry.'

'They are; bloody angry. They've been beaten. No army likes that. It's being treated as a kind of victory here, plucked from the jaws of defeat, all that stuff, but they've been there and back. The beaches were hell but it was hell even getting through to them. Many of the chaps feel betrayed. Some of the officers left them to fend for themselves while they saved their own skins. A soldier expects to be led and when he isn't he turns nasty. He expects to do his job and his officers to do theirs. An army in retreat like that, without order and discipline, is a mob, a rabble, violent and confused, looting, raping. . . .'

'I've never seen British soldiers behave like it. . . .'

'You've never seen them in war, and defeated. All armies are like that in defeat, and victory too. There were nasty scenes as we withdrew and began the evacuation. Not everyone of course. Some units marched on board as if they were on the parade ground.' He upended his glass. 'Nothing's been said here. . . . And you mustn't say anything either. To the rest of the world it's got to look like a heroic and orderly withdrawal, not a rout, or Hitler will be down our throats even faster.'

'Faster?'

'Oh he's bound to try and invade if we don't chuck in the sponge. The French will give in quite soon.'

'We won't, will we?'

'Not now Chamberlain's gone. What about another gin if I can twist the barmaid's arm?'

She watched his back in the neatly fitting jacket that was only slightly creased, going away from to the bar and leaned back against the black leatherette of the settle, half closing her eyes.

'You look done in. We'll have an early dinner and get you to bed.'

She felt as ever comforted and protected by his concern, even though slightly guilty that she ought to have been the one who was worrying about him.

'How's Ailsa?'

'She's fine. I had a letter this morning. She says she's got a new friend called Lennie.'

'Lennie?'

'I think he's an evacuee who comes to see her.'

'Does the school allow that sort of thing?'

'Oh I don't think there's any harm in it. Just a bit of hero worship. She's only nine after all.'

'But going to be rather a stunner like her mother?'

'Harry, if the war goes on . . .'

'It will, unless we're beaten.'

'I want to do something.'

'Do something?'

'To help.'

'I can't see you as a nurse, Daph.'

'No. I don't mean that. I wouldn't be any good. So messy. But there must be something I can do.'

'The WVS?'

She pulled a face. 'Too much tea making. No, I want something more active. After all you're in the thick of it.'

'What about Ailsa?'

'She's perfectly all right with the school looking after them and if it gets rough I expect they'll all be packed off to deeper country . . . Wales. She doesn't need me. I can't just sit by and twiddle my thumbs. It's so dull at home with you away and everything out of bounds or closed.'

'What will you do then?'

'I can drive, which is more than a lot of women. There must be something I can do with that.'

It was time to be going yet still he lingered. What was left of the French army was drawing back from the open city so that its rape would be as swift and painless as possible. He must get to one of the channel ports soon if he wanted to be taken off from this sinking ship to start again somewhere else. Yet he still lingered. The streets were full of carts, bicycles, anything with wheels that could go or be pushed, piled and slung with pitiful goods, just as the streets of Warsaw had been, with refugees heading for the country, except that there they had scurried away between piles of rubble and the smoking ruins of their past. Paris would avoid all that and he couldn't blame her. Their devastation had done them no good: it had merely made the suffering greater while not postponing the end for as much as a single day as far as he could see.

The July sun was ironically warm. The trees in the little gravelled squares with their iron and wood seats, where the black-frocked nursemaids had watched their charges playing, waved their arms in the light breeze as to unheard music and the doves and classical façades he had come to love, to see as a second home, seemed to be dissolving under the veil of dusty sunlight.

Karol thought that all the activity of flight would stop, that a strained waiting silence would fall before it was broken by the marching stamp of the victory parade and the thunderous rumble of tanks shaking the old foundations. He should have gone with the rest, as a naval attaché he should have been in the government train. Government? Government-in-exile as it already was, recognized by the British and French, the allies who had failed to save them. He beat his hand against the stone parapet above the river where the bouquinists had opened their portable cases under the sun and he had stood turning the pages of a thick ivory-papered Flaubert as though the sky wasn't falling, tumbling as swiftly as Warsaw herself had, so that there was no time for rescue.

What was the point of retreating further, carrying the myth of Poland over the sea to a cold damp island that had been unable to save a continent. Poland had ceased to exist, split in two like a ripe peach and the two halves devoured by the black birds of prey. The people had become serfs in their own country. If he had stayed he would have already been dead or deported to one of the concentration camps word was beginning to filter through about.

'That it should come to this, not two months,' Hamlet had said. Even that was too long. Six weeks it had taken from first to very last while those of them who were already in Paris had watched with impotent fascination, told to stay put until there was nothing to be done but leave again, taking the split and splintered baton Mościcki had passed from internment in Rumania to Sikorski in Paris, in an attempt to preserve the fiction of Poland's continuing existence. He wanted to stop running away, to die as the first German soldiers entered the city, to run at them with arms flung open so the bullets would thud into his chest, into his heart. Yet he knew the origin of that desire, could see in his mind's eye the ship putting in at Hamburg, himself going down the gangway slicked and pressed for an evening out, the seamen's bar he had thought he was entering and the bleak room where the pale young Protestant had taken him for the first time.

They had deserved what had fallen to them: they were arrogant and archaic, their twenty years as an independent republic merely a gloss on a deep-grained feudalism, their Jewish deputies little cork figures bobbing on a sea of anti-Semitism. They had sat too late on the terrace café of the Europski Hotel gossiping and smiling while the string orchestra played the faded tinsel airs of a half-forgotten operetta until it was time for the cavalry to ride out against the tanks and planes.

He continued to stare down at the river while the broken images flickered past in silent picture show cranked by a mad projectionist. Suddenly over the trundle and creak of wheels and the calls of those in flight Karol heard the distant drone of aircraft. The refugees had heard it too. A woman's scream rose above the traffic sounds. The wheels were stilled. The drivers stared up at the sky. It couldn't happen: Paris was an open city. Yet in war no one, no pact could be trusted. The noise of the engines bore down on them and stopped in a tight cascade of sound. Tattered figures threw themselves down on the hard stones like rag dolls but Karol stood up straight. Perhaps this was the way it would come, out of the sky from the hand of some black angel, his fair hair hidden in a tight skin cap and his blue eyes cold behind their goggles. But as he stared the planes reared up and he saw the sky-pale bellies and tricolour roundels of the British fighters. The others were getting to their feet and waving.

'Not yet,' the rat voice gnawed in his skull. 'Not yet. Now it is time to go.' The wheels were turning again; wearily he joined the crowd flowing towards the sea.

Rua leans her back against the upright of the tree crotch she is sitting in and bites on the hard woody shell of the milk pod in her mouth, cracking it with her strong teeth. She spits out the wet

35

slivers of shell and then the sticky inner envelope holding the white beans she is breakfasting on, smearing her face with milky latex as she munches. Her younger brother, Houmi, is crunching pods in the next small tree with half an eye on her to see when she will become bored with this food and move on. Since their mother died last year he follows her everywhere, even sharing her nest at night.

She gazes out across the valley over the gallery forest tops towards the lake, lying calm in its shawl of acacia and bamboo. Then she turns to look the other way where the strange noises have come from, silencing the usual chatter of colobus and hornbill and the barks and screams of the baboons. She is bored with the milk pods, now that dozens of shells lie scattered at the foot of the tree but she is uneasy. The hair rises on her head and she hoots quietly to herself. Houmi stops feeding and watches her intently, feeling her restlessness and fear. He has heard the sounds too, but he will take his cue from her and go where she goes. Curiosity is drawing her towards the strange happening, winning against her fear.

Rua has heard something like the noises, sharp cracks as of hard wood branches snapping, before. She knows that they are bad sounds made by the smooth apes who come hunting with thundersticks and kill the people, especially the mothers, and carry off the young ones. When they come it is best to run away and hide because they are afraid of nothing. Then why doesn't she do it today? She puts her arms around herself and rocks gently. She should take Houmi and hide.

Instead she climbs down from the milk pod bushes and follows a narrow path uphill through a tangle of vines, past clumps of tall miombo trees. The leaves are still glazed with dew the sun will gradually burn off as it climbs the blue arches of tropical sky. For a moment she stops to pick a handful of ripe palm nuts and rolls one round in her mouth comfortingly. Houmi begs some from her and because she wants the reassurance of his company she gives him one to chew. Then she moves on, out from the security of the trees into a sparser cover of tall grass and scrub towards the peak of the ridge where a single dudu tree lifts its silver trunk. From the top of this she can see far away towards where the sounds are coming from.

Houmi squats unhappily whimpering at the foot of the tree. He has understood that he isn't to follow her up but to wait there. At the top she bends a few leafy branches together to make a quick day nest to hold her while she watches. But there is nothing to see. She concentrates on listening instead.

There are dull thuds interposed with the sharp cracks of the thundersticks. She feels the trembling of the air from their percussion. If she were nearer she would feel the ground shake. She isolates two sets of sounds, each answering the other as if two great males were beating their chests or pounding trees in fierce display. Now she knows why her fear was overcome by curiosity. They are busy with each other and only if one succeeds in driving the other away might it turn on her and Houmi.

Rua snuffs the breeze. She smells the strange smell of the thundersticks which is quite different from anything else in the forest and even from the smell of the smooth apes who carry them, which is an animal odour like any other and a good thing for the people because it warns them when the smooth apes are about, before they can be seen or heard. They are mainly black smooth apes but sometimes there are one or two pink ones and they smell differently. Their sweat is more acid from eating much meat, like the people's when they have caught a young monkey or bush pig. After they have eaten it their sweat and their droppings, both liquid and solid, have the tang of the animal's flesh and brain. Rua's mouth waters at the image of meat passing through her consciousness, last in a series which began with the prey straying unconcernedly into her group's ambit.

She abandons the nest and climbs down. Houmi is relieved to see her and to feel her fears calmed. He throws his arms round her and she hugs him close. Then she leads him down the ridge towards the valley. There is a termite mound she wants to inspect. It is deep in the undergrowth which is why none of the others have found it yet. She leads the way in through a dense green tangle to the little clearing where the mound sticks up like a wart. Rua puts her ear to the heap. She can hear activity inside and smell the rich concentration of insects. She picks at a tunnel entrance with a hard fingernail until it is large enough. Then she plucks a long grass stem and pokes it into the hole. There is a moment's pause before Rua draws it out coated with clinging delicacies. Houmi is very excited. He pulls a stem for himself and tries to poke it into the tunnel but the stem bends and creases and he gets nothing. Still he goes on trying while Rua digs herself out another tunnel to fish in.

After an hour's termiting Rua feels a need for more company. It is very hot now and time for a rest and a little mutual grooming among friends. But as soon as they leave the thick leaf cover and come up on to the more open hillside Rua is aware of the sounds again. They walk along the valley to a large fig tree where a small group is already resting. The glossy young Karka approaches to see if Rua is in season. She presents submissively but he merely sniffs, pats her and ambles away.

Tondi and her baby are lying in the shade. Rua goes up cautiously but Tondi is glad to see her and they sit side by side searching each other's fur gently with their long nails while the young ones tumble together. Rua finds the older female comforting now that she no longer has her own mother to turn to. The feeling of her long careful fingers combing through Rua's hair is soothing and pleasurable together. Rua feels herself growing relaxed, contented. She would like to doze but that would be rude.

Suddenly Tondi lifts her head and growls. The others look up too. It is the silence that disturbs them. They have grown used to the background rumble and crack of thundersticks. Now they have ceased. The forest holds its breath. Everyone listens. The smooth apes have stopped fighting.

Hilary looked out at the flat potato fields beyond the carriage windows, stretches of dull green the colour you most often seemed to end up with in your paintbox when you were a child, flecked with the insignificant white florets stretching to the horizon under the heavy hazy sunshine. With luck the siren would go when she reached the station and she could get out, cross the footbridge and climb into a train going back again into London instead of continuing on for the first lesson of the week. That was the rule she had invented for herself or rather bent out of the school's guidelines that they weren't expected to travel back in an air raid.

It was hard to concentrate anyway after the long hot

summer holiday spent between the back garden, the pictures and the shelter, turning on the news for the latest tally of planes shot down. When the holiday ended her mother hadn't wanted her to go back.

'You might as well stay here and then at least we'll all be bombed together,' Lil had said. 'Fancy evacuating a school to a place between two airfields. Where was their sense?'

Her father had smiled bitterly. 'They thought Jerry would bomb the cities instead of going for the airfields. Well they still might. There's a long way to go yet.'

Even so early the carriage was stifling and smelt of sweaty metal, old cigarette smoke and dust, yet she knew that if she opened the window and leaned out to watch the engine as the front of the train came into sight, meandering unaccountably since there wasn't a bump for miles as far as the eye could see, she would be clouded by rancid steam and her face pocked with smuts in an instant.

Small silk bows of cabbage white zigzagged from potato plant to plant. Her mother used the stirrup pump they had been issued with against incendiaries to spray their beans and tomatoes with soapy water against the caterpillar and aphid. The Anderson shelter took up the end of the garden with its hump on which nothing but nasturtiums would grow and where small beetles with irridescent metallic shells scuttled. She turned her eyes back to the First Reform Bill and tried not to think of home.

The train puffed on through the two dimensional fields, heading towards the deep East Anglian plough that had slept under the high wide skies for centuries until its very flatness had made it the ideal place for aeroplanes to take off and land. Once coming back in her new green mac Hilary had heard the rat-tat of machine-gun fire zipping towards the train and had debated whether to get down on the floor of the carriage as they'd been told, but the mac had been bought dear, not at the Co-op but with hard-saved money in the Harrods of the Broadway, and she stayed upright in her seat rather than risk the undoubted grime of the floor.

Today, her heart sinking, they drew into the little station without incident. Hilary picked up her case of clean clothes and her satchel, let down the window and turned the sooty outside handle. Few people got out but she recognized Marion Elman who had also been home for the weekend, in her meticulously neat uniform topped with the blond waves, blue eyes and cheeks that always looked as if she had been walking against a fresh wind. Marion was the only one who ever beat her at History but not fairly, because she had a photographic memory and could recall not only the page upon page of notes Smithy dictated but their place on the sheet and the page number. It wasn't even that English history interested her very much since her grandparents had come from Lithuania. It was simply that her mind absorbed facts and then spat them out again with incredible accuracy, undigested but also uncontaminated. Marion wanted to be a doctor. She had special dispensation to leave school early on Friday so that she could have finished her journey before the Sabbath fast began.

The siren went as they reached the top of the High Street.

'Blast,' Hilary said daringly.

'Shall we run for it?' Marion asked doubtfully. She was short and plump and found games hard work.

'I don't think we run.' Ten minutes before, Hilary thought, and she could have gone home again but she wouldn't admit this to Marion. They swung their cases boldly as they walked with ears searching for the drone of aircraft. Suddenly there they were above them, a wave of grey, thick-snouted bombers, plunging down it seemed towards them, then overshooting the little town.

'They're going for North Weald.'

'Or Hornchurch. Look there are the fighters up above.'

'Where are our lot then?'

The crump of falling bombs sent shock waves along the layers of heavy air, across the sullen fields of potato and sugar beet: 'Root crops' they learned to call them in Geography, rank with earth and leaf mould like the dead. Everyone said the sweetness of beet was different from cane, bringing a tang of its origins to all that it touched. Even against the grocer's dark blue bags it wasn't as white and fine as that from the sweet sappy stalks that had put out their pampas leaves under the tropic sun day after day. Hilary remembered bread and sugar in bed on Sunday mornings when she had crept in between her parents 'before the war'. The phrase had taken on a meaning heavier than the sum of its three words. It had become the equivalent of the Golden Age, Lost Eden, the Never–Never Land.

An ARP warden cycled past on his bicycle, a tin hat chin-strapped to his head. He blew his whistle at them angrily, holding on with only one hand so that the bike wobbled dangerously.

'Take cover you girls; the siren's gone!'

They continued to saunter, swinging their cases, gas masks bumping against their hips in the beige cardboard boxes.

'Look, there are ours,' Hilary pointed up at an echelon of fighters diving to intercept.

'How do you know?'

'They must be.'

The two girls stood still in the empty High Street, staring up into the hazy bowl that was like the shell of some huge egg: auk or roc or a great bird flown out of *The Thief of Baghdad*. At any moment the genie's foot would come down to crush them under its ridged leathery sole and serve them right for loitering. But instead, as they gazed, the sky was daubed with little puffs of seemingly harmless cloud and the soft snow-ridges of contrails. The distant rattle of gunfire was a toytown exchange. Hilary knew she should feel excited but she felt nothing. It was all too far away, too like a mock joust of model planes.

Suddenly one of the small crossed specks upended above them and began to tumble down. As it fell closer they could see the red leaves of fire sprout along the stem and a black bloom of smoke break out behind.

'He's got him; he's got him!'

'Is it one of ours or one of theirs?' Marion asked. 'I can't look.'

'It's theirs of course. It's going to crash.' They heard the thud and without consultation turned and ran together back towards the station and up the wooden steps on to the footbridge. Far out over the potato sea a plume of oiled smoke wreathed upwards, reddened at its base with flame.

'Serves him right,' Hilary said fiercely, exultantly.

'There's another one. Look a parachute.'

'And another. But where have all the rest gone?' The sky

41

was suddenly empty, apart from the drifting mushroom canopies with their helplessly dangling puppets. If this were the school stories she used to read, she and Marion would be racing towards them through the knee-high greenery, armed with pitchforks for their arrest but Hilary knew better. She was grown up now. Next year they would be taking Higher; 'war permitting' she said inside her head and crossed her fingers in her blazer pocket.

'We'd better find someone to tell,' she picked up her case. Marion followed her down the steps but as they reached the bottom a truck roared past with two uniformed figures in the back holding their rifles upright with one hand while the other clung to the canvas side to steady their swaying bodies as they swung out of sight round a corner, and Hilary remembered her first day of evacuation and the sound of feet marching below her strange bedroom window. She had got out of the narrow camp bed and gone to lift a corner of the blackout to see below her a column of men in helmets and capes with shrouded lanterns going away from the barracks to embark for France, and the truck that had overtaken them with stern square eyes set in the middle of its blackened headlamps, glowing like the great dog's in the story of the Tinder Box.

If they came tonight, in whatever shape, parachuting out of the moon, the bombers' moon or dropping their destruction from the sky, they was ready for them. He hoped Lil was alright. She had gone off early to firewatch, leaving a note on the table, propped against his tea, slices of corned beef and a quartered tomato between two plates, with another of neat shavings of white bread and a scrape of butter. She had gone to practise putting out fires, she wrote.

The bombers had been coming now for days and nights but nothing had reached them as yet though he knew it was only a matter of time. Each raid, the noise of falling bombs and the line of fire and destruction moved, it seemed inevitably, towards them. It was the softening up bombardment before they came over the top. Oh he recognized it alright for what it was though he never let on to no one, especially Lil. They didn't tell you in the papers or on the news of course because they didn't want to start a panic, but he reckoned that by now the French coast must be stiff with helmets and guns, and fringed with landing craft waiting for the word or the right tide. If they ran true to their form in Poland and Holland and all the rest, they'd come by sea and air at once. He looked up at the moon as he made his way through the darkened street to the corrugated drill hut. Yes, it could be tonight.

Well they was better prepared than in the beginning. Now they had the Bren and a rifle between three by courtesy of the Yanks.

'You take one, Wilf, and see if you can sort it out,' they had said when the wooden case was opened revealing the long gunmetal shapes in their rack. 'Then you can show the rest of us.' He had picked it out of its nest. 'That's all got to come off for a start.'

'What is it?'

'Bear grease I expect.'

'Go on. Looks like vaseline,' and they had all laughed.

'Do you have to do that here?' Lil had asked when he had covered the kitchen table in newspaper and laid the dark barrel on it.

'Got to get it done, Ducks.'

'Ugly thing. All that grease.'

'Not as pretty as the Lee Enfield but better than what we've had up til now, which was nothing.'

And it had all come back to him as he had handled the gun, the weight of it, the mass balanced between cheek and shoulder, the kick and the noise and stink of war as he stripped and cleaned, checked the barrel and the bolt action, and finally peered through the aperture sights that he had to admit gave a better view than the old U and blade he had fought with, before they had set him down behind a machine gun.

'What is it, Daddy?' Hilary had asked.

'It's a Yank rifle: a Winchester.'

'Like in the Westerns, cowboys and windybums?'

'That's right.'

The Lee Enfield had a stock of polished walnut and a barrel as smooth as a silk handkerchief. These were frontier weapons.

'What do you reckon, Wilf?' they asked when he took it back.

'It's off balance. Look.' He held it at the trail and the muzzle came up. 'So you have to allow for that on parade. Now let's see what it fires like.'

They had followed him out to the improvised range and watched as he loaded with precious ammunition from the metal box, smelling of pear drops, they had cut open with a tin opener, took aim carefully, snuggling it up to his body for the best fit, and fired.

There was hardly any kick at all. You could have held your horse with one hand and let off with the other it was so smooth. And accurate. After all these years he'd been able to plug the target with a crack that smacked hard home. He knew how it would thud into a man's flesh to the very heart and the deadweight sack, cowboy or Indian he never knew which side he was on, topple from the careering horse, over-hanging rock or palisade. In the same way he hadn't hated Jerry the first time round. They were all poor buggers together conned by their rulers and bosses for no good purpose. This time he saw was different. The whole of Europe was gone and we were next. This was no matter for an armistice and both sides going home again. If Hitler came he would stay and the Yanks would do a deal on spheres of influence.

And Russia, what would she do? He no longer knew, except that like everyone else they would look after number one. That was the law of the jungle, the law we had to follow too, now that we were up to our necks in shite. That knowledge would keep him going, not the rhetoric the old warmonger was filling up the masses with, a new opiate for the people. He didn't need it, never had. Every animal defends its own territory and he would see to his. It was easy for him because he wasn't afraid to die since his boy's ears and eyes had been stuffed with it, his nose rubbed in it. He had died twenty years ago and walked about ever since in borrowed time.

Now here he was a sergeant again. 'Right, we'll take a gander at the yards. Take a couple of rifles and the Bren.' He had his own of course. The rest had to share one between three. 'Watch the blackout as you go. We'll have time for a quick one on the way back.'

The moon was a clean white plate racked above the sweaty streets. 'We'll stand still until we get our night vision back.' He heard Johnson coughing quietly. He always coughed when they went out on patrol. The siren had gone an hour before but the night was quiet. They set off in a loose file, two abreast. The sound of a piano leading a singsong came from a street away as they moved towards the silent yards. It would be a good place for a drop. Would they try to land on the capital, perhaps out here on the edge and move in, surround it from every side, drifting down on park, common and waste until the land was snowed under with them?

He could make out the others' faces now that his eyes were used to the moonlight. They ranged from uncooked cake mixture to knobbly spud and their necks were too scraggy to hold up the metal mushroom domes of their helmets, either not yet filled out enough like Johnson or grown scrawny like himself. Chalky White, who was always unhandy, stumbled against the kerb and dropped a precious rifle loudly in the still street.

'Sorry, Sergeant.'

'Pick it up. Is that what you're going to do with it when Jerry gets here, chuck it at him?'

'Sorry, Sergeant.'

The house was very quiet when she let herself in; the staircase well, as she climbed, full of shadows. They had given her a key which showed they trusted her. And so they should.

'Feel like one of the family, Tilde,' Dr Fentiman had said. 'It's all behind you now. You must try to forget.'

But how could she? Anna-Lise's last letter was growing furry with much reading, and worn at the creases until it had fallen into four playing card-sized oblongs to each page. By now in any case she knew it by heart.

'Don't worry. Mama was allowed to take an extra quilt with her in case it was cold where they were going.'

From this distance she could see so much better what it all meant, that she almost laughed out loud in the gloomy house, a harsh laugh that would sound like a raven croaking out death. Not that the English understood in their little island.

No it was distance not them that had made her able to see what they hadn't, still couldn't, understand at home: that no one would ever come back. Because it had seemed so polite, so . . . so normal: the knock at the door, the salute, the typed official list, the suitcase and warm clothes that were permitted to be taken.

And the alternative was so unthinkable that the human mind couldn't encompass it; it was simply beyond possibility, that you should go away and never come back, that somewhere out there were places where people died; were killed, some said who were prepared to be called alarmist. She felt the knob of pain in her chest, the stone heart that choked her with its hard mechanical beat filling her ears so that she expected it to stop any second and she would be flooded with pain until she dropped like a stone itself on the landing.

The Fentimans would find her and all his doctoring skill would fail to raise her from the grave she fell into in slow motion every day. She laughed again at their long faces bent over her in concern. How would they explain it to the bobbies in their ridiculous hats. This young girl, this refugee, seems to have died of a broken heart. She began to climb up the tall house again. Beyond the glass of the landing window was an English garden; a little gate in a neat hedge and a street, or road, as she must learn to call it.

'Street is for the city, Tilde,' Frau Fentiman had told her. 'Here where we live they are called "roads".' Or avenues or gardens or the close.

'What is a close?'

'It's the part near a cathedral where the clergymen and their families live.'

They were English first, the Fentimans, and Jews second, whereas at home all of them had been, had had to be, Jews first and now nothing second. They weren't Germans. Germans were blond and tall, like Anna-Lise or her young lover in the drama club who was indeed a Fritz. She almost laughed again.

She had reached her room at last and opened the door into the little box whose lid folded down on each side like the peasant's hut in an illustrated book of folk tales they had had as children until it had seemed wrong for them to be reading about the Black Forest where the Aryans had their roots and Mama had put it away in the bottom of a cupboard.

This had been the maid's room before she had been called to work in a munitions factory, leaving the Fentimans with no one, so that they could offer work, domestic work which was all she was allowed to do. She must hang up her coat and put on her apron to get tea ready. The Fentimans ate English, except for Kosher occasions like Passover. Frau Fentiman would come home from the centre where she organized comforts for the poor who would be bombed that night, to her tea with milk and dull cake in slices that Tilde had learned to bake. When she had sighed for a little choux paste lathered with cream and glazed with dark chocolate, Frau Fentiman said it was the war but Tilde didn't believe her. It was England, the taste of Protestant puritanism in food and sex. How else could a nation have invented anything as dull as their madeira.

'Say your name is Tilly Goodman if anyone asks,' Frau Fentiman had said when she had first taken her to the centre, dressed in her hard hairy suit and beetroot hat like a Bavarian. But nobody did ask. She helped to clean the tea urns and make sandwiches which would all have curled by the time the next wave of homeless came in. Some of the night before's refugees still lingered. They smelled, the English poor. Their clothes hung baggy with age or stretched shiny because they had been made of cheap cloth. The women's blouses were clean where they hadn't been smirched with mortar and brick dust, and so were the aprons they seemed to wear all the time but their other clothes, the men's suits and their overcoats, were fusty with years of sweat, tobacco and the grime from coal fires that filtered unceasingly through the city air.

The people were short and misshapen; the children like dwarf sprites with their heavy boots on their dirty legs and their pointed pallid faces. The smaller ones whined and their noses were always candled. The bigger ones chased each other in their big hobnails striking sparks from iron halfmoons hammered into the soles and letting out harsh goblin cries she couldn't understand. She had never seen such poverty except as illustrations to a translation of Charles Dickens.

On the other side of that narrow sleeve of water Hitler was waiting to come and draw up new lists on which Tilde and the Fentimans would both appear, she first and immediately because she was a traitor as well as a Jew but the Fentimans, who thought themselves so English, their turn would come too. They would be so shocked. She laughed a little again. And now there was nowhere to go unless you could beg a passage to America and risk being torpedoed like those poor wretches on the *Arandora Star*. She wondered if she'd known any of them, but even if she'd been given their names and recognized them she knew she would have felt nothing because of the stone in her chest.

They had been going to Australia, about which she knew little except that there were kangaroos with babies like pouched puppies. Was there safety there: Australia a warm pouch she might creep into? When she had looked it up on the map it had seemed uncomfortably close to Japan who was Germany's friend. Wouldn't the Japanese be told what to do with Jews or, if not, would any of them survive a rule so alien? England, Britain she should learn to say, was an island at the edge of the world from which there was no escape except across thousands of miles of sea. She had finished with running. If the Nazis came she would die this time before the knock on the door and the salute as the list was brought out from under the black overcoat. She wouldn't wait to be sent back in a cattle truck, not even to lay her bones beside those whose living faces she knew for certain she would never see again.

'Tilde, Tilde, is the kettle on?'

The sweet gush of relief as they crossed the coastline was like coming, and he must do something about that soon if he wasn't to die a virgin. Funny how you only ever thought about dying on the way back; never on the way out. Bombing barges was a piece of cake, a milk run that's why it was called the Blackpool Front from Ostend to Calais. You couldn't miss: they were jammed so tight, side by side like pleasure boats for a row round the lake. You went in as low as you could, and dumped the lot as close as you could. Then you got the bloody hell out of it because even if most of their night fighters were off with their bombers to London there was still Archie blasting away and the lone night-prowling Messerschmitt 110 ready to pounce.

He'd been disappointed at first that he wasn't to be a fighter boy and fly a Spitfire but consigned to lugging an unwieldy bomb platform around the sky hour after hour, one of the many as they were being called, not the glamorous few. Now he saw he was temperamentally more suited to the long voyage into the dark reaches of sky rather than the quick dash at the sun, the sharp encounter. There was something almost soothing in the navigator's constant checking, plotting, little nudges that moved them through the air over rivers, mountains and towns, through frontiers that didn't exist up here where the only barriers were aery mountains of cloud, invisible fronts held by the giant guardians of squall and thunderstorm. He could hold course and dream until the next adjustment was given him.

As pilot he didn't have to kill anyone either, except by default or incompetence, and then the victim would probably be himself. The rear gunner had to try to knock down the attacking fighters, the bomb aimer dropped his indiscriminate shit on whatever or whoever was unlucky enough to be underneath; he just flew.

The navigator was at his ear now. 'Base reports they're completely socked in. They've given us an alternative.'

Alan felt fear suddenly claim him. It had been perfectly clear when they'd left what seemed such a short time ago. They were unlucky and that was bad. He told himself it was the same for everyone who'd gone up that night; that it was nothing special. But he would have to let down through cloud, searching for an unfamiliar beacon and flare path, flying blind with all the others depending on him. He turned on to the new course and checked the instruments. Up here there were still stars but he could see in his mind's eye the long breakers of fog rolling across the flat fens, hiding the dykes and canals that lay in wait for the unwary, or unlucky. He pushed the thought away. The navigator was telling him it was time to go down.

The stars went out. There was nothing beyond the glass nose but a clammy swirling phlegm of fog. They were plunging down uncontrollably. The ground was coming up to hit him. Sweating he willed himself to ignore the sensation and concentrate on the instruments. He was aware of the others waiting anxiously behind him in the long narrow body of the Hampden. Suddenly he felt the metal skin pressing in upon him and a terrible urge to struggle out of the pilot's confined seat in the cockpit to leave the controls and just get out. The wet banks of cloud looked solid enough to walk on. Surely he could just open the door and jump to the ground below. He strained against the harness tethering him to his responsibility. He couldn't go on: someone else must take over, but there wasn't anyone else or rather it was his job and he couldn't funk it now.

'We ought to be getting the beacon soon.'

'Not a ruddy sign.'

He stared down into the clag. A thousand feet. Where the fucking hell was it? Eight hundred feet. The altimeter unwound inexorably.

'What's that?'

'A light.'

'It's a fucking farmhouse. Well at least we know where the ground is now. I'll start a square search.' The fog closed down again but he felt a surge of relief. That sign from a human habitation had restored his sense of reality. All he had to do now was follow the rules.

'They've got a fix on us. They say we're very close.' For two minutes he flew due south. There was still nothing but the flocks of fog pressing against the aircraft. He turned on to the western leg.

'How's the juice?'

'Going fast. They sent us out short as usual, mean buggers.'

It was hard to keep flying level. Every instinct tried to force him up away from the dangerous ground or down where he might be able to see. His throat was sore and he felt sick and hollow. His frozen hands sweated in the silk gloves under the leather mitts. He turned on to the northern leg. A minute later he heard the navigator yell.

'There it is, there.'

He strained forward. There was the beacon letting out its series of flashes.

50

'Give them our signal.'

Now he could see the flare path. Resisting the urge to go straight down he began to turn on to a wide circuit. He must keep his eye on the height and speed. If he came in too high and too slow they would stall and go in. If he was too fast, he would overshoot without enough height to pull up and go round again. The navigator switched on the landing lights but the sharp pencil only lit up the swirling white clouds below. The flare path dazzled and danced in front of him. He glanced at the instruments. He must hold on to what he had been taught: undercarriage and flaps, a touch of throttle, of right aileron to stop her yawing. Hold it steady, cut the power. They were sinking down with the first flares. He felt the wheels touch, racing as he kept her lined up in the centre of the path. They were down, down. He hoped he wasn't going to throw up. There would be bacon and eggs in the sergeant's mess and beer later; then tomorrow, if their luck and fog held, a trip into town and the chance to look for a girl. Fleetingly he wondered if he would ever write another poem.

'My dad was in Norway. He said it was a terrible mess.'

'You mustn't say things like that.'

'Why not, if it's true?'

'You don't know if it's true.'

'I do if my dad wrote to my mum and told her so.'

'Perhaps he didn't understand what was happening.'

'Yes he did. He said we didn't have the right clothes for a start.'

'What sort of clothes?'

'Warm clothes and them white ones so's you don't show up against the snow. The Germans had them, and skis. We never had nothing.'

'I don't want to see you again if you say things like that. It helps the enemy.'

'How does it?'

'It's like careless talk costs lives. Our headmistress explained it to us. He shouldn't have written it and she shouldn't have passed it on to you. That's the way rumours are spread.'

'It wasn't a rumour. I told you: he was there.'

'Why didn't the censor cut it out?'

Ailsa produced this triumphantly but Lennie, as she knew he was called though she seldom used his name even to herself, threw it as triumphantly back.

'There you are, that shows there was nothing wrong in saying it, that it was the truth.'

'I think I'm going in now. I'm getting cold.'

'You're running away because you're wrong.'

'You're bossy. Just because you're older than me and a boy, it doesn't mean you're always right and you can boss me. I don't have to meet you at all and I'd get into trouble if anyone found out.'

'Alright then, don't.' He stuck his hands deep in his shorts pockets and turned away. His legs below the grey flannel were brown and stitched here and there with long scratches. The trousers were cut down from a pair of his father's he had told her. He seemed to be proud of it.

'I didn't mean it,' she said to his back. 'I've got something to show you. Come with me. But you must promise not to tell anyone.'

He turned round slowly and faced her. He didn't want to go away and never come back. He liked her, and he didn't seem to get on with the others like he did with her, neither the vaccies he had come down with nor the local swedes. Her way of talking, which was so different from the rest, he would have taken the Mike out of rotten if he'd heard it from anyone else, but with her it seemed right.

'Where's your father then?'

'I can't say.' She didn't know exactly. Her mother never mentioned it in her letters. Sometimes she made things up to tell the other girls. She knew only that he had been at Dunkirk and come back safely. Her mother had told her that, had come down to take her out to tea just to tell her. She had felt very proud of that. Since then she had been told nothing. She would ask in her next letter. 'Let's not talk about it any more. Come on, I want to go to my secret place.' She turned now and moved away, hoping that he would follow. Without looking round she could hear him coming behind, as his heavy boots snapped a twig or scuffed in the dry dead leaves. It was going to be all right.

'I hope you aren't wasting too much time when you ought to be reading or playing games with the other girls. I do want you to get into one of the teams before you leave,' her mother had written. It had been a mistake to mention Lennie in her letters home; she knew that now.

'What is it that's so special?'

'Wait. We're nearly there. Then you'll see.'

The other girls weren't interested in the war. They hardly seemed to know it was going on. When she tried to talk about it they didn't answer but just stared as if she were some strange animal or, worse, a human outsider. None of them would have talked to Lennie or be taking him to her secret place; none of them, she was sure, had a secret place.

'Now we have to go through there.'

'Where?'

'There.'

'It's just a bank.'

'No it isn't, silly. It's a sort of wall of rock with a little tunnel you can just squeeze through. Look.' She parted a curtain of ivy and bramble.

He hung back. 'It's alright for you. I'll get stuck.'

'No you won't. I'll go first to show you.'

She bent double and crept into the dark gap in the rock. He watched her disappear like a hermit crab drawing up its dangling limbs into its shell to hide.

'Come on.' Her voice came hollow out of the hole. *The Zombie*, he thought. He would have to try to squeeze through or he'd look a sissy. He lowered his legs into the gap and then quickly pulled them back again and went down on hands and knees. Taking a quick breath he stuck his head into the blackness.

'The black hole of Calcutta,' he said aloud to give himself courage, his voice booming in his ears. He couldn't see a thing and the rock threatened to crush him. It smelt of old earth, of the grave.

'It gets bigger.' Her voice came out of the darkness. He pushed forward and plopped into a large chamber, on to a rock floor sprinkled with soil and leaf mould. Opposite he could see the silhouette of an arch with the girl standing in it. He stood up and went forward.

She led him out into the green daylight. They were in a large circle bounded by the wall of solid rock, impressed at regular intervals with the upright coffins of round-topped niches in which stood rain-worn and lichened statues as if the last trumpet had sounded there turning old gods to stone.

'What's this then?'

> 'Deep in the shady sadness of a vale
> Far sunken from the healthy breath of morn,
> Far from the fiery noon, and eve's one star,
> Sat grey-hair'd Say-turn, quiet as a stone,
> Still as the silence round about his lair. . . .'

She pointed at an eroded figure, sitting with chin cupped in one hand. 'I call him Say-turn.'

'That's another name for the devil.'

'I know but I don't think it's spelled the same.'

'So what was it for, this place?'

'I don't know. Perhaps they had balls out here in summer.'

The grass under their feet was close cropped enough for a springy dance floor.

'Or perhaps they had sacrifices here like witches.'

'Don't say that. You'll frighten me and then I shan't be able to come here alone.'

A bird began its autumn evening song from somewhere outside. Suddenly she shivered. 'I'd better go. It must be teatime.' Standing there in the middle of the stone circle she looked to him like the princess in the tower but how or from whom he had to rescue her was beyond him.

If he did not always understand the wardroom jokes it was his own fault for being there of course, on a British ship when he could have applied to serve in one of their own with a Polish crew, among his own people, speaking his own language: HMS *Garland* for instance which had been lent to the Polish navy. But he had deliberately avoided that and this strangeness among strangers was the price. Even so, it was worth it. He had realized very quickly that he couldn't live with his countrymen and their passionately alternating despair and hope. He needed the calm of the British if he was to survive. The others were braver than he was: they could confront and experience their own emotions. He couldn't. He needed to overlay them with the officers' jokes he didn't quite understand but understood the purpose of. Even the British ratings were the same, as if it was something that seeped into the national character in order to endure the climate. That would almost qualify as an English joke. Perhaps in time he could learn. He had already learned some of the strange names they had for different jobs: 'number one', 'yeo', 'swain'. At first he had understood only 'commander' and 'pilot'. Then painstakingly he had added 'guns' and 'torps', and at last one of the subs, seeing his bewilderment had taken his education in hand.

The boy was slight, dark and Welsh, a phenomenon Karol hadn't come across before. He guessed that he too was to some extent an outsider in the destroyer's wardroom. The British class system was much more subtle but also more all-pervasive than the one he was used to. There were no true peasants in England, although there were, clearly, the poor. And there were no Jews, at least not that he could recognize as such, though looking through the London telephone directory he had seen Cohens and Levis listed in abundance. This too was perhaps part of British subtlety. They pretended to pragmatism and a surface phlegm but underneath he sensed a structure strong, complex and tensile as a wire mesh holding everything in place.

After he had expressed his preference for a British ship when he had presented himself to the Admiralty in London and had been examined and passed fit, he had been told how to get a uniform to replace the one he had left behind in Paris in case he should be stopped, and ordered to report to HMS *Pembroke*. Fortunately the officer in charge had taken pity on him and explained that this meant Chatham barracks. With his shaky English Karol had managed to buy a blue raincoat and a cap in which to report for duty. At the same time he bought himself a dictionary. Every night he tried to add ten words to his vocabulary and blessed his mother for her insistence that he should be taught English as well as the customary German.

'One day,' she would say, 'when you are grown up you can take me to England to shop in Harrods.'

Even as she was dying, lying against the pillow while the sun beat on the shutters, she had reminded him of this dream.

55

One of his first expeditions in London had been a pilgrimage to the store but he had been glad she wasn't there to see the windows crisscrossed with sticky brown paper against blast, the denuded shelves and above all the air of contrived frivolity of both assistants and shoppers.

He had been shown to his 'cabin' by a sailor, a rating as he had quickly learned to call them, which was a perfectly ordinary, if cramped, room with two beds in it. As the man had been putting down his battered suitcase there had been a shrill whistle and the sound of a voice from some address system. It was, the seaman explained, the call to mess, and he had pointed Karol in the right direction for the wardroom. Karol had asked about the pipe.

'That's the drummer, sir,' the man had answered with a grin. When he had gone, giving Karol a chance to look up the word in his new dictionary, he had been mystified rather than enlightened to find it described as 'one who plays a percussive instrument'. He had asked the first person he had found in the wardroom to explain.

'What are you drinking? I should try a pink gin,' and he had directed the messman to pour one out for Karol. 'What were you asking? Oh yes. The piper being called the drummer. It's traditional. Goes back to the days of sail when you went to action stations to the beat of the drum. Then I suppose someone thought we might get mixed up with the army so they gave us the pipes instead.'

How could they expect to win with such fantasies, childish games where barracks were ships and pipers were drummers? He knew how his compatriots would laugh at first, and then rail. In London he had managed to find a Polish restaurant to eat in. Here in the wardroom he would have to get used to English food. It was heavy but there was plenty of it and wine to drink if you paid. They explained the system to him carefully.

The toast to the King was drunk sitting down. They explained that too but by now he was finding the explanations increasingly hard to follow. When he reached his room the air was shaking to gunfire but Karol fell asleep at once. In the morning the summons after the bugle call was completely unintelligible. He supposed that, clogged by sleep, his English wasn't working yet.

'Call the hands, Call the hands. Heave ho, heave ho, lash up and stow. Show a leg, show a leg.'

He had been assigned to HMS *Hausa* with the rank of lieutenant. The voyage up the east coast had been mercifully uneventful as it had taken him all his time and energy to learn his duties and the strange life of the ship which went by rules as archaic as those that had governed his family estate. Gradually he had come, if not to take these things for granted, at least to cease to be continually amazed by them. Scapa, when he finally reached it, was reassuringly busy, with dozens of ships lying at anchor which had saluted the destroyer as she had passed through to find her station with others of her kind and the smaller craft, hospital, depot and repair ships up Long Hope.

'Suitably named,' the number one had muttered to Karol. 'A lot of this anchorage can't be used because of the clag on the bottom. Over there,' he pointed with his binoculars, 'is the *Royal Oak*. At certain times you can see her from above, flying over I mean, just lying down there. We're invited for drinks tonight in the *Ashanti*, and there's a tidy little golf course on Flotta if you play.'

Play, there it was again. He would ask the torps about the *Royal Oak* when he got a chance.

'U-boat got into the Flow and sank her while the rest of the country was still enjoying the phoney war. Nearly a thousand went down with her. Sometimes I think I should have gone in for submarines.'

A thousand men just like that, and their coffin resting quietly on the bottom could be seen, a perpetual memorial or warning inside their own back door. Karol shuddered, finding in himself a will to live that he had thought was gone perhaps for ever.

It was dark by the time the party reached Hull on Sunday. They had left Yarmouth in the morning and changed at Crewe to get another unheated train that ambled north through the bitter countryside.

'Me bleeding plates is frozen.' Fred stamped on the carriage floor. 'I shan't need to paint me snoz red if this goes on.'

'I'll knit you a nice thick pair of socks and a scarf dear,' Juanita Passmore said, as her fingers clicked away the slow miles. 'Call me Jean,' she'd told Vi when they all met for the first time on the platform at Victoria but Vi preferred to think of her by her stage name. It made it easier when her own turn came to go on, and it helped her not to scream as the needles clacked monotonously, reproaching her own idle hands. Juanita's scarlet nails darted among the tendrils of wool like the small pointed beaks of parakeets.

'I laid in a store of bottles when I realized war was about to break out, on professional grounds of course. I knew I couldn't dance properly without it.' Her toenails wore the same livid enamel. 'I always keep to the one colour: a sort of good luck charm. Don't I Ron? I hope I've got enough to see me through to the duration.'

Rodrigo, her husband and partner in the exhibition tango, stared across the darkening fields through the mesh on the windows. He was hungry. There had been nothing to eat on the trains and the thermos of Camp coffee and currantless yellow buns had had to be offered round in a spirit of camaradarie.

'I hope to Christ we get some decent digs. Here, if you're cold Violet, my little flower, you can come in with me tonight.'

Vi smiled politely, knowing that if she had taken Fred at his word he would have been the one discomfited. It was just a line: what men were expected to say to girls and what girls were expected to fend off without giving offence, like the wolf whistles of labourers on scaffolds or in repair trenches or in concert from the backs of open trucks of squaddies. If you didn't blush or smile you were a spoilsport, stuck up and would end an old maid. Anyway it wouldn't do to offend Fred or the Passmores. They all had to get on together since they were now The Beltones and bound to each other, day and night for ever, or at least as long as the tour lasted.

The others were professionals and used to this way of life. Vi tried hard not to show her ignorance, and to keep her mouth shut and her ears open like the posters told you to. She was still in a state of amazement that she should be here, and tomorrow would get up and sing and dance before a crowd of people in one of the factories or camps she might have been in as a mobile woman if her mother hadn't heard about the auditions.

'Go on Vi. Have a go.'

'But I'm not good enough.'

'How do you know? That's for them to say.'

It had been raining when she'd arrived at Drury Lane with her hair in rats-tails. She'd felt lumpish and dull.

'Think of Deanna Durbin,' her mother had said, citing her favourite.

Vi knew she wouldn't be as good as Deanna but she had been the best in her tap class. Madam Vera had always given her a solo in the shows she put on to drum up trade and she was always made to sing at weddings and family parties. This was different, of course. She waited with the others who were called for that morning, trying to appear unconcerned. When she walked out on to the big stage she could only just distinguish the three shadowy figures of the auditions committee sitting in the stalls in the otherwise empty cavern of the auditorium. For a moment she thought she heard gunfire but it was muffled as if it wasn't real but simply noises off, and no one else seemed to take any notice.

'Right. Miss Violet Queen, song and dance. Have you given Bill your music? Over there at the piano.'

Her legs ached with fright as she crossed the huge stage, her taps clacking loudly on the boards. Shaking she leaned over the pianist.

'Don't worry,' he grinned without dislodging the cigarette from the corner of his mouth. '*Painting the clouds with sunshine*, of course I know it. I'll give you a three-bar introduction. Just tip me the wink to start.'

It seemed she was crossing acres of boards back to centre stage. Her voice wouldn't come out; her legs were filled with ball bearings.

'Ready Miss Queen?' The voice floated impatiently up from the anonymous figure on the right. She nodded. Bill struck up. And suddenly it was all right. She could almost see the one-strap black patents she had worn to class at Madam Vera's carrying her feet through their routine. Her voice sounded a bit thin, empty, but she remembered not to force it into a squeak and to keep the tempo steady but lively. At the end she sank into a curtsey and then bobbed up eagerly. The heads were conferring.

'Right Miss Queen. If you can't wait we'd like to see you again at four o'clock this afternoon. Next please.'

'That means you're in with a chance,' a voice said as she walked off. It was a young man who'd been watching her from the wings. 'I've been called back too. Let's find a pub.'

She had never been into a pub with a man alone before but Vi thought she was managing rather well, sitting down on a bench while he went up to get her tomato juice and his Scotch.

'What do you do?'

'I'm a magician.' He produced a card which read *Miro available for private and public occasions*. 'I wanted to go into the RAF but failed the medical. Weak chest.'

She looked at his thin face and the two bright spots high up on the cheekbones, understanding the euphemism. Her cousin Maggie had died of TB in her twenties, and afterwards Vi's mother had stuffed her anxiously with jars of malt and poured Bournvita into her before bed. Once she had burst out when Vi had complained, 'I don't want you going the same way as Maggie.' When Vi had told her she had been given a contract after the second audition she had been pleased at first, after all hadn't it been her idea, and then apprehensive.

'It'll mean not getting to bed til all hours and no proper food. You'll have to look after yourself because I won't be there to look after you.'

Already that seemed like years ago, and then again like only yesterday. She had been told to work on her act, that she would be one of a small touring concert party, that she would get seven pounds a week which, as her mother pointed out, was more than her dead father had ever earned. To celebrate she bought a new silver container of Tattoo and a Max Factor pancake. She had practised to the wind-up gramophone on her tap board laid over the stone floor of the scullery.

'I used to do a bit of walloping,' Fred said when she told him what her act was. 'Old ticker wouldn't stand it now. Keep an eye on your wardrobe or the buggers won't put it on the train and then you're in shtook.'

'What about you?'

'I can always get by with a bit of paint. I never let that out of me sight. Look.'

He had opened a wooden box on his lap and shown her the surprisingly neat compartments of slap, cold cream, brushes of every thickness, hair powder, cotton wool. 'That's me, the real man, in there.'

Vi had stared down at it, breathing in the heavy greasy smell. 'Will you show me how to use them all?'

'Course. But you won't need it. Young and fresh, that's your line, not some made-up glamourpuss. Wait til you get to her age and you've got no option.' He lowered his voice and nodded across at the Passmores who were supervising an elderly porter's efforts to unload their theatrical basket of costumes.

'Here's what we'll do.' Fred had found them a carriage together. 'I'll go on first to warm them up. Then I'll introduce Juanita and Rod, then you Vi, and we'll end up with a singsong.'

'Who's going to accompany us?'

'They're supposed to lay on a pianist at least. If we're lucky we get a band.'

The stop at Yarmouth had been to visit a bomber station, a chance to get used to each other. The station band had been laid on. Vi hadn't quite been able to tell anyone it was her first really professional engagement. They'd changed behind curtains with empty ammunition boxes for dressing tables. Beyond the curtain proper she could hear the audience assembling, the rumble of men's voices and the tramp of feet on the boards of the wooden hut that served as cinema and theatre. She felt sick and remembered reading somewhere that if you took a deep breath it helped. She took several.

'All ready?' Fred's face appeared round her curtain. It was the first time she had seen him made-up; there hadn't been a chance to rehearse. She was amazed. His usually rubbery features were given a new definition by the clown's mask under the straw boater.

'Do I look all right?' She patted her hair nervously and smoothed the short skirt.

'Like Shirley Temple with knockers. They'll love it.'

Young, bored, frightened, eager to be pleased, they had, of course, whistling and stamping for an encore, unwilling to let the sight of her go.

'I say, what a smasher!' someone had called out of the blue cloth sea when she had run on. She'd fumbled once or twice in her routine and the singing she knew was a little breathy but she'd done it.

'I'll be better next time,' she told the rest of the Beltones as Fred had christened them. That night in her chill hard bed at the boarding house she'd gone through it all again and again while the sea slurred along the beach and filled the air with its sweet saltiness. They'd been an easy audience for her first. Now would come the hard bit, the keeping on when she was tired and cross and the others were too, and so perhaps the very people they had come to play for.

The train dragged itself into the station. Fred stood up.

'This is it: Hull.'

'How do you know? There's nothing to say.'

'Once seen never forgotten and anyway I feel it in my bones.'

Juanita was carefully folding her knitting, stabbing the diminished ball of wool with thin steel needles. 'I hope there's a good supper wherever we're going.'

'How will we get there?' Rodrigo asked.

'They said we'd be met. You two go and look for our stuff. Vi and I will see about the transport.'

She had followed Fred into the gloomy station hall where every kind of uniform had gathered to wait, some accompanied by girlfriends or mothers. Under the lighting, subdued for the blackout, they were drained of colour, reduced to a series of barely touched etchings in tones of grey. Fred led her through the Way Out into the black street.

'Christ how will we ever find anything in this?'

A figure stepped forward out of the gloom. 'Are you the Beltones? I've got your transport.'

Their eyes accustomed now to the thicker darkness, they looked across the street.

'Christ,' said Fred again. 'It's a bleeding hearse.'

*

So ended the period of our innocence which some, many of my colleagues among them, would see rather as ignorance, a wilful blindness that was heavily punished. They would argue that by our policy of appeasement and neglect of the armed forces we encouraged Hitler to believe we would not oppose him and thereby endangered our country and the world. However the stance of 'I told you so' has never seemed to me either attractive or helpful. Anyone of any sensibility was sickened by the First World War which had been endured largely as the war to end wars. To rearm in the early Thirties would have been tantamount to admitting that it had all been pointless and would have seemed like a betrayal of those who had died.

For the first few years after the Great War we existed in a state of shocked relief. To rational and sensitive minds a repetition of what Europe had just been through seemed unthinkable, morally unacceptable. This was the correct reaction. What was to make it historically invalid was the advent of Hitler, the last tyrant in the classic mould whose reality the British mind could not at first grasp. The trouble was that we had not had a tyrant of our own (I use the word precisely) since Oliver Cromwell and even he had hardly prepared us for Hitler. The French understood better because of Napoleon. We merely thought both Hitler and Mussolini were funny fellows whom their countrymen could not possibly take seriously. If we can be said to have sinned in the pre-war period our sin was more the monastic one of *levitas* than the classical *hubris*. No rational person or nation could want another war, therefore either they or their intentions could not be taken seriously.

Some may argue that we are a nation of petty tyrants and that is why we do not have or need a supreme one. Almost any of us, or all of us collectively, will do and that is how we gained and ran our Empire. I am prepared to admit that there may be something in this charge which is also related to the popular belief that an Englishman's home is his castle. Coupled with our insularity which springs from the geological accident of a rise in sea level, it distorts our sense of the reality of what is happening over the water and enhances the universal inborn tendency to pursue tribal superiority.

Our leaders are chosen by a kind of political natural selection from a pool of possible aspirants, to reflect the national temper. Before the war when what we wanted was peace, we selected Chamberlain and kept him until the last possible moment when war was unavoidable and had to be prosecuted single-mindedly, at which point we replaced him with Churchill. Chamberlain cannot be blamed for embodying the collective will to peace and appeasement. If he had not done so he would have been replaced earlier. This does not mean that we are always right. Merely that we get the government we deserve, that is want. For the same reason Churchill was kept in the wilderness until he was needed.

Above all we did not want to fight another war in Europe. It was Hitler's threat to invade, and then his bombing of our cities that, ironically, stiffened the British resistance just when we should have been intimidated after the evacuation from Dunkirk and the fall of France. We went to war unwillingly, in half-hearted defence of a piece of the continent, because we had at last begun, almost unconsciously, to perceive Hitler's intention of making a Germanized united states of Europe, which could reduce us to an overcrowded offshore island dependent for its sustenance on an Empire separated by thousands of miles of ocean both from us and from its different parts, and constantly menaced by all those European colonies which Germany would acquire along with her continental conquests.

This is to give the most cynical explanation of our action in supporting Poland but human and even national decisions are rarely so simple and the urge to defend our economic interests was at least compounded with the perception in the national mind that we must, at last and however unwillingly, fight for some concept of freedom. We were saved from invasion certainly by the

Battle of Britain but also by the temperament and practice of Hitler himself. He was used to quick, overwhelming victories and to ignoring pockets of resistance in pursuit of his main objective. Yet beyond Britain there was no objective. Perhaps the island could be ignored while he gave his attention to the Germanization of Eastern Europe, an essential part of his expansion plan, which Britain was not.

For the last time perhaps in our history our isolation behind a narrow strip of water saved us. Operation Sealion was called off: he turned away.

. . . And what an error to believe that England is personally too much of a coward to stake her blood for her own economic policy. The fact that the English people possessed no 'people's army' in no way proved the contrary; for what matters is not the momentary military form of the fighting forces, but rather the will and determination to risk those which do not exist. England has always possessed whatever armament she happened to need. She always fought with the weapons success demanded. She fought with mercenaries as long as mercanaries sufficed; but she reached down into the precious blood of the whole nation when only such a sacrifice could bring victory; but the determination for victory, the tenacity and ruthless pursuit of this struggle remained unchanged.

. . . The state is a means to an end. Its end lies in the preservation and advancement of a community of physically and psychically homogeneous creatures. This preservation itself comprises first of all existence as a race and thereby permits the free development of all the forces in this race.

. . . If physical beauty were today not forced entirely into the background by our foppish fashions, the seduction of hundreds of girls by bow-legged repulsive Jewish bastards would not be possible. This too is in the interest of the nation: that the most beautiful bodies should find one another, and so help to give the nation new beauty.

Mein Kampf   A. Hitler, 1924

II *Iron*

It had been a funny old Christmas. Last year, in the beginning, the war had hardly made any difference. Now it was everything and everywhere, seeping into the furthest corners and under things, a peasouper that wouldn't let you see a hand before your face as if this was the natural state and what had gone before it, was merely a time of waiting, not peace but simply before the war. That summer world where she and Sylvie had played tennis had become insubstantial, a lost dream of childhood where she could sometimes hear their voices or catch the sound of ball on racquet. For her father, Hilary knew, it was different. He had always been at war.

Lil fretted over the Christmas cake.

'Don't worry about it, Ducks; we can always do without. As long as we can get a drop to drink.'

'It wouldn't be Christmas without a bit of cake. Besides I told Cousin Bet we'd bring that, and the pudding.'

Sensing a crisis, Wilf had laid aside the *News Chronicle*. Hilary had been home that weekend. 'I'll have a look round in Burntwood. Sometimes they have things off the ration there that we don't get here.'

'At least there'll be a bit of cream at Bet's. That's one advantage of being married to a milkman.'

'The recipe in here says use raw carrot in the pudding,' Wilf offered from the pages of the paper.

'Cut that out Daddy please.' Lil got the scissors from their nail on the side of the overmantel.

He snipped neatly round the printed oblong and passed it over.

'It comes to something when we need a ministry to tell us how to make a pudding. At least they're giving us extra sugar.'

'Propagoose,' he had said, shaking the pages into alignment before he assumed his intent reading of them.

'If the raids are too bad I shan't want to leave the house.'

'He'll stop them for Christmas.' Her father always knew about such things.

He had proved right of course: so there they had been on Christmas morning, getting out of the underground train at the end of the line where it ran up into the daylight, and climbing the wide shallow stairs to the entrance hall, whose pale green and cream opaque glass walls were trellissed with brown paper ribs.

'What about something to warm us up for the walk?' They had gone into the buffet where there was just a lone railwayman in his dark blue uniform, features etched sharp in the white skin with weariness, sitting staring into his tea at the end of a shift. Lil had found a seat with the bags while Hilary and Wilf went up to the counter. 'Three coffees please and three drops of whatever you've got.'

'I've got some rum in.'

Hilary was always to remember the rich black treacle steam as she bent her head over the cup, and the rivulet of hot spirit that seemed to pour through her veins.

Her father coughed loosely. Lil looked at him, her voice harsh with anxiety. 'You alright, Wilf?'

He nodded and drew a gasping rush of air through his blue lips. 'Just caught the back of me throat.' He pulled out a handkerchief to spit into and wipe his mouth delicately. His cheekbones were white prominences as if touched by frost-bite. The unspoken rule was that Hilary and Lil would talk to each other while he fought for breath, covering his weakness with inconsequential questions and answers.

When they were ready to leave, Hilary had firmly picked up their conker-coloured cardboard suitcase and held the door open for them both. Wilf's hands were deep in his mac pockets. The tops of his ears showed red smooth curves below his cap. She could hear the mucous bubbling in his chest. The road ahead lay long in front of the station but there were no slopes before they reached Bet's, pacing slowly, their breath three cloudy haloes against the hazed sunshine.

The rest were already there: Wilf's sister and Bet's mother, Edie and young Wilf, her quiet son, Bet's husband, Cyril, back from his early morning round, and their two children: Leslie and Margaret. Lil went into the kitchen with Bet while

Cyril unscrewed the top from a quart of light and then another and poured the grown-ups each a glass, with a gin and lime for his mother-in-law whose apple-dumpling face Hilary had never before seen without a smile. It all seemed so normal, so like it always had been.

'Cyril's had his papers, haven't you?' Edie said.

'No more deferment. I've got to go. They're bringing back Alf Edwards who retired last year. I'm relieved in a way. It was beginning to look a bit funny, me still being here. Mr Service says he'll keep my job open for me to come back to.'

Wilf drew on his pint. 'He's got no choice, not like last time. He's got to do that by law not just by rights.'

'I don't know how Bet'll manage on a soldier's money with two children. Me and Young Wilf will help her out of course. Good job he's in a reserved occupation.'

'They wouldn't have me anyway; said I was more use making boilers, with my chest.'

'Runs in the family,' Wilf laughed.

'They'll be calling up the girls next,' Edie said, not believing it. 'If it keeps on.'

'Oh it'll keep on, don't you worry about that.'

'Come on now please: dinner's ready. Hilly and Young Wilf, you bring two chairs,' Lil ordered from the sitting-room door.

'I'll just make up the fire.' Cyril hefted the coal hod from its place behind the brass fender, the flames playing redly on his shining face. Sometimes Hilary thought that Bet must have married him because he looked so like her mother. It was hard to imagine him away from his family, in uniform.

'Do you know where you're going?'

'I have to report to Catterick on the 3rd of January.'

Bet had managed to get a hand of pork and some sausages in return for cream which, Hilary noticed, her father refused, but then he was always fussy with his food, preferring fish or cheese and picking in a token way at everything else.

'How old are you now then Hilly?' Edie asked while they waited for Bet to bring the pudding from the stove.

'Seventeen and a bit.'

'You might get called up then, if it goes on.'

Hilary saw her mother put down the gravy boat she had picked up to take to the draining board.

'What's all that about?'

'Cyril's got to go after Christmas,' Bet said. 'But we won't talk about it now. Margaret get the plates. Cyril, light the brandy.'

The dark pudding had flared blue for a few seconds while they cheered. Hilary chose the lemon jelly to go with her moist slice rather than the thick sweet cream she only ate at Cousin Bet's and always found too rich. They had discussed being called up in the sixth form common room at break, drawing on the forbidden passed-round fag that made them feel every one a Bette Davis. She hadn't really thought about it much but now she would have to. It was only fair: if boys had to go girls should too, although she knew instinctively that her mother wouldn't agree.

'Lovely pudding, Aunt Lil,' Cousin Bet said, raising her spoon. 'I don't know how you've managed it.'

'Ah, that's my little secret.'

'I know I was sent out with a jug for a quart of old ale.' Her father had got his breath back enough to joke. 'She's a little mivvy when it comes to a pudding.'

'What's all this soft soap?' Lil cried. 'You know what my mother used to say: "Kind words butter no parsnips". He must be after me money.' She laughed harshly to cover her embarrassment and the others laughed too.

'Me? I've got plenty of dough; more than I know what to do with. You want a bob or two, sweetheart, you come to me. I wouldn't want you to go short.'

They were all used to her parents' rituals; it was part of the small coin of family gatherings. Later while Cyril and the children washed up and the rest dozed by the fire, Hilary turned again to what she would do. Perhaps she wouldn't have a choice but would be directed like Cyril. She was ashamed to find the idea exciting. Looking round at the slumped familiar figures she saw that Cousin Bet and Aunt Edie had their mouths pursed while her father's was slightly ajar. Lil catnapped. At any moment she might open an eye, wink at Hilary and close it again as if in a deep sleep. Cousin Wilf's chest hardly rose and fell, he slept so quietly, his family face a faint engraving from her father's. A line drifted through her mind out of one of their Higher School's English set texts, *The Metaphysical Poets* they all found so difficult:

Or snorted we in the Seven Sleepers' den. . . .

Edie's mouth opened and she began to snore gently.

Later they had woken to cups of tea and jelly with more cream, followed by her mother's cake under its mantle of ground soya and almond essence, bright yellow marzipan, bedizened with a handful of sugar flowers and leaves her mother had managed to scrounge, and piped with *Merry Christmas* in chocolate spread. Then the glasses were brought out again, and the bottles opened.

'Come on, Aunt Lil,' Cousin Bet said as they had all known she would, 'give us a tune.'

'Alright.' She took off her best apron and folded it over the back of the chair before sitting down at the mahogany piano. 'But you must tell me what to play.'

She struck a series of chords to flex her fingers and then: 'Here you are Daddy, here's one for you,' and she began the chorus which they all took up at once, except for Leslie and Margaret who were crouched over a game of lexicon on the rug in front of the fire.

'If I/you were the only girl in the world
And you/I were the only boy
Nothing else would matter in the world today,
We should go on loving in the same old way.
A garden of Eden just made for two,
With nothing to mar our joy,
I should say such wonderful things to you,
There would be such wonderful things to do. . . .'

Lil's voice, perfectly pitched but with the hard edge of the music hall or pub singer, rose above the pied keys where her hands moved, the fingers thickened with years of scrubbing floors and clothes until her wedding ring was embedded between soft pads of flesh so that, as she sometimes said, if she died tomorrow they would have to bury it with her. Hilary heard her own voice joining in and her father's crooned descant accompanying the higher voices of the others as if their singing could hold up time for ever. It had certainly been a funny old Christmas; almost like normal.

So after two months of pushing and shoving it all boils down to this: nothing. That's what the desert is: miles of pale sand like water, a sea of sand where we've crawled like flies while the flies crawled over us all day drinking our sweat until the blasting sun goes down and you can lie out under the stars in a bit of blessed peace and quiet, hearing the sandthorn twigs crackle under the billy as Archie brews up our holy char. Nothing or nothing to write home about.

I never thought a cuppa could come to mean so much, even though it's out of a tin mug. I think sometimes of cool, smooth china, of a cream-coloured tea set Mum had, not for best but everyday. The grate of metal on metal, spoons on plates, meal after meal, sets my teeth on edge. Everything's hard like the sun and the heat, rancid, metallic from the hot sides of the truck to the hard leather of your dried-out boots. The sand itself is flinty sparks, gritting away your skin like emery paper.

Funny that I was never one for the Boy Scouts and that sort of caper and here I am living the outdoor life, camping and making fires, sleeping in tents when we've got them or on the ground under the sky when, as most often, we haven't. Now the fighting's over for a bit it's hard to remember what it was like with the old ticker thumping in fright most of the time. I suppose that's how humans keep going, by forgetting the bad bits and only remembering the good. I remember the spot of leave in Cairo, not the coming back on the Blue with the prospect of being shot or shelled to atoms.

In some ways it was too easy, rolling up the Eyties like old carpets. Not that they didn't fight but their hearts wasn't really in it. They're happy enough behind the wire, sitting on their POW patched backsides like the blue-arsed baboons, chattering and smiling and boiling up their macaroni that smells better'n our bully. That one who slipped me a couple of bottles of Chianti in return for some tins of fish when we was on conner guard seemed a decent enough bloke. Reminded me of Giuseppe at the chip shop.

You can't feel hatred for them. They didn't ask to be here any more than we do. It was just the Duce wanted a bit of old glory, a crack at empire-building. Now it's come unstuck and we've pushed him out of Africa, they'd all like to go home to the wife and kids, which it's a shame we can't let them. It's the monotony that gets to us now. I never realized how much there was to look at in Hammersmith, especially the old river going under the bridge. This morning on parade I suddenly thought of Boat Race day, not the crowds on the towpath but the water, gallons of it white, blue and grey unwinding itself down to the sea and when I looked up it was out across the mardam, with a distant blue dazzle rising up from it like a lake where three blokes was walking looking for scrub for the fire and all split up by the mirage, ten feet tall and their bodies, arms and legs broke off from each other like dolls.

It's a nightmarish world that seems as if it will go on forever. The old soldiers are the ones to copy. They keep their nuts down and use their loafs. They've got a language all their own we've learnt to speak because somehow it makes it easier to keep going. There's different words for everything and everyone, like being in jug, or thieves' talk. The talk holds you all together when you're sitting round for a gripe session or lying with a fag nattering or on a stag in the darkest hour before that slash of grey in the sky lets you rouse the other lads and get your own head down for a couple of hours' kip.

The lucky ones are the readers who can pass the time with their nose in a book. I've never been a great one for that. I'd have done better at school if I had but I've had to give it a try since I've been out here and I find it comes easier with practice. Reading and kipping take you out of the desert better even than leaf in Cairo because there you know you've got to come back, no matter how blind you get or what bint you find to shack up with; it's only for a few hours or days, whereas with reading you can get away from it all any time. I still can't decide whether to try a wog bint or whether I should go on being faithful to Millie in the hope she's being faithful to me.

The other lads think I'm a bit of a fool but then from their tales I reckon they don't enjoy their trips down the Berka much, and a lot of them just seem to stand around in the houses taking a shufty at the bints without laying out their twenty piastres. The desert even knocks that on the head. The best part of leave is the pictures, and going from club to club, the YMCA, up the Empire, down the New Zealand, on to the Tipperary, gormandizing and guzzling as much as you can while you can, before it's back to desert rations and burgoo for breakfast instead of ham and eggs. There we eat like lords, better than I've ever ate in me life and likewise most of the other chinas.

I wonder how they're feeding back home, Millie and the boy. He'll be alright in the country but in her letter she said she'd moved back to look after our tackle. Three months for a letter to get through and then just one side of the page, telling you nothing really except that they were alright that long time ago and might be dead by now. They'd let me know that, wouldn't they? If they knew themselves that is, and who would tell them? They'd notice she wasn't drawing me pay: that's how. Three months don't mean nothing and we're all the same out here, all waiting on mail, on Jerry, on the brass, on leave, on the next brew up.

You could end up like that scorpion Archie found in his blankets last night and leaped out shouting blue murder. Surrounded the little bastard with a ring of petrol and set fire to it. The beast kept running at the burning circle trying to find a way through until at the end it lost heart upended its tail over its back and stabbed down into its own body. Hari Kari. I almost feel sorry for them when they do that, though like everyone else I dread the finding one in me boot or bedding. But they haven't a chance in the flame and they're only obeying their own nature when they creep into something snug. Like the rest of us really.

Here comes Archie with the billy. The stars are so big you could reach up and pick them. Funny they called our show Compass. I'll never understand how they think up the names they do for ops and such. Sidi Barani! Sounds more like a music-hall turn than a place.

'We're invited to dinner.'

'It's very kind of your sister.'

'She's short of a man. She asked me to bring someone presentable so I thought of you. She hates people who throw the bread about if you know what I mean.'

Karol didn't. However it was best to smile in pretence. 'But I am on watch.'

'Change it. Get one of the subs to do a swap.'

He wondered what the boy might have been intending to do himself. Find a girl at a dance probably. Which was why he hadn't been too worried; one night was as good as another and there would be plenty of time while *Hausa* was refitting.

'She'll pick us up. Betty always manages to wangle some petrol. It's black tie but we're quite perfect as we are of course. Everyone loves a uniform these days.'

Number One, Jimmy, had been kind or perhaps helpful was a better word. He had treated him with uninflected casualness which in his terms, Karol realized, meant as an equal.

A large black saloon was waiting with a fair-haired woman waving and calling behind the wheel. They left the city behind and drove into the still unspringing countryside. Sitting in the back behind brother and sister, Karol found their conversation too muffled by the engine and too allusive to follow. He stared instead out into the hedged fields. A short clear shower beat on the windows and was gone, leaving translucent liquid tadpoles to squirm up the glass. The narrow lane seemed to run with blood and looking again he saw that the earthbanks were now a dark red mud stitched with the mint green and yellow of small glossy flowers. The car turned, climbing steeply through an open white gate and along a drive to a square pink and black brick house, veiled by trees on the point of breaking into flower or leaf, and flanked by outhouses with, he thought, stables beyond. Suddenly Karol realized how much he had missed horses. Even when she learned that the Radziwills had bought a motor car his mother had kept her carriage. Three dogs in assorted sizes and colours ran barking out of the door and he realized too how much he had missed dogs although his mother's elderly and stately retainers would never have given tongue.

'They're all quite harmless.' His hostess turned towards him, 'just rather loud. They'll calm down in a minute.'

'It's good to see them again. You don't get them on a ship.'

'Only seadogs,' Number One said and the pair of them laughed.

'Gerry will show you to your room,' his sister said.

Karol looked at him in surprise. 'I'm sorry I thought . . .'

'All Number Ones are Jimmy. Don't ask me why. I'm afraid my own name is Gerald. And yours?'

'Karol. In England you only have it as a girl's name I believe.'

'Lord yes. Drinks downstairs when you're ready. Can you find your own way?'

He found his way by the noise of voices vying in conversation. He hoped his English would be up to it. His French was better but the English didn't seem to speak French. Gerald, as he must remember to call him, Gerald's sister came forward.

'Now let me introduce you. I'm sure I shall make a mess of your name. Karol Michalowski. How's that?'

'Splendid.'

He couldn't assimilate the names he was offered in return but found himself eventually beached on a sofa with another pretty fair-haired woman. 'You are the sister of Gerald also?'

'Heavens no. I'm just a friend. Betty and I were at school together. I'm down for the weekend, resting from my labours.'

'Your labours?'

'I drive an ambulance in London but I've run away for a couple of days.'

'It must be very frightening.'

'Oh but nothing to what you do. I really shouldn't have said anything. Betty says you've been escorting convoys in the Atlantic. All very hush-hush, I expect. My husband's doing something so hush-hush even I don't know where he is.'

'Hush-hush?'

She put a finger on her neatly reddened lips. 'Shh! Don't tell. Careless talk costs lives: all that sort of thing.'

'Ah secret! I don't think what we have been doing is very secret. The more the enemy knows we are there the more he will keep away. We do not wish to be brave and sink him, only to be like the English nanny and keep our little ones safe.'

Gerald had joined them at that moment. 'You two don't look much like Nanny to me,' the woman said looking up at him.

'I see you've managed to collar the prettiest girl in the room. She wouldn't look at me you know. Went and got spliced to a brown job.'

'He means my husband is a soldier. Look we've drawn each other for dinner. You must tell me about your home.'

It was difficult to manage the different obstacles presented by each course and English conversation at the same time but he was able to tell her something about his mother and his childhood.

'It must be terrible for you not knowing what's happened to it all.'

'It will have been sequestrated in my absence. But it is not so terrible for us as for some people. Poles are used to exile. We have been occupied so often. That is why there are so many of us all over the world. I am only glad that my mother died before it happened.'

'But does that mean you're quite alone?'

He smiled to soften it. 'I suppose it does, or did. Now I have the *Hausa*.'

'And a girl in every port.'

Afterwards when they were leaving and Gerry came to take him away she said, 'You must come and see me when you've got leave in London. We could go to the theatre. I'll give you my telephone number. Gerry, I've decided your friend is a count in disguise.'

'Are you?'

He found it impossible to lie. 'Something like that but in Poland it means nothing. They are ten a penny.'

'You seem to have made a hit with Daphne Pearmain,' Number One said as they climbed the brow. 'She's quite bright, although like all women she's inclined to rattle on. I rather fancied her myself for a time as one does one's sister's friends. I should look her up if I were you. All's fair in love and war. I must say my brother-in-law's got a good cellar. Just as well they got hitched in time to put one down.'

When he reached his bunk Karol wished he had drunk rather less of it. They seemed to have run into a force ten gale that was plunging the cabin sickeningly up and down. Whenever he closed his eyes he seemed to be drowning and when he eventually fell asleep his dreams were of walls of green and white water, cliffs of ocean falling towards him while Daphne Pearmain, he knew it was she although he couldn't see her, laughed, lorelei, beyond the curtain of sea.

The row nearly killed you at first. You thought your eardrums must go because it was the sort of noise you weren't used to after being at home for years alone all day; even some blokes would have found it hard, him for instance after nothing louder than the traffic and the ting, ting of the bell. It hit you like a blow to the head, the clanging of metal and the stuttering roar of the machines. You couldn't hear yourself or anyone else speak until gradually you began to get used to it and it died into the background like everything else, even that, that the other girls seemed so keen on.

How crazy she'd been for it when they was first married. Then the boy come along in all that blood and pain and it had turned her right off. And he wasn't one to press, she sensed that, even though she knew he was still keen, he wasn't going to carry her up the stairs like Rhett Butler, leaving her singing in the morning til he came in and made out he was sorry and spoiled it. That would have been him alright. He'd have cried after if he'd ever had pluck enough to spill the milk. Not that she was wanting him to, not really.

The other girls talked about it all the time one way and another and when they could make themselves understood above the din, laced morning and afternoon with *Music While You Work*. But in their break or on trips to the toilet or queuing for the bus home the turbans wagged, the Tattoo-ed lips pulled on a fag and they laughed and rolled their eyes and their tongues round the forbidden words. Sometimes Alfie the foreman would overhear and blush while the sharpest grinned openly in his face and pulled his leg for being such a stick. Some of them were as common as muck of course, but then you were bound to have to mix with all sorts because there was a war on. And they did make you laugh even though there were things, words you wouldn't have entertained for a minute in the old days. They were good enough sorts underneath it all, would lend you a fag or a few bob. They all stuck together in their story, against the foreman and the bosses and the people they brought round with them from time to time to show them the happy workers singing at their lathes.

When she was really going first thing in the morning, she could knock off two plates a minute. Pick up one, place it on the jig lined up with the markers, bring down the drill, press the power pedal, bore the hole, raise the drill, reverse the plate, bring down the drill, press the pedal, bore the second hole, raise the drill, chuck the drilled plate in the box, pick up the next. Your mind goes for a walk by itself while you're doing it over and over again for ten hours, with just the two breaks for a cup of tea and the longer one for dinner, to look forward to. No wonder some of them give up and tried for the forces. But she wouldn't fancy that, in barracks and being ordered about. At least when you come out, even when it's dark again and the whole day seems to have wasted away, with nothing to look forward to but two penn'orth of chips and a joey's worth of rock eel if you're lucky, and the nine o'clock news to cheer you up, at least you're your own boss in your own place til you clock on again next morning. And there's always Saturday night.

They all longed for it, married and single. Friday, no matter how tired, she felt she must wash her hair. Then she could get to the butcher's queue early Saturday morning and after look for a new blouse at Barbers with those coupons she'd bought off Grace, something smart to go with that skirt Grace'd run up for her out of a remnant of blackout material. The stuff was on the thin side but it fitted her so tight it couldn't crease. She knew she looked a bit tarty in it and he wouldn't have approved but then he wasn't here to see, and neither was his old mother who would have given her a piece of her mind if she'd seen her all dolled up of a Saturday. Now there was only them upstairs and she didn't give a bugger about what they thought as long as they didn't poke their noses in and start writing him letters about what she did or didn't get up to.

Roll on Saturday and if they wanted her to come in to work in the morning she wouldn't, even though it meant losing the extra overtime. As it was they worked all the hours God sent, so when she put her head down at night she'd still be boring into them bloody plates with her eyes shut until she dropped off. She must remember to post the postal order for the boy's keep in the morning and he needed new boots he'd written to say. Well as long as there was enough left over for her fare into the palais and a couple of gin and limes she didn't care, even though she and Grace might have to dance together half the evening. It was so good just to stand up in the music under the slowly revolving globe of little mirrors that was like a turning world of light, and quickstep away all the worry and pain.

*

He pushed open the swing door and tried to adjust his eyes quickly from the brightness outside. Like night flying. There were several indistinct figures in the gloom and then the bar with a neat unbarmaidly bun-haired woman behind it.

'A pint of Younger's please.'

Alan took his jug to a corner table and got out a copy of *Poetry Quarterly* to hide ostentatiously behind while he cast an eye over the inhabitants.

'You go out dear. It'll do you good. I've got plenty to keep me busy,' his mother had said. On the kitchen table was a pile of khaki, grey and navy knitted palms and backs of hands to be stitched into pairs of gloves, a quicker method than the intricate fashioning of fingers on four needles.

He had left her guiltily, taking the train to Charing Cross and walking up towards Soho through squalidly busy streets, thronged with uniforms and eager girls, whose painted legs below their short skirts, red succulent mouths, and jutting conical breasts set the words tumbling through his head for the first time in weeks. Others managed to keep writing, *Poetry Quarterly* was full of them, so why shouldn't he?

He was sure this was the pub they all came to, a latter-day Cheshire Cheese where he might learn his trade by having the magic of contiguity rub off on him. Writers, especially poets, had always met to drink and talk together. After all the months of chat about ops and girls this was the stimulus he needed. Perhaps, though, he was too early. There was an elderly woman drinking bottled guinness beside the bar and a tall man leaning on it in a long camel-hair coat with a silver-topped cane propped beside him. His hair flopped poetically over his forehead and from time to time he would push it back with a gesture at once contrived and careless.

Alan was wearing his school mac over his uniform as a compromise. It was a useful nondescript grey that didn't proclaim its origin. The door opened behind him. He took a nervous mouthful of bitter and wished he had positioned himself better to observe newcomers. It was too late to move now without making his intention obvious. As the figure came into his line of sight he was relieved to see that it was also in uniform, the rough khaki serge of a private. The soldier approached the other man and was clearly acknowledged.

Almost at once they were joined by a fair girl in grey slacks and white blouse with her shoulder bag swinging provocatively to outline a breast or bump against a hip. She too was known and greeted with kisses. Next a short plump young man with brown curly hair above a stained raincoat joined them, and two more girls or rather, Alan corrected himself, one was a woman with long bobbed hair and an alert pixie face while the other had the uniform glossy red lips, eyebrows plucked into a pencilled arc and piled swags of clean brown hair in front, falling away behind in a glinting shower Alan longed to plunge his hands into up to the wrists.

It had become a party he prayed wouldn't move on until he had got himself invited to it. If he finished his pint and went up for another there might be an opportunity to speak. He emptied his glass and stood up, undecided whether to leave *Poetry Quarterly* marking his spot or to take it with him. Then he saw himself dropping it like a glove or handkerchief, bending to pick it up, stumbling, a red-faced fool and decided to leave it. He sauntered over to the bar. The group talking loudly now conveniently blocked his way to a refill.

'Excuse me.'

'Give the password,' the pixie-faced woman smiled at him. Was there a hint of menace?

'I'm afraid I don't know it.'

'Then you must invent one and we'll decide if it will do.'

Alan's mind went blank. He longed for some shaft of brilliance to strike him so that he could astound them all.

'Your time's up. No password, no booze. Which is as bad as being shot. Do you agree?'

Desperately he said: '*Horizon.*'

'The enemy!' the camel-haired man cried and the fair girl raised her hand with finger pointing and shot him dead.

'Bang.'

He clutched his chest dramatically and let his knee sag. His heart was pounding with fright.

'I bet he's a bloody poet,' said the soldier. 'We don't want any more bloody poets here. The profession's overcrowded already.'

'I think he's nice.' The fair girl licked her lips making the gloss shine wetly. 'You can buy me a drink.'

'With pleasure.'

'One for all and all for one.' The plump man upended his glass and stubbed it down on the bar.

'What'll you have? Everybody.'

'Let him wash away his sin in liquor.'

He didn't care how much it cost him. They would have to talk to him now and anyway wasn't this what he had been saving up his pay for? The bun-haired barmaid came from behind her mahogany battlement to switch on the lights and put up the blackout shutters, cutting off the outside world.

By half past ten they were all best friends though he still wasn't sure of their names. 'Drink up,' the camel coat cried. 'This dump is closing. We have to run down the road to the Highlander where they stay open til eleven.'

There was a rush for the door. Alan found the fair girl hanging on to his arm. 'I don't want to lose you,' she said laughing.

Outside it was pitch dark and cold. He was glad she was with him or he might have been left behind and never found them again. He was aware of other passers-by as they stumbled along. An L-shaped streak of light showed briefly the outline of an entrance.

'Put that light out there,' the girl called, giggling. They lunged at the door which gave way, enmeshing them in the heavy curtain behind and letting a flood of noise pour over their heads.

'Come on,' the girl dragged Alan forward. 'There they are.' The group was nearly submerged in a sea of girls almost identical in dress to the one who had now let go of his arm. Among them bobbed the occasional uniform male or what seemed to Alan mere schoolboy, in tweed sports jacket with leather elbow patches.

'Who are they all?' he shouted.

'Film-makers for the Ministry. Like me. Get us a drink before last orders.'

Alan fought his way forward. All London must be packed in there trying to get served with a final tot of oblivion. The girl pressed in behind him until they met the others who had already, he was relieved to see, wrung their drinks out of the harassed barmaids.

When last orders rang out the girl downed the dregs of her gin and lime and passed him the glass. Again he fought his way through the press. He felt awash with beer but pride demanded that he sink another pint as she drank her gin.

'Let's go back to my room. I've got some salami. We won't bother with the others.'

Her name, he at last ascertained, was Liz. Shushing him and giggling alternately she half dragged him again up a dark staircase on to a landing smelling of Lysol where she opened a door with a Yale key. There were a couple of letters pushed under it which she picked up and propped unread on the mantelpiece above the gas fire. 'Have you got a bob for the meter?'

The jets popped into flame and warmth as she put a match to them. 'Food, I'm starving.'

Alan admired the line of her back and buttocks while she crouched down to a tin safe below the table and brought out a dog-end of bread and a piece of red sausage in a grey skin. She sliced the salami and the loaf, wrapped a piece of one round the other and handed him the chunk. He watched as she bit into her own and pulled a piece of skin out between her teeth which were very whole and white like small peeled nuts. Alan crammed the sandwich into his mouth. It tasted salty and spicy together. His mother would never have approved. He suspected that the meat wasn't even cooked.

Liz found two tumblers and sloshed some red wine into each. 'Here's to us. It's time you kissed me.'

His lips were numb with the booze but he pressed them to hers and felt the slight greasiness of her lipstick. He put his hand behind her head and pressed their faces together. She smelt pleasantly scented and her skin was very soft. Her breasts were hard against him. With one hand he opened his jacket to feel them better.

'Take it off.' She began to remove it. He felt himself hardening. She led him over to the divan. 'Let's be comfortable.' She lay down and he knelt for a moment beside the bed until she half pulled him on top of her. He pulled up her skirt and saw the tops of her stockings and the hard rubber and metal suspenders on their elastic straps. He was going to do it and she wanted him to but he didn't know how to move next

85

without fumbling and spoiling it all. He rubbed his hardness against her through the rough cloth of his uniform trousers. Then he was aware of her hand undoing his belt and fumbling at the buttons on his flies. When her hand closed about him easing him through the slit in his pants he almost came at once. He would have liked them to undress further but there was no time. He thrust himself through the wide leg of her knickers and forced himself down on her and up, up inside as she arched a little to help him. He only had time to move once, twice before he was coming in a fierce rush that had him grunting and gasping.

He couldn't tell whether she was angry or not or whether he should feel ashamed or proud.

'Pass me the tea towel over there,' she said. He got off the bed pulling the limp moist flesh back into his pants as he did so. He handed her the tea towel.

'You have made a mess.' She began to wipe herself and the dark stain on the bedspread. 'Next time don't be so hasty.'

He looked round at the room, trying to memorize the details but his mind registered only the orange-white, purple-white, crocus colours of the Penguins ranged on the windowsill. And the alarm clock. With horror he saw that he had missed his last train. 'I have to go.'

'Why don't you stay the night? Next time I might have some fun too.'

'I've missed my train.'

'Ring up.'

'We're not on the phone.'

His mother would have gone to bed but would still be listening for him even though she wouldn't call out or show that she had heard him come in. 'I'll have to try for a bus.'

'Give me a kiss before you go.' She opened her mouth forcing his open too and let her tongue tease him before she pushed him away. 'Where do you live?'

'Ladywell.'

'Ladywell, Ladywell fly away home
Your house is on fire.'

He almost fell down the dark stairs, found the catch and let himself out into the cold night. 'This is the last one,' the conductress said as she pulled on the bellwire. 'New Cross garage only.' He felt she could see what he had been doing. She was old enough to be his mother with greying curls frizzed out from her navy cap. The smell of his own spunk seemed to cling to his skin.

He left the bus just before it turned into the depot and set out past Goldsmiths' College along Lewisham Way with its wide grey pavements, his eyes accustomed now to the faint starlight, and then left down Tressilia Road to the small sloping common of Hilly Fields. A plane droned far up. Was there a raid on? He didn't know. The conductress hadn't mentioned it but then she and the driver, a gaunt man in his fifties Alan had glimpsed high up in his cab, had been wanting home and their beds.

Pausing under a scrubby tree he lit a cigarette. If Jerry came now, one of their bombers dropping its load on him as he had done on Mannheim last week, his life would be completely rounded, replete. He had done it at last. Tomorrow he would put the whole experience into a poem and send it to her or better still go and find her and give it to her. After all he still didn't know her surname and he wasn't all that sure of the address.

Rua stares up at the shining things in the blue sky. Houmi hugs her legs to comfort himself. The others have all stopped munching on the fig leaves and are gazing up too, some of them hooting softly. At first they had ignored the flying things when they had passed over high up taking them for birds sailing the thermals. Then they had noticed the strange droning noise of their wings unlike the usual predators that glide soundlessly in order to stoop in surprise on the unwary. As a rule they didn't bother the Forest People but very young babies were carried close clinging to their mother's chest hair just in case, their weakness protected by the bulk above.

Now the loud birds are coming lower and there is clearly something wrong with them. They hold their wings rigid as in a dive but they scream and roar as if in anger or pain as they fly across the tops of the forest so that the sound echoes for miles and everything else is silent. Even the waters of the lake seem to tremble under the strokes of their noise. Then suddenly they are all going away into the distance, going as far as the eye can see; gone.

The forest still holds its breath while the people whimper a little, waiting. Even though the number of strange sounds and happenings has grown greater over the past few months they are still not used to them. They know that somehow they are all connected to the smooth apes who have gone towards the great water. When the rains were falling they passed northwards while the people watched them hidden in the trees and ready to run away. They had thundersticks with them. Some were walking and some went along in great nests that would hold several at once. Some were brown and some were pink, as the smooth apes are. The smell of them passing through in such numbers was rank and oppressive. It was several days before the rain washed it all away and the air was clean again. Every morning Rua came out of her night nest leaving Houmi safely inside and snuffed the breeze to see if the smooth apes had come back, before she would let Houmi out. Once, soon after, they heard the noise of big thundersticks and then all went quiet again. Gradually they were able to relax, to go farther afield for food and to eat in peace.

Now the smooth apes, for who else can it be, are back with a new noise and a new strange smell, oily and acrid at once, unsettling their stomachs and making their hair stand on end. The noise is like the thundersticks and unlike the forest noises of bird and animal, the swaying of leaves and branches. The smell, too, is unlike that of even the smooth apes themselves but like the smell the great nests make moving along. Like the noise, it is not just different in intensity but different in kind, in its nature, from the rest of the world. That is why they know it comes from the smooth apes who fill the air with their loud stinking farts that seem to cling to the leaves and hang in the clearings like mist.

Karka is excited by the hard birds. As soon as they disappear he stands up and drums with one hand on his chest. Then he seizes a vine and shakes it wildly, screaming and stamping defiance. He looks both threatening and handsome with the sun glinting off his dark hair. The Boss has seen him however and feels his position threatened by Karka's display. He stands up menacingly. Karka quietens down and pulls a handful of fig leaves to chew.

Rua knows that he is looking sideways at her from time to time as she feeds. She would like to go off into the forest with Karka but it won't be easy. There is Houmi who never leaves her and there is the Boss who might take exception to their going. He too looks at her from time to time and she is aware of her seasonal pink blooming behind and letting out its own odour of enticement. She shifts a little on her swollen buttocks. The Boss stops feeding and stares at her. She keeps very still. He begins to amble over.

As he approaches she turns to present herself. She can feel his breath on her neck and hear his murmurings as he puts his arms around her. She feels the swing of his large balls against her, the quick plunge of his mounting. Then with a couple of thrusts he lets her go, pats her and ambles away.

While it was going on she could see that Karka was getting excited and that Houmi was on the point of intervening. Only his fear of the Boss kept him from rushing between them. If she went off with Karka he would follow and Karka would have to accept him. She moves a little closer in her feeding to the young male. The Boss, satisfied that he has exercised his rights, ambles towards a large miombo tree, shins up to the crotch and composes himself to sleep, propped between the two branches. Rua moves farther away, ostensibly to pluck a fluffy yellow flower and pop it into her mouth. After a moment or two Karka sidles after her. Houmi looks up from a milk pod, spits out the pips, grins anxiously and pads up behind.

Further and further she goes from the clearing followed by the other two until they are beyond the Boss's ambit. Rua knows where she is heading. There is a quiet leafy valley beside the lake where couples go to be alone. It is a recognized retreat and the group doesn't go there to feed. She will lead the others there and then see if Karka wants to stay with her. And Houmi too of course. That is understood.

Her hands shook. She tried to hold the paper steady but the pages rattled like dry bones. Harry was somewhere in the middle of it all, she knew although he hadn't told her. And it was going badly. Her years of experience as an army wife had taught her to read between the lines of what everyone else was told and she could see that beneath all the bravado of 'falling back in strategic withdrawal', 'successful re-grouping' and now 'carefully planned and executed evacuation' lay a retreat, a rout perhaps like she'd seen after Dunkirk with an angry rabble of beaten soldiers. She wouldn't even know if he was safe or *dead*. She said the word to herself, confronted the sound of it but it meant nothing. She couldn't believe in his death, wouldn't ever believe, she knew that.

They had been to Greece for a holiday, a second honeymoon, a cruise between the islands before Ailsa was born. She wondered now how they'd afforded it on a captain's pay, though of course her mother had helped. It had been bliss. Day after day of that extraordinary purple sea meeting the almost vulgar blue of the sky, like a bluebell wood: something that only nature could get away with.

'The wine-dark sea,' he had said as they leaned on the rail, 'and look there are the dolphins. That's lucky.'

'Really good luck or lucky to have seen them?'

'Both. They only accompany a lucky ship.'

They had arched their dark muscular shapes out of the skin of water until her eyes had begun to blur with staring at them against the intense backdrop riddled with sunflecks. Did the sun still shine there in April and the dolphins run beside the evacuation ships?

At night in their cabin with the smell of the sea washing in through the porthole he had seemed like a sea god in the darkness as he arched above her. It was better than their honeymoon when they'd both been nervous and tried too hard. It was something she'd been able to set against the dreary semi-detached house in Camberley, the other officers and their wives they dined with, who always seemed gauche beside Harry. They had said he should do well in the staff college and then the bloody war had come. She resented its shattering of her dream. Instead of the white islands awash in their bowl of blue she had to see troops and guns, broken villages and the tramp of boots on the stone quays. The bombs and shells would pound the fishermen's cottages to splinters, as every morning now they had gashed and gouged out bits of London she saw, as the fires dwindled to smoke and ash, a veil she drove home through that couldn't hide the bitter scars and the blackened shocked faces of the survivors.

Because she understood more about what was going on it was hard not to feel both despair and resentment that life, her life, should be thrown away, all the sweetness and expectation gone. She had needed her couple of days' off at Betty's. It had been hard to come back to the dreary servantless house that had begun to smell of neglect, however she tried to push half-heartedly at the dust which sifted down in a perpetual delicate rain of discarded cells. She was glad when it was time to shut the front door behind her for the night shift.

The sky showed the pink of old brick above the city as she drove to her station. She hoped that interesting naval lieutenant she had met at Betty's would look her up, if not (she suspected he was shy) she would seek him out. He must be rather lonely. He had certainly looked it. His foreignness made him interesting, romantic. Betty had said he was a count. There was no harm in it. She was only trying to cheer someone up who was a long way from home. He had seemed intelligent, someone you could talk to more than most men.

She missed Harry, missed his unruffled common sense, his dry intelligence. You felt he knew what it was all about and, as long as he did, everything would be all right. He would have told her why we had been so badly beaten, thrashed in the Balkans and what should happen next. She had put the newspaper down and then took it up again, looking for comfort, a morsel of good news among the advertisements for Brooklax and Carters' Little Liver Pills in the only paper she had been able to pick up, a tabloid mixture of laxatives and exhortatory propaganda, braces for body and spirit.

Every night now seemed to be worse than the one before. They were lined up in the station yard for a pep talk. The siren sounded even as the officer briefed them. He would be gone soon and one of the girls promoted. As she half-listened Daphne wondered which of them it would be and whether she wanted the stripe and the white boiler suit that went with it. They were given their sections and the latest information on closed streets. As they broke ranks and silence, heading for the tea wagon in the lull before the first bombs and the first call she wondered for a moment where he was. Not Harry, the lieutenant, Karol she now remembered he was called. At sea again? Or drinking in a pub in the port? He had said the refit could take some time. If he didn't materialize soon she would have to wangle another trip to Betty's and hint that her brother and his friend should be invited to lunch.

Once upon a time Gerry had fancied her himself and she'd had to slap away his hands when he'd tried to rip her clothes off in the front seat of his car. Fortunately the steering wheel had come to her rescue because, although she found him quite attractive and his lust exciting, it was always awkward with a school chum's brother though not as difficult, of course, as with a randy father. Some papas were frightful lechers and always tried to get a hand up your skirt if you were left alone with them for a second. At least a boiler suit inhibited that.

She wondered as they tramped into the asbestos-covered post for their urn-stewed tea if the others suffered in the same way. Not Mrs Adams of course who in spite of rationing still managed to look like a cottage loaf and had learned to drive her father's greengrocery van when she was a girl. Or Miss Morris who was a maths teacher by day with Eton-cropped hair and rimless spectacles below her tin hat.

Count Karol would be a perfect passionate gentleman who kissed her hand and sent her flowers; two areas in which Harry was defective. She wasn't being disloyal to the dear old thing in admitting this to herself and he was only like every other man she knew, never able to remember a birthday, even hers, unless she reminded him well in advance to avoid the embarrassment of his forgetting. And as for Ailsa's! Of course that was a woman's job, remembering such things. The child had looked rather strained when she'd taken her out last. She had seemed to be worrying about Harry. She had had to remind her that soldiers' daughters had to be brave and she'd looked up and said, 'Don't get killed by a bomb Mummy, I should die,' the words tumbling out of her small white face.

Her engine was giving trouble again. She would have to get Dennis to swing the handle for her. The drone of aeroplane engines and the crump of bombs sounded far away.

'Here we go.' Miss Morris put down her cup. The hut trembled slightly as the explosions drew nearer. Daphne had been surprised at first that none of them seemed afraid. Then she had discovered that she wasn't either. She supposed it was having something to do. In fact if she was honest she had to admit it was rather exciting and much better than sitting at home alone. She turned the key and the engine roared satisfyingly. Someone must have changed the plugs. Dennis came out into the yard with a sheet of paper.

'First call Daph. Casualties in Chant Square for the Royal Free.'

He was always better when the warmer weather came. That winter had been a bad go. After Christmas he thought he'd never get up again. Lil had made him get the panel doctor in and have a week off work. At least you were paid for sickness now. When the big raid had come, Jerry making up for Christmas, he'd stayed in bed while the girls went down the shelter, too poorly to get up, feeling the house shake. He hadn't been able to turn out at night for three weeks and by the time he'd rolled up again they'd all decided he'd skived off for the duration and Chalky White was leading the section.

'Am I glad to see you,' he'd said. 'I was worried sick Jerry might know you was away and pay us a visit! Look what's turned up. We didn't dare open them hoping you might be back. Number 36s they're called.'

Wilf had picked one out of its little flat case and balanced it in his palm, his fingers seeking automatically for the lever at the side and the serrations of the dark hard fruit. 'Whatever moniker they've give it now it's a Mills bomb.'

'And we're getting uniforms too, proper ones. We've all got a greatcoat. Yours is waiting for you, hanging up behind the door.'

It had weighed heavy when he had first tried it on. How had he ever marched about in one with a full pack, rifle and trenching tool? He must have been a young man then.

'I must have been a strong young feller the last time I put one of these on.' He heard the wheeze deep down in his chest, a sign of warning. But he was getting better.

'Do you reckon he'll come in the spring?'

'He might but not if he knows you're waiting for him Chalky.'

They'd been standing to in a sense ever since that weekend in September when the signal *Cromwell* had been passed down

93

and Johnson had pouped his britches with fright. He'd had to take him aside and cheer the boy up, tell him thousands of men had done the same under bombardment in the trenches and there was nothing to be ashamed of in that, to just pull hisself together and he'd be alright. And he had. But Jerry didn't come.

Then this May, when you'd have thought it just the time, there'd been a lull while they digested what they'd gobbled up, Greece and Yugoslavia. Even the blitz had gone very quiet. They were leading up to something. The brass hats knew it too. That's why they'd been given the sten guns, utility mobsters' Tommy guns for running and fighting with a quick burst from the hip, and the Northover for lobbing grenades at tanks.

He was stood down tonight so he could study the manual, bone up on tactics for guerrilla warfare. Now his girls had gone off to the pictures he could concentrate in peace. First, though, he'd douse the tomato plants with soapy water using Lil's stirrup pump to combat the aphids. He filled a bucket and went out into the hot twilight. The chickens murmured sleepily in the henhouse. Lil had cleared it out that morning but the smell of fowl droppings was still strong in the heat. The hens were off laying at the moment, which meant there were few propitiatory fresh eggs for the neighbours in return for the scraps of cabbage leaves and potato peelings. He squirted the stream of small cloudy bubbles at the black and greenfly clinging like lice to the plants, and rolled a thin cigarette between thumb and fingers to a perfect cylinder, unwilling to go indoors while there was still light.

No one else seemed to be out. He drew his watch on its gold chain from his pocket and flipped up the case. Inside it read *Watch Case Co. Illinois USA*. His father had brought it back from one of his voyages and had worn it til he died when his mother had passed it to Wilf as the eldest. He had carried it ever since. It had a loud comforting tick, a steady pulse against his ribs and it gained a minute a day. Now he saw it was nearly nine o'clock. He'd better go in and listen to the news, then put in an hour's study before the others came home.

Afterwards when he'd switched off, he sat back to think it

all out. So Hitler had done a Napoleon and invaded Russia. That was why it had been so quiet here, and why he had had to have the Balkans sorted out so's no one could stab him in the back. Had he decided we were done for and could be ignored, mopped up later when he'd starved us out by cutting off our food from around the world or did he think we were too tough a nut to crack and Russia would be softer, a last underbelly of Europe for slitting, a backward nation of peasants his modern equipment and methods could run all over as he'd overrun the rest, and then he would turn back to us? If he succeeded he would rule a third of the world and there would be just three monoliths facing each other in an eternal triangle: America, Fascist Europe and whoever won in the east, Japan or China.

We would be nowhere, our Empire which we'd got by blood and oppression broken up, given the independence by others we should by rights have given them donkey's years ago. If you waited long enough the wheel came round, for empires that was, Greeks and Romans, Charlemagne, the Austro-Hungarians all fell in their time and now it was our turn. Hitler wanted his own because the Germans had felt done down by the Versailles treaty, that was how he'd managed to put one over a whole people and get himself elected, that and because he promised an end to despair and work for all.

Discipline was what the masses needed and if there wasn't any from inside in the end it was imposed on you by circumstances like now. We'd needed a government to keep us in order and put us to work, a system same as Russia and Germany had or the Army. He'd been best off then, he should have signed on after the war but Lil had wanted him out and said she couldn't be a soldier's wife living all over the world in married quarters. He didn't regret it. He'd had what he wanted: her and Hilly though he'd have liked a boy to go drinking with and teach to be disciplined and fit, not tipping his cap to anyone as he never did or rather as he did to everyone, the one-fingered salute in greeting to people he knew and to every passing hearse.

We'd had no sense of the British people: that'd been our undoing, only an idea of England and the Empire which was all imagination not real.

> If England was what England seems
> And not the England of our dreams. . . .

His dreams had been revolution, to see the top hats tumble in the dust. If Hitler beat Russia it would never come. Fascism was a perversion of his truth of 'the world is my country', the words he had lived by although he had been duckshoved into fighting for England once before and would do it again; the negation of Tom Paine's 'to do good is my religion', just as capitalism had perverted the American Revolution and had poisoned the air we breathed and the water we drank with its waste.

Its time would come too, to decay and fall, though he might not live to see it, had to come, to be the light at the tunnel's end else what was it all for. The gutter press said there were forced labour camps and mass purges in Russia, that people went in fear of their lives but then they always had for hundreds of years under the Czars. It took time to change, to pull millions of starving peasants up off the ground. They had to have time. And discipline. The masses didn't know what was good for them. They were like little children easily deceived with brightly coloured toys, circuses, when they should have been asking for bread. Without discipline people fell into the rule of the mob and the mobster and then into every man for himself.

He got off the hard chair he preferred to sit on and took out the *Pears' Cyclopedia* 1930 edition from the sideboard where the booze and the books were kept. Inside the front cover were the small coloured oblongs of the flags of the Empire with their postage stamp Union Jacks in the top left-hand corner. Bypassing the Dictionary of the English Language, General Information, Prominent People, Classical Mythology and History, the Office Compendium and the Dictionary of the Nursery he came to the Atlas of the World and turned through Mercator's Projection, heavily outlined in black lead pencil where Hilly had traced it off for school, through the departments of the British Isles and on across Europe his fingers following in Hitler's footsteps as he turned each page as if Hitler had had the same atlas open before him, leaving aside Italy and Switzerland, until he came to the green bulked map labelled *Russia in Europe and New Baltic States*.

There was Minsk, still designated White Russia on the map. Obviously Jerry would head for that, in a dead straight line for Moscow, with pincer arms north and south, attacking on three fronts and fanning out through the country. And the Russians would fight with every man and woman for Holy Russia, Mother Russia. The old warmonger had said in his broadcast that we would give our aid to any nation that fought Nazism. How that must have stuck in his gullet but he was a cunning old bugger and knew where his bread was buttered in wartime.

They'd tried to destroy the revolution, sending British troops against the Bolshies after the last war, but they'd failed and now we were all in it together. He tore a thin strip from down the margin of the *Chronicle* to mark the place before he put the *Cyclopedia* to one side. He would be able to follow progress, to look up the cities in the Gazeteer of the World that came after the atlas and he needn't bother to study his Home Guard manual tonight, at least not the section against enemy invasion.

'The news isn't good I'm afraid, Tilde.'

She stood in Dr Fentiman's study where Frau Fentiman had summoned her and twisted her apron with its insipid flowers into a wrung dishcloth. So what was new? How could the news be good? Did he expect her to be surprised? She would never see any of them again. At most her heart of stone might crack a little for Anna-Lise and for Fräulein Blumberg who had taught them English literature. Mama she had already buried under the stone and couldn't weep for. Anna-Lise had been so trusting and Fräulein Blumberg so rational, both were probably dead too but she couldn't quite inter them yet. She had learned that word from Shakespeare via Fräulein Blumberg. The English she had noticed didn't use it except in 'interment' where it softened the fact of burial. 'Inter', *in terra*, to put in the earth, where good in the form of green shoots might sprout from it like the buried head, potted, that nourished Isabella's basil along with her tears. . . . Fräulein Blumberg had been eloquent on this work of a dying young man, the contemporary of Goethe. She must pay attention to Dr Fentiman in his dark brown study. He was waiting for her to speak.

Downstairs in the basement his panel patients waited too, wheezing and coughing into their rags of handkerchief. They walked from their slum streets nearby where it seemed to be always raining soot, treading very carefully as if they might break, to sit on benches in the draughty basement passage of the house, double-fronted behind its privet hedge, and wait to be called into the gloomy surgery to hear bad news. The private patients called Dr Fentiman and he went to their houses, doing his rounds after the early morning surgery at a time most convenient for them. Then in the evening came those who had taken their ills with them to work all day and now exchanged them with each other while they sat in the passage. They were there now. She must speak.

'Yes?'

'Do you have friends in Poland, in Warsaw?'

Perhaps her ex-lover, the young Fritz, but she wouldn't mention him to the Fentimans.

'Why?'

'They have been forced to build a wall, it isn't quite clear, to enclose a part of the city, and all the Jews must live inside it and not go out without permission.'

'A ghetto. We are used to them.'

'In the Middle Ages yes. But now. What could be the purpose, except an evil one? But there is worse. In Vichy France they are claiming that the Jews plot to spoil the relationship between France and Germany. Thousands are being arrested and sent to labour camps in Germany. Something is happening in country after country which I don't understand.' He put his hands to his face with the heels of the palms in his eye sockets as if he would rub them out. 'The Germans are civilized people. Think of Beethoven, Schiller, Goethe. You are a German. Explain it to me.'

'There is no such thing as a German Jew, in Germany that is. There is only a Jew who is permitted to live or to die there.'

'But you were born there, grew up there. You must understand them.'

'I thought I did. I no longer understand anything.' For the first time she felt not anger but pity for them, the Fentimans and all the other lost sheep. But that was dangerous for she might come to feel pity for herself and then she would be lost too. Her shell must be kept intact while it grew inwards, calcifying the still soft interior until the shell met the stone heart at its core and she became like the pumice people, left behind in the ruined city after a volcanic eruption with the tide gone out for ever from the ashen shore.

'We had friends in Nice. We used to go and see them in the summer. Perhaps they will be all right.'

She didn't answer. They were still deceiving themselves and she refused to be a party to it: she was tired of playing Cassandra. Instead she said, 'I should like to go to evening classes.'

Dr Fentiman looked at her uncomprehendingly, as if indeed she were mad. 'Evening classes? To go out alone, in the blackout. Where would you go?'

'I would go to the City Literary Institute on my afternoon off. I should have an afternoon off.'

'Of course, of course you should. I ought to have thought of it or Evie should. And a whole day, Saturday or Sunday, once a month. What would you study?'

'I should study English literature.'

'That would be good: to improve your English.'

'Do you think it needs improving?'

He spread his hands out placatingly. 'No, no. Except that of course we can all improve. It's very good, much better already. But Shakespeare, would that help?'

'It would help me.' It would remind her of beauty and timelessness and Fräulein Blumberg. She had enjoyed the sex with Fritz and other young men but she had loved Fräulein Blumberg.

'You don't find the work here too hard?'

'It keeps me from thinking.'

He stood up from behind his desk and looked at the grandfather clock in the corner. 'I must go down. So many poor sick people needing attention all the time. You will always remember to scrub the waiting-room floor with strong Lysol once a day won't you. Even if it looks clean there are invisible germs. Dr Harris has been called up you know. Half his panel patients are to come to me and the others are to go to

99

Dr Macdonald who is seventy-three already. Why don't you take the afternoon off tomorrow once you have washed up after lunch? I will tell Evie that is what we have agreed.'

'And Sunday?'

'Oh yes. Next Sunday too.' He had scurried away.

She would be free to walk about, to go into the park and look at the fat grey barrage balloons tethered at their moorings and the empty terraces and cages of the zoo, to travel into the centre of London on a bus and find the City Literary Institute and look for the shade of Fräulein Blumberg among the English poets.

Souls of poets dead and gone. . . .

Somewhere there was still poetry and music. She had read that there were free concerts on Sunday afternoons. She would find one and go to it, let the strings throb through her before she finally became stone. Was it disloyal to think of music and poetry, to go on at all? No, they had sent her away to survive and remember them, as a walking memorial. Perhaps the words and music would make a crack in her shell but that was a risk she had to take.

'My mother drives an ambulance rescuing people from bombed buildings in London.'

'Mine's in munitions making bombs and shells.'

Ailsa considered for a moment. Which was the more important? 'I don't know where my father is. I don't think Mummy knows either. I think she's worried about it.'

'My dad's in the desert. Mum had a letter from him. It took months to get to us.' Even in the sunken road under the heavy canopy of leaves it was hot. He still wore the same shorts and shirt he had worn in the winter, with his sleeves rolled up. She was hot and sweated in her heavy purple blazer over the mauve and white gingham summer dress but she knew that to take it off would make her feel naked. 'I could leave school at the end of the summer term and go out to work but me mum signed a paper for me to stay on. That was before the war but she said it still counts. If I left I'd have to go back to London with her but I don't think she wants that.' He kicked at a dry twig across the path sending it flying into the bushes.

'What do you want to do?'

'I don't know. Sometimes I think I ought to leave.'

'What do your teachers say?'

'They want me to stay. I can take School Certificate next year and then maybe go into the navy when I'm sixteen.'

'You could be a midshipman. Why don't you go into the army like my father, and yours?'

'The navy's better for boys when you're only sixteen. We had someone came to talk to us about it the other day. If I do well in School Certificate I could be a midshipman like you said. That's how Nelson started. There's nothing like that in the army.'

The girl opened her mouth to defend but shut it again. She was sure he must be wrong but she couldn't quite see how.

'Anyway the navy's doing better than the army. They sank the *Bismarck*. And the navy had to rescue the army at Tobruk. They had to get through the enemy planes and ships with food and ammunition or the army would have starved to death or had to give up because they'd run out of ammo. I think that's where my father is.'

'You don't know.' She wanted to argue with him because of what he had said about the army.

'Rommel's a brilliant general. Better than anyone on our side.'

'You're a traitor saying things like that.'

'No I'm not, if it's true.'

'My father could be a general one day and he'd be brilliant too.'

'Go on. There's only a few generals. Not every officer can become a general.'

'My father's very clever.'

'I'd rather be an admiral.'

'You've got to be a captain first.'

'You just want to argue with everything I say.'

'You're the one who's arguing.'

'You started it.'

'I'm going in.'

'You always say that when you're losing. Anyway I thought you said you lived in Camberley.'

'We do.'

'Then how can your mother drive an ambulance in London?' He wasn't at all sure where Camberley was but he knew it wasn't London.

'Well she does. I expect she drives up there first.'

'Women drivers are all rotten.'

'My mother's a smashing driver. My father says she's better than he is and anyway he has somebody to drive him and she's a woman too.'

'I expect my dad's driving a tank by now.'

'That's easy. You can't run into anything in the desert and if you do it doesn't hurt. You can kill someone with a car. I shall learn to drive when I'm seventeen. Mummy says I can.'

'I shall be in the navy by then.'

'The war will be over by then and we shall have won. . . .'

'Maybe. If we get some better generals.'

'You're a traitor if you doubt. You have to believe.' She felt the sweat trickling down her neck under her dress until it was soaked up by the line of her vest. She was aware of the two bumps that had appeared in her chest that were sometimes tender if she accidentally banged them in games or gym. Her summer dress was really too short and too tight for her this year but Mummy said there were no coupons to spare for a new one. He had to believe. Passionately she needed him to, otherwise it might all go wrong and we wouldn't win after all. Only if everyone believed hard enough would it all be all right.

'And ice mast high
Came floating by
As green as emerald.'

'What is that?'

'It's a poem we read at school. It may be the thing that made me join the navy. It's about a ship.'

'The Welsh are like that sir,' said the helmsman, 'all singing and poetry. You don't have to take no notice.'

The green glass crags shone away to the north under the unflecked blue sky. Wandering opalescent floes of loose pack ice butted the hull and sheered away. The ice was on the move, growing towards them every day since they had left

Hvalfiord and the air within the Arctic Circle was bright and cold. Karol was used to freezing, Polish winters. He had wondered how the British would take it after their damp warm island climate but they seemed to respond well, increasing the layers of clothing (the captain was rumoured to wear two pairs of silk pyjamas under an assortment of heavy top clothes of which only the jacket belonged to naval uniform), and grumbling as they always did but cheerfully. The ratings, he found, were allowed the same mixture of complaints and jokes which would only be checked at some invisible point too fine for him to gauge. There was less formality among the crew themselves, especially now they were at sea, but an immaculate presentation in port, governed by the strange high piped calls that had puzzled him at first but whose meaning he now understood automatically.

The shapes of the other ships in the convoy were clear black silhouettes against the dazzling dish of water, easily identifiable at the eight knot speed of the slowest, a lumbering tramp that wallowed under the weight of its cargo of crated planes. Around them were staged the slim destroyers and corvettes of the escort that *Hausa* was part of. High up above their bobbing screen of towed balloons a shadowing aircraft added its metallic whine to the bass notes of the ship's engines and the hiss of bow waves.

Karol was officer of the watch while the captain slept in his sea cabin. There had been sudden fog the night before, the nights were lengthening rapidly as the summer receded, and he had been up fretting that the ships would lose station in the dark and fog, edging away from each other nervously to avoid collision against their orders to stay on course. He had been right to worry for, in the morning when the sun slowly sucked away the mist, they could see that the convoy had lost shape and had to be rounded up again.

The sun, though it exposed them to the shad planes, made it possible to get an accurate fix on their position and correct the compasses unsettled by their latitude north. It would be fatal to drift too far north or south of Bear Island, towards the advancing ice or the German bomber airfield at Banak on the tip of Norway. The captain had hung on for an hour or two after the fog came down, catnapped until dawn, been on the bridge until they had gathered the other ships and taken their position and then retired to the narrow cabin with its high-sided bunk. The freezing fog had coated the ship's super-structure in a glittering lichen it had taken the sun a long time to pare away.

It was peaceful on the bridge in the bright light. From time to time Karol raised his German binoculars to his eyes to track across the ocean for the periscope of a submarine. What was he doing on an English boat, taking arms to Russia who had split Poland with Germany until she had been attacked in her turn? The whole world had become unreal, a shifting phantasmagoria of loyalties and values. He might as well be here, where there was at least order and discipline, and the boy's narrow dark face with the large brown eyes screwed up against the light, a Caravaggio child under his peaked cap.

'What was you in civvy street Taff sir?' a rating had once asked the sub.

'I wasn't old enough to be anything. I thought I might become a teacher.'

'Why do they call you Taff?' Karol had asked.

'All Welshmen are Taffs; the Scots are Jocks, the Irish Micks or Paddies.'

'And the English?'

'The Americans call them Limeys and the Australians call them Pommies. But the rest of us just call them "them".' He laughed. 'Oh the Scots call them Sassenachs when they remember.'

'Do you have a home in Wales?'

'Yes. I have a mother and father and a sister there. My mother is dark like me. She's from north Wales but my father is from the valleys and he's fair like you. My sister is dark. That's the two types of Welsh, the dark and the fair. My father is a steelworker. My mother misses the north and the farm she was brought up on where my grandmother still lives. I could have gone into the steelworks too but I wanted to join the navy.'

'And see the world,' the helmsman had joked.

'Tell me more about the poem.' Karol liked to hear the boy talk in his half-sung English that was unlike the rest, either officers or ratings.

'It's called *The Ancient Mariner*. It's about a ship that brings bad luck on itself and is becalmed. Only the sailor telling the story survives and he has to go on telling everybody he meets because it was all his fault. He killed the albatross that was following the ship.'

'Like our albatross up there,' the helmsman jerked his head at the plane.

'Do you know *The Flying Dutchman*?'

'No.'

'It's an opera by Wagner.'

'Wasn't he a fascist?'

'Not in today's terms.'

'Look what's that?' The boy pointed out towards the south. At the same time there was a shout from the masthead voicepipe.

Karol bent his lips to the bridge pipe that connected with the sea cabin. 'Sorry to wake you sir. Enemy aircraft approaching from the south. Not our usual chap. Three Heinkel 115s I think.'

'Sound action stations. I'll be right up.'

The warning began to squawk out above the noise of the oncoming engines. The captain scrambled on to the bridge, pulling on his jacket. Their two gun turrets swivelled towards the planes. Karol was flung against the side of the bridge as the guns crashed out together. From aft came the sound of the smaller AA guns pounding at the aircraft as they passed over, heading for the centre of the convoy. Now guns were firing all around. The air was filled with flashes and smoke and the stink of explosives. One plane took a direct hit and burst apart in midair. There was a cheer over the intercom although no one could say who had hit it.

Then the remaining two had dropped their bombs and passed on. The guns ceased. There was a sudden silence. A messenger came forward with a scribbled note. One of the merchantmen had been slightly damaged but could still go on. The captain smiled.

'Keep a sharp lookout in case they come back but I doubt it. And break out a tot all round. They've deserved it. Our first blood.'

*

'What silly bugger dropped us in this shit?'

'Met men: we'd be just as wise reading tea cups.'

'Where the fuck are we Digger?'

'Somewhere over Germany.'

'Well at least we've hit the right country.'

'Look at that bloody cumulus. Did you ever see anything like it? It's the bloody Himalayas.'

'You're supposed to be looking for Mannheim on the chart not gazing out of the sodding window.'

'Trust an Aussie not to know the way.'

'We make bloody good navigators.'

'It's all that trolling around in the bush.'

'Go on they daren't go out without an Abo to guide them.'

'Shut up you lot and look out for fighters.'

'They won't come out in this.'

'Neither should we.'

'Can we go home now, please Skip?'

'Not until Digger finds us somewhere to drop the bloody bombs.'

'I'm going off for a slash.'

'At least we've got a bog on these Hallybags. Not like the old Hampdens.'

'I dunno. I miss the old piss bottle.'

'Remember the time that erk tied a knot in the hose and we had to go all the way home with our boots paddling about in Digger's urine? Hey Dig why is your piss so rank?'

'Comes of feeding the babies on kangaroo milk.'

'I've got it Skip. I've found out where we are.'

'Can we please go home? I'm cheesed off with stooging about up here.'

'You see that river: we follow that along. . . .'

'There's a fucking great thunderhead in the way. I don't know how high up it goes. If we try to go through it or over it we'll lose the river.'

'That's the way to Mannheim.'

'Alright then, hold on. I'll put her down and we'll go under it.'

'Why isn't there anyone else about? I thought this was supposed to be a big show.'

'They've all gone for the big one itself.'

'Gone home, more like.'

'Stop wittering and keep your eyes peeled. Anything could drop on us out of that lot.'

'Trust us to get the longest bloody trip.'

'That's the end of the river. Where to now?'

'90 degrees to port. Straight on for twenty minutes and we should hit the Rhine at Mannheim.'

'Someone's lobbing a lot of tracer about over there.'

'Some poor bugger's catching it.'

'Maybe we're better off with this one. They'll concentrate their fighters over Berlin. Bound to.'

> 'We are the heavy bombers, we try to do our bit
> We fly through concentrates of flak and cloud and shit
> And when we drop our cargoes, we do not give a damn;
> The eggs may miss the goods yard but they fuck up poor
>   old Hamm!'

'Shut up Clapper. You can't sing a note.'

'That's it Skip, ahead. The Rhine.'

'Where's the Rhine maidens?'

'Due north for Mannheim. Eyes skinned now. Ten minutes to OT.'

'Get ready to drop our shit and get the hell out as fast as we can. You ready Clapper?'

'Nobody's dropped us any lights.'

'Don't worry, Jerry'll probably switch on for you.'

'Here they come.'

'Looks like Blackpool illuminations.'

'Put that light out there.'

'Hurry up Clapper.'

'Steady as she goes. Hold it, hold it. Pressing the tit now. Bombs gone.'

'Let's go.'

'Well we hit something. Look: bloody Guy Fawkes.'

'Do you think that was Mannheim?'

'Course it was fucking Mannheim.'

'Fighter coming in on the starboard wing at seven o'clock.'

'Keep him off Chug. I'm going for the cloud.'

'Do my best Skip. Come on you bugger. I've got a little present for you.'

'Fighter closing. Can you see him?'

'He's a crafty one. He's keeping out of my sights.'

'Give him a burst anyway. Show him we're awake.'

'Will do.'

'Good shooting. He's sheered off.'

'I'm going for the cloud now. Hold tight. Let's hope we don't bang into him.'

'He'll never follow us in.'

'Which way home Dig?'

'If we follow the Rhine we'll run into everything the others have stirred up over Berlin and Cologne. Better go back the way we came.'

'Where's that bloody fighter? I can't see a sodding thing in this soup.'

'Steer due north Skip, til we're out of it.'

'I hope the bloody compass isn't u/s. How much fuel have we got Chug?'

'Just over half. Enough to get back if we don't hang around.'

'I can't go through this muck much longer. I'm going down for you to get a fix Digger.'

'Okay Skip. I reckon that fighter's given up and gone home.'

'Going down now.'

'Christ look at those fucking anvils.'

'There's the river.'

'How do you know it's the right one?'

'Because it looks right.'

'They all look the same to me.'

'That's why they didn't let you navigate.'

'Look at that archie right across our route.'

'That's not archie. It's bloody lightning. And there's no way round it.'

'What's it going to be: under or over Skip?'

'I'll take the kite down to 100 feet. With any luck we'll be under the clouds and the radar. If anyone pounces we can just hop up into the nearest cloud.'

'Piece of cake. Watch out for high tension wires and low-flying bats.'

'I didn't want to join the Air Force.
I didn't want my bollocks shot away
I'd rather hang around
Piccadilly underground
Living on the earnings of a high born lady. . . .'

'Christ what was that?'
'You missed us, you fucking bastards!'
'Belgian border coming up.'
'Keep going Al, keep her going.'

From this night's raids thirty-seven aircraft failed to return.

'I went round to Chadwell Road school today to register. It looked very sad without any children in it. All the classrooms empty. The desks covered in chalk dust. Nobody to clean them. It brought it all back, how I used to sit there. I could see myself and the others going in through those gates when we were children: me, Carrie, Cissie and little Dot through the *Girls and Infants* and Stanley through the *Boys*. Now there's only me and him left. I can still feel how high the steps seemed climbing up to the back of the class when you'd done well in the spelling test or mental arithmetic. They've turned the downstairs hall into a rest centre. Little girl Sedgeley was sitting on an infant's chair with a cup of tea in her hand. I asked her what she was doing there and she said a bomb got them last week. Must have been a hit and run 'cos there was no warning. They've nothing left. They were all in the shelter. When the cat come home three days later it couldn't find the house. They'd gone back to look for it every day. They're looking for somewhere nearby to rent now.' Lil wiped a knitted string dishcloth over the enamel draining board, wincing slightly as it snagged on the rough edges of the black fingerprint chips. 'This cloth needs boiling in soda. Reach me down the old saucepan, Hilly, and light the gas ring.'
    'What did they ask you?'
    'What I did before I was married. I've to go round to Baileys down West Ham Lane on Monday, a little furniture factory making mainly for children: cots and high chairs and

playpens. That sort of thing. I suppose so many get destroyed. It'll be a bit peculiar being back at work after all this time but I suppose we'll manage. When have you got to go?' She dropped the powdery lumps of soda into the boiling water and added the string flannel.

'I don't know. I filled in the form and sent it off.'

'You could find a reserved occupation. Go to college and be a teacher. That's allowed for women.'

Hilary heard the unspoken plea. 'I don't know, Mummy.'

'You must do what you think right. Good job I'm going back to work. The place won't have so long to feel empty to me.'

'I can't decide between the WRENS and the Land Army.' She saw dismay in her mother's face swiftly covered over. 'If I went to college I'd have to go away anyway. But I don't think I could settle to just studying until it's all over.'

'It's heavy work on a farm. I remember during the General Strike Grandfather Stebbing went down to the country and worked on the land until it was finished and the works opened up again. He was glad to get back, though he went home there to die in the village where he'd been born when he retired.'

'What will Daddy say?'

'He'll say you'll become a swede.'

'Perhaps it's coming out in me.' She tried to joke her mother's pain away.

'My mother's father was a blacksmith, a tradesman not a labourer.'

The distinctions were fine and infinite. They covered the whole of life with a crocheted mesh of what was permissible, holding everything in place against anarchy and degradation. It was being torn in places now but the net was still there. Certain things might be given a dispensation, like married women going out to work, but that didn't make them right . . . just 'for the duration'.

'What do you think Daddy?'

'How can I say? You have to make up your own mind Ducks.'

Lil had queued for eels that morning and now the succulent black-skinned segments swam in the white sauce flecked with parsley green, beside ivory banks of mashed potatoes on their two plates. Hilary eased the spine round with her tongue as she disengaged the delicate flesh from it. Sometimes the vertebrae had sharp tines that stuck in the gums if you weren't careful. She mashed some potato into the white gravy and forked a moist mound into her mouth.

'Make the most of it,' Lil had said as she left. 'You won't feed so well when I'm back at Baileys and can't queue for extras.'

'Your mother would like you to go on to college.'

'I know. I should be applying now if I'm going next autumn. Perhaps it will all be over by then.'

'Don't you count on that. This one's got a long way to go yet, as long as Jerry doesn't knock us out.'

'He couldn't could he?'

'Churchill might make a deal; leave Hitler free to conquer the Russians in return for an armistice in the west.'

'He couldn't.'

'Who's to stop him?'

'He'd look such a traitor.'

'Who to? A load of Bolsheviks. Anyway, politicians are used to that. He turned coat once before don't forget.' His cynicism rasped away her will to believe. She saw him working with his file at a piece of metal, the cat's tongue blade paring down until her ideals were ground to a uniform sameness and she could no longer hold on to the rough-edged truth. He called this process 'teaching her to think'.

'Doesn't matter what you do. If you was a boy it'd be different. You don't have to fight.'

'If I joined the women's forces I could be sent abroad. Even if I didn't fire a rifle I might drive a truck or help man a gun or even learn to fly.' Hilary had long ago accepted that there could never be anything for him like that last war and the terrible camaraderie of men about to die together but she felt deflated, her femaleness an inadequacy that cut her off from him.

'Your mother wouldn't like you to go abroad.' He was the enforced traveller of twenty years ago. Lil had never been further than the tip of Southend pier. 'She'd worry herself sick.'

She and Sylvie had discussed it after school during a prep period in the sixth-form room. Sylvie had decided to become a nurse, or a Windmill girl. 'I think they're ever so brave.' They had agreed that the ATS were out.

'They say they're nothing but legalized camp followers for the army,' Hilary had said, hoping that she wasn't blushing as she let the words out daringly.

'Then you might just as well be a Windmill girl.'

'You couldn't really take your clothes off and go out on a stage starkers, Sylve.'

'I'd probably funk it at the last minute. Anyway I've put meself down for nursing now. But what about you? What about college?'

'That'll still be there when the war's over if there's anything left, and if it isn't nothing will matter anyway. I can't say it to Mummy of course because she'd be hurt but I want to get away somewhere on my own.'

'You always said the WRENS had the smartest uniform.'

'I know but somehow being evacuated down here I've begun to feel different. You know when we had to go harvesting in the summer holidays I really liked it.'

'You liked Alan, that RAF pilot who spent his leave helping out for a few days.'

'Oh he was alright I suppose but it wasn't that. I really liked it even after he went.' It had seemed as if briefly nature had been making up for man. The sun shone; the ripe fields were as golden as in the first picture books she had got from the public library. A little wind cooled them when they were too hot.

They had got up at five, washed their faces in cold water and eaten plates of fried bread and baked beans in the farm kitchen before riding out in the cart to spend the long day in the fields, stooking the prickly sheaves whose loose seeds and wisps of beard worked their way through their aertex shirts and down their dungarees to scratch the soft townee skin. She had ached all over after the first day and fallen heavily asleep as soon as she lay down on the thin mattress on the attic floor. The second day had been torture as her muscles protested and she had felt a leaden somnolence all day in head and limbs so that nothing really impinged on her, the external world came mediated through a quilt of numbness that seemed to envelope her. By the end of the fifth day she had never felt better in her life.

They had been driven to a dance in the village hall in the

evening and there she had met the RAF type, Alan, spending a few days' leave on another farm. He had taken her off the wallflower bench by the wall and when he discovered she was good at English and was doing Higher next year, he had said he was a poet and had talked to her all evening about her set books. She had liked talking to him, been proud not to be left sitting while the others danced the night away to the unlikely combination of a piano played by a large lady who had once accompanied silent films and a whiskery old man on a squeeze-box who might have been a beached seadog. The dances were necessarily a little out of date too. They had laughed together at them and Hilary had felt very sophisticated.

He had said how hot it was after a couple of dances and indeed he was sweating in his thick blue uniform, the trickles running down from the high sideboards beneath his forage cap to the points of his jaw. He was a sergeant, he said, a pilot though she wasn't sure if he was shooting a line. Outside in the dark under the obligatory harvest moon they had walked round the back of the hall while he lit a cigarette whose red tip glowed sporadically as he drew on it, lighting his face. There were, she had noticed, nicotine stains between his first finger and thumb but only faint ones.

When he had backed her against the wall of the hall which throbbed with the heavy beat of music and feet she had felt a faint excitement. This was it. Her first encounter. She had expected the sensation to grow as his face came down on hers, his mouth on hers and then the lips parted to let his tongue feel out her lips and teeth but nothing had happened. The sensation had died rather than grown and she was disappointingly aware of other shufflings in the night, the tobacco and beery tinge of his breath, the roughness of the stubble on his cheeks and the smell of haircream. Her head seemed to be a detached observer of her body. She had murmured that they had better go back: she didn't know what time the van that had brought them in was going.

He had taken her to the pictures the next night and the kissing had been repeated. He had even fondled her breasts a little through her cotton frock because the neck was too tight to get a hand in easily and her bra was an added protection or barrier: Hilary couldn't decide which. Back on the hard mattress with the others breathing in the stifling dark she had considered her own lack of reaction. She was excited by the idea of what he might do but when he did it nothing happened inside her, passion refused to gallop her away. She had been almost relieved when his three days' leave was up and he had to go, leaving her his name and address to write to.

'Fifty years of neglect,' her father had said, 'letting the land go to waste while we imported from all over the world and now they're digging up the parks for vegetables and getting in women and children to bring home the harvest. You know what I'd have done: if the gentleman farmer didn't work the land I'd have taken it away from him, leased it out to those who would. That's what should have been done years ago, not have to wait for a war to push us into it. What a way to run a railroad. You go and help them out sweetheart.'

'Now Wilf don't spoil the girl's holiday with politics before she even gets there.'

'At least as a Land Girl I wouldn't be sent abroad. Mummy would like that, but I don't know. Maybe it's the only chance we'll ever get to travel. Unless you do become a Windmill girl.'

Sylvie had sighed. 'I don't suppose I really will.'

Afterwards he would try to remember what he had been doing the day the world changed. Making a little bread for Christmas coming. Hustling for a few bucks with his horn in the evenings and on Sundays at funerals, toting stuff around by day whatever any dude would pay him to tote: baggage, sacks of feed, flour from the mill, coal from the railroad. He must have been standing around for hire that morning. Yes brother, that was for sure. He could see himself now in the faded, patched duds he wore for toting, with a sack of shit on his back in a line of other cats all similarly loaded coming and going from the open railcar to the waiting wagons when somebody shouted: 'The Japanese have bombed Pearl Harbor. We're at war.' Every last man stood still with his sack on his shoulder and his mouth hanging open catching flies. Then as if at a whistle they'd dumped their stuff on the ground where they stood and was hightailing it to the nearest tonk to get the news hot. Up until then they hadn't paid it much attention. Whitey was having his war over in Europe wherever that might be, too far away to be any business for us to mess with. Even when they'd introduced that Selective Service shit there'd been no need not to stay cool. It was a numbers game and maybe your name would come up but first would be the death or glory boys out of Westpoint and points east. They wouldn't rush to saddle themselves with a parcel of untrained niggers. Stay cool and keep your head down and no one would notice you.

Now suddenly it had all been different. Little yellow men had attacked Whitey and caught him with his pants down, lambasted his arse like Black Betty. Now he would need all the black childs to help him out. It was plain as day that he wouldn't be going it alone when the shit started to hit the fan. There would be a nigger draft and Beale would be near the top, courtesy of his clean living, taking it easy all this time on the snow and the juice, unlike some of the other musical cats who kept theirself thumping and blowing through the night with magic potions. He'd only ever needed the music to keep him going. Whenever he sagged and the smoke and the press of the dive wore him down the next break would lift him, his horn soaring and singing while the others wove it in back there, a carpet of sound he could stand right up on and fly away.

But there would be no more flying except by courtesy of the US government for some time to come. He'd be offered the army or war work. He thought about it carefully and then decided there was no sense hanging around, that was just unsettling. It was better to get down to the draft office and sign on. That way at least a man knew what he'd be doing and since he liked flying, though there would be more dough staying home and working in a factory, he thought he'd at least be around aircraft and maybe sometime get a ride in one. So he put in for the air force and walked back up town, seeing the street cars and the boys on the corners and the girls on the steps calling out to the Johns passing by as if it was for the first or the last time.

*

'It was Christmas Day in the workhouse
The wind was howling loud. . . .'

'Bring on the crumpet!' someone shouted. The uniformed figures began to stamp and whistle, their impatience at the leaveless Christmas translating itself into anger with the performer.

Vi, listening in the garrison theatre wings, recognized the signs. Her problem was what to do about it without offending Fred. Though they didn't even know she was there it was her they wanted, ached for as the antidote to the fear of dying young and soon. She knew her job now, she wasn't afraid any more. Fred was hardly making himself heard above the din. She took a deep breath and a decision and ran on to the stage with her best ingenue trip. There was a roar that threatened the roof. She ran up to Fred, took his arm and kissed him smackingly on the cheek whispering, 'A bit of father and daughter routine to get them quiet. Then I'll sing to them.' They were still, waiting for her to speak.

'This here's me daughter.'

'And who are you? Old Mother Reilly?' There was a satirical cheer from around the speaker.

'If you don't behave yourselves I'll send her to bed and won't let her sing to you.' There was another cheer.

'Oh dear Daddy let me sing for the young fellers.' Vi went down on her knees in supplication.

'Oh go on Daddy,' came the chorus.

'All right then. I can't refuse her anything you know.'

Vi stood up and nodded to the pianist.

'I've made a postwar plan for someone and me
I'm saving for one certain soldier. . . .'

'Wot about the navy,' someone shouted.

'Shut up!' called several voices.

Vi sang on.

'What could be better than a life full and free
For me and that one certain sailor. . . .'

The audience roared its approval at the change and then caught by the song and the singer were silent to the end.

'And so I know through all the lonely hours I'm spending
That all I save and lend will help to send
A happy ending. . . .
We'll find a peaceful world where love is the key,
For one certain sailor and me.'

Now they were with her she brought Fred forward and they sang together:

'When can I have a banana again
Tell me mother do . . . ?'

bringing the audience in with an 'All together now', for the second chorus.

Then Vi chanced the naughty Florence Desmond number, *The Deepest Shelter in Town*.

'Don't run away mister
Oh stay and play mister
Don't worry if you hear the sirens go, though
I'm not a lady of the highest virtue . . .
I wouldn't dream of letting anyone hurt you . . .
If you hear the siren call
It's probably me . . .
When it comes to shelters
Nowadays it's all bunk . . .
I won't even be wearing a frown
So you can hang around here until the all clear
In the deepest shelter in town. . . .'

There was a barrage of catcalls and wolf whistles that carried her and Fred into *Follow the White Line all the Way* while they stumbled blindly round the stage bumping into each other in an imaginary blackout, imitating that outside in the darkened camp. Finally they got off stage to *Goodbye Now* and Rodrigo and Juanita burst on behind them for their exhibition medley. The audience, good humoured now, stamped and clapped in time and whistled at the sexier moments in the tango. When it was all over and the Passmores had run off hand in hand the applause went on with calls for Vi to return.

Gathering her last remaining energy she walked out front of curtain, and began what she knew they were waiting for:

    'You are always in my heart
    Even though we're far apart. . . .'

At the end there was silence before they began to cheer.

Sometimes she wished she really had someone to sing about or to but their way of life, constantly travelling from engagement to engagement, falling exhausted after the last performance into a narrow lodging or hostel bed, gave little chance for her to meet anyone. Her mother had at first been disappointed that she wasn't coming home for Christmas.

'If there wasn't a war on I'd probably be in panto somewhere so I'd still be away from home.'

Tonight was different; tonight because it was Christmas they'd been invited to the officers' club after the show and however tired she felt she was going. She caught herself wishing she would be going alone without the rest of the Beltones but that couldn't be helped. At the stage door was a dark-haired boy in naval uniform who stepped forward and said he was their escort. She could tell at once he was a Taff. He shone his dimmed torch at their feet, lighting them along the cold tarmac, damp with a salty mist that got into her lungs and made her cough. They hurried across a parade ground and through an arched doorway, bumping up against each other as they'd done in the song, before the door was closed behind them and the light switched on in the long hall. Eager to begin the evening Vi refused the offer of a cloakroom.

'Now Ron,' Juanita said, 'I don't want you cramping my style with your green eye.'

They followed the young fellow into a noisy room crowded with dark blue uniforms.

'I'm dying for a smoke,' Vi said.

'Here,' said the boy, 'have one of these.'

'What are they? Not Capstan I hope.'

'No they're American: Camels. I picked them up on our last trip to New York.'

From the unpublished memoirs of
Captain later Brigadier Harry Pearmain DSO, MC

    Hindsight tells us now that Hitler had gone away for good but we had, at the time, no means of knowing this. To us he had merely called off the invasion for the months of bad weather. With the spring he would be back. The renewal of the blitz in March after a remission in the worst of the winter seemed to be the softening up preliminary to landing. It was at this time that the iron began to enter our national soul.

Looked at dispassionately we were the people best fitted to be placed in a position of solitary opposition to a triumphant enemy since our chief virtue, which at times of course is also our chief vice, is endurance. We will continue long beyond the point at which it is rational to do so and in this case we believed, against all the evidence, that we could not be beaten. Endurance is thus a kind of passive arrogance. It is particularly dangerous when confronting the impossibility of a nuclear war since its effect is to diminish the threat. We cannot rid ourselves of the belief that we should survive, we of all people, that endurance would be enough again.

Even so we came near to breaking, not in London itself with its homogeneous population, bound together in a street culture propagated by the music halls which had given it a consistent image of itself, but in more volatile places like Liverpool which came near to panic and indeed to riot. The deliberate attempt to destroy civilian morale and bring about internal collapse almost succeeded. It was defeated not by an iron fist but by the appearance of our emblematic rulers among the still-smoking ruins, by the development of a concept of equality in suffering which had not existed as a national idea during the Thirties and the Depression.

Endurance was also the chief virtue of our soldiers who at the beginning were, except for the core of regular army, underequipped and physically poor material: the adult counterpart of those evacuee children who had so dismayed the country people who had to receive them in their undernourished and verminous state, the result not of parental neglect but of poverty and bad housing. We had not an army but a horde of green civilians many of whom were eating and sleeping better and able to keep themselves cleaner and better clothed than ever before in their or their parents' lives. It is perhaps not surprising that Marx's extreme principles were developed with the example of the English industrial peasantry all around him. He could not of course have understood that such conditions would breed not revolution but endurance.

Faced with what they saw as an untrained, and some began to believe untrainable, undisciplined rabble of clerks and porters without any military, or indeed in most cases civilian skills, unable to shoot or to drive a vehicle, some commanders began to long for the Hitler youth, and it was some time before the further-sighted were able to make use of the qualities which this hastily assembled militia actually possessed, and learned that the men were better at being led than commanded, and responded to attempts to keep them informed about what was going on, rather than to demands for blind obedience. The soldiers in fact saw what they were doing as a job and rather admired Jerry than hated him, especially the German commanders like Rommel.

Our civilians on the other hand became pitiless as the only way to survive. They needed small doses of revenge, the bombing of Germany, the quick commando raid, the sinking of named capital ships to prove that the enemy was not indestructible; the initial success in North Africa. We lived, breathed, ate war with every lungful and every mouthful. There was no escape from it except briefly at the cinema, concert or dance hall or in passion, real and simulated. We could be taken out of it for an hour or two but it was the reality to which we had to return whether in the desert or in the factories and shelters. In its absorption of civilian life it set the pattern for all later wars.

When Hitler invaded Russia instead of us we knew at once that he had made a terrible, for him, mistake. We did not believe that he was greater than Napoleon and we knew that if he did not succeed at once he must be defeated by the size of the country and its population, and by the winter. A burden was lifted from us: the burden of being the only European country still unoccupied and at war, even though we had of course been supported by our distant colonies and those who had escaped from the occupied territories, and were not therefore, technically speaking, completely alone. Our isolation was psychological, compounded by the initial unwillingness of the Americans to involve themselves in another European war.

However it seemed at first as if history was not to be repeated, the German advance into Russia was so rapid. For five months they swept forward while we held our breath and waited for them to be halted by frost and snow. War is a succession of 'ifs', that is what makes its study so fascinating. All our games are imitations of it. Afterwards it is possible to analyse and reconstruct the chain of cause and effect but at the time the players must make their moves largely blind while convincing themselves that they are following the correct strategic rules. Often tactics and strategy are at variance and defeat each other. As with all games, the psychological element is as important as technical skill and standard of equipment.

Not only the weather defeated the Germans in Russia but their own psychological error in treating the population in the areas which they had occupied with great brutality, just those territories, White Russia and the Baltic States, where with a softer touch they might have persuaded the inhabitants to throw off Bolshevism and join the Axis by establishing a pro-German state. Instead, the besieged inhabitants of Leningrad preferred quite literally to starve to death rather than surrender, thus buying valuable time for a Russian counterattack and tying up valuable resources of men and equipment.

The Germans made a further mistake in declaring war on America after she had been attacked by Japan and thus dividing the world into two opposite camps. It is still debatable whether the USA would have declared war on Germany even at this stage, although had her people fully understood Hitler's plans for the Jews they would probably have forced their government to do so later in the war. The Japanese looked for space in the east as Hitler did in the west, to extend the Japanese empire and sphere of influence by driving out the white colonists while they were busy elsewhere and unable to send reinforcements in time down such extended supply lines. In this they succeeded brilliantly: the whole world was now at war.

Some Aspects of Fighting in Built-up Areas

The ground. *No other battlefield includes ground both so open and so close. In every street are coverless stretches affording ideal fields of fire. Bordering every street are numerous protected firing positions, hiding places and sources of ambush. It follows that fighting will nearly always be at close quarters, casualties high, and the nerve strain for both sides heavy.*

When a built-up area is the scene of a prolonged period of fighting, however, many of its characteristics will be modified. Buildings are liable to become heaps of rubble and fields of view thereby increased. When a whole sector of a town is reduced to rubble, the piles of debris render the whole area analagous to close country providing much cover; and they will also restrict movement except on foot.

Darkness. *Owing to the restriction of movement outside buildings by day, much fighting in towns will take place at night. Streets can be crossed, small parties can stalk past defended houses, and it will be difficult to distinguish between friend and foe. Darkness is the ally of the attacker rather than of the defence.*

Fire (the element). *Used intentionally fires produced by one's own side have a very heartening influence and a proportionately depressing effect upon the enemy. Nevertheless, clear orders concerning the use of incendiarism are always necessary because it is a double-edged weapon which can do more harm than good.*

Principles of Home Guard defence

Defence is final. *A defended locality must fight to the last man and the last round. . . .*

Defence must be concentrated. *Seeds not soldiers survive distribution in penny packets. It is fire power that stops an attack. . . . The German methods of total war against soldier and civilian alike can only be defeated by total defence.*

Concealment and Deception. *There is nothing more obvious than a sparrow's nest or the eggs it contains. The fecundity of the species allows it to survive all casualties. Probably that is why its concealment is so imperfect. In Britain, however, there is a shortage of manpower, and Home Guard must be less careless (when on active service) than sparrows.*

Home Guard Instruction No. 51

For issue down to section commanders – two copies for each section.

GHQ Home Forces

III *Papers*

It seemed strange to be setting out on Boxing Day with the memory of our Christmas dinner fortunately receding as the western gale buffeted the leading ships. It was a long uncomfortable night. The blessed were those who could get their heads down and sleep as if tomorrow would never come but some of the troops were painfully and stinkingly seasick. We seemed to be plunging on into the blackness forever like some benighted Flying Dutchman. I managed to wedge myself in an angle of bulkhead to stop from pitching about and dozed on and off until the word came that we would make landfall in thirty minutes at seven o'clock. I roused my party and made sure that everyone had his full quota of equipment before we assembled to tranship to the ALCs. The navy opened up its bombardment and the RAF laid on a smokescreen to cover this always very vulnerable moment of scrambling from one vessel to another, especially when both are bobbing about on a brisk sea. My party made a successful transfer and our boat set out full speed for the shore. One of those unfortunate accidents that are the little ironies of war now took place when an ALC abeam of us suddenly burst into flame from a phosphorous bomb released from one of the screening RAF planes which had been hit by German gunfire. Men, crouched in the open metal craft which had become a floating oven, were burning and screaming before our eyes. The rest of us could do nothing but press on.

There was no element of surprise involved now and I heard Jack Churchill's bagpipes playing his lot ashore. Fortunately for us the naval bombardment had been most effective on our quarter and our two groups ran into the island without even being fired at. The garrison of our objective seemed quite nonplussed and we were able to put the lot in the bag without any difficulty. The others then went on to clear their second objective, the factory, while we covered their rear. However it now became obvious that the main group was having a harder task than anticipated in taking the town and we soon received a signal to join in. We set the explosives with time-fuses designed to wipe out the main buildings and gun emplacements as soon as we were safely off the little island and embarked for the mainland port. I called our party together and outlined our procedure. This was the first taste of street fighting for some of them and I knew it would be slow and if we were not careful there might be heavy casualties.

The plan was for us to advance from the dockside clearing the buildings until we made contact with troops of the main party who were fighting their way through from the other side. I afterwards learned that there were more enemy troops than expected in the town because some were spending their Christmas leave there. Snipers had holed up in the warehouses and had to be winkled out. Usually we could spot and deal with each in turn but one cunning fellow let some of our party pass his position and then began shooting them from behind as they pressed ahead. Sergeant — was shot three times in the back before we could turn enough fire power on the window the sniper was using and silence him.

Then we resumed our slow advance from house to house. At the next there was a very rough defender. I put my head cautiously round the door and we both fired at each other almost simultaneously. Fortunately he missed but so did I. I ordered grenades to be thrown in to blast him out but he merely appeared at the door out of the dust and smoke and returned the compliment with a couple of stick grenades before retiring inside. After our previous experience I was unwilling to go on and leave him in our rear as a very substantial threat and I allowed one of my officers who was already wounded to have a go at him with a Tommy gun. The German shot him but he was able to walk out. Then one of the troops ran in with a burst of Tommy and sprayed the inside of the building but the Hun merely shot him in the thigh.

This was proving too costly a hold-up, both in time and men. I therefore decided to burn the sniper out. I detailed one man to stay behind and wait for him to emerge, threw petrol in and set fire to the building before we went on our way, continuing to fight from house to house with more casualties until we got through to the other troops who had been clearing their own path towards us. By this means the town was cleared and our objective gained with the destruction of the docks and other key points.

We also destroyed all the shipping in the harbour and the battery. Overall hung the stink and black smoke of burning fish-oil factories characteristic of every strike in Norway. Another bizarre element was provided by the presence of Army Photograph Staff snapping us as we went about our business.

We then began re-embarking as daylight was beginning to fade at two o'clock, taking the wounded, our prisoners and some Norwegian volunteers back with us. Although we had suffered some seventy casualties we nevertheless felt a great sense of achievement in having carried the war into the enemy's camp instead of passively waiting for him to turn his attention to us. In however small a way it seemed to redress the appalling defeats we were suffering everywhere else.

Report of Captain Harry Pearmain

Dearest Bet,

I don't know whether this will ever be let through to you but it helps me to write it. Everything here, though I can't say where, is as bad as can be. I know we're not supposed to be defeatist but sometimes it's important to face the facts and I know you're strong-minded and not likely to go under because of anything I say.

We are anchored just off the port as an evacuation ship. It seems unbelievable but it looks as if this place is going down and I only hope we are allowed to leave in time and don't go down with it. Really it's unthinkable, like the *Titanic* all over again. Thank God at least they have stopped the nightly dances at the Raffles. Even after the sinking of *Prince of Wales*, and *Repulse*, they were still holding the usual tiffin dance on Sundays and laying white cloths and silver for dinner with the bodies from the last air raid lying unburied in the streets outside. The native population goes into a blue funk every time a Jap plane comes over while the planters still can't seem to grasp what is happening. Karol says in some ways it reminds him of Warsaw before the fall, which isn't a good omen. Ironically we are sitting here in the harbour with the great guns pointing at us on fixed sites unable to turn or raise their trajectory while the Japs gallop down the peninsula behind. The island is stiff with troops and yet I feel that it's doomed.

Our real problem, and that's what did for Phillips, the Vice-Ad. commanding *Prince of Wales*, is that we have no air cover and the Japs have. Some of the Hurricanes our convoy brought in were destroyed even before they were uncrated, by Jap bombers, because most of the coolies had run away from the docks. Also they didn't seem to have trained our chaps for jungle warfare believing it couldn't be done, apart from a few of the Scots who are mad anyway. Even so I wish I felt we could put up a real fight. If Malta can hold out, this place could too, if we only had some air support. That's what's keeping them going of course. A carrier would do it. At the moment the little yellow men seem unstoppable, going through the effete Westerners like the proverbial dose of salts. It's some consolation that the Yanks aren't doing any better, after all the hopes that were built up when they joined in. You can say it was all our fault for training the Japanese navy so well in the first place.

If we get out of this mess we should be due for a spot of shore leave, in which case I hope you'll invite us and dear old Daph down for a naughty weekend. I'm working to fix something up between her and Karol – unless you fancy him yourself of course. I always thought Harry P. was rather a stick and not worthy of her, being a brown job. Anyway in wartime we all have to seize what's going, in case there isn't likely to be any more. I could see she rather fancied him. I know that look in her eye of old. I suppose I'm clinging to this because everything here looks so hopeless.

Personally I don't know why anyone would ever want to live in Malaya. The climate is absolutely lousy. You feel whacked all the time which is probably why the residents here are such a wet lot. They've had a pretty lush time here playing the sahib and it's sapped their ability to think let alone act decisively. I think they thought they were quite safe in their tight little island fortress and that the Japs were just another bunch of natives who couldn't really pose a threat to this outpost of empire. They should have asked the Chinese. They think it's all like Gilbert and Sullivan still and not to be taken seriously. I suppose it will serve us right if we do get our noses rubbed in the shit by the Nips.

All this sort of thing becomes much clearer now out here. Like everybody else I've never really thought about these things as you know. We weren't supposed to. Just took things like the empire for granted. It used to be quite fun coming to places like this in peacetime and one never thought about how it was all kept up, like a theatrical set, a painted illusion with no substance to it, if you know what I mean. You can blame the war for your brother becoming a bit of a philosopher and treating you to this rather ponderous letter.

Continued later.

I had to break off because there was a buzz for us all to go to the wardroom. The old man was looking very grave. We sail tomorrow. Apparently the navy are pulling out and blowing up the base, leaving the brown jobs to carry on as long as they can. Ours not to reason why but it does seem a rotten trick though I suppose someone has decided it's hopeless and that we and the base aren't to fall into enemy hands for which I'm thankful. It seems that things are going the same for them in Burma and the old Moulmein pagoda is no more. I wonder if we shall ever be able to watch *The Mikado* again.

Karol and I went into town to try to pick up some stores. I had never seen anything like it. Some of the Aussie troops from upcountry have effectively deserted their units and stagger about the streets looting the abandoned liquor stores. There are queues of people outside the shipping offices desperate for any sort of bottom to get away in. There are horrifying stories of rape and murder by the Japanese troops. Did you know their army, the infantry that is, travel by bicycle? They have pedalled their way down the whole peninsula wearing lightweight uniforms and soft shoes while our poor squaddies are weighed down with packs and greatcoats. Rain pours down unceasingly but it's so hot that everyone sweats and steams like a Turkish bath. It still isn't clear what will happen when we go, whether they will fight on to the last man or just cave in through weariness and despair.

Where will they strike next? The obvious places are India once they have finished with Burma and then Australia. All the Aussie troops which are being wasted here should have been evacuated to defend their own country and perhaps the Indians too but without our cover it couldn't be done. As it is we're bombed and shelled several times a day. Karol is very cool. I suppose he's seen it all before. I like him better the more I get to know him.

Meanwhile I hope you're all right and there haven't been any more raids in your neck of the woods. I'll post this the first chance I get. Then you'll know that at least we got away from here before the curtain came down.

> Your loving bro,
> Gerald

This letter was rejected in its entirety by the censor and never reached its destination.

*

20 March 1942

Today I begin my English diary, partly to practise my English and partly because I have something at last I want to record. Last night I went to the Polish club with Eva whom I have met at Mrs Fentiman's centre, helping with the tea urn. She had had terrible news and wanted distraction. It seems that every day thousands are taken away from Poland in cattle trucks never to be seen again. For her this is new and distressing. She and her brother escaped as I did and came to England. He is in the Polish Air Force. Talking to her and to others at the club I realized that I am different even from them. They speak together in their own language but even although many of them have very good German we did not speak it. Perhaps in private we might but in public it might be overheard by the English who would perhaps be angry.

This I can understand when I go out into the city. Although we do not have the big raids every night now but only the little hit-and-run raids, so much damage has already been done that everyone wonders how it is to be rebuilt. Already in some places the weeds are beginning to grow over the first bombed sites, tall purple flowers, very graceful, that the English call fireweed because they say it grew first after the Great Fire of London in the seventeenth century. In other places walls are propped up with pieces of wood. You can see into half a house and know people are still living in the one next to it. Everywhere there are broken buildings and what are not broken are grey with dust from the others, their windows shuttered and boarded waiting renewal. The city goes on. The people get up and go to work also in a grey relentless way. Every day we hear that the RAF is bombing Germany. Hamburg of course is a necessary target, all the streets and squares I remember as if in a dream that becomes a nightmare. To bomb is all that the British can do because everywhere they are defeated in ordinary battle, in the desert and the jungle, and by the U-boats at sea.

It is clear that Germany whatever the outcome (I like this word which I have looked up in a dictionary I found in a secondhand bookshop). Even to buy a German/ English dictionary is difficult. The man in the shop was very stooped and scholarly with little half-moon glasses. I felt I had to explain as I brought it forward from the dusty, dark shelf where there were the works of Goethe, Schiller, Heine, that I was a refugee. He was very kind, very civilized. He said that he had thought about leaving the books there and then had decided that they were not responsible. Nietzsche he has withdrawn for the duration. Inside the dictionary which was only sixpence is a bookplate from a school prize-giving with a girl's name in it: Ada Collins. German Literature Prize, 1931. *A Good Book is the Precious Lifeblood of a Master Spirit*. It reminds me of the Master Race which I was not a member of. I have lost my sentence but I shall not go back.

Last night sitting and talking in the club in English, it came to me that I am no longer a German and that whatever happens I shall never return there. The Poles will go back to Poland one day but perhaps I shall never see Hamburg again and if I do, it and I will be utterly different. But also last night sitting at the long table with the European faces and uniforms all round me I suddenly became convinced that I would live; should live perhaps I mean. All this time I have been grieving with no sense of personal survival but last night there was one man who talked to me very earnestly, who asked if I would go to the cinema with him on my next evening off and for the first time I felt the stirring of sexual desire, my body remembered, as if after a long illness, and I said yes I would go out with him if he is still here next week. Perhaps we shall speak a little German in private. Can I make love in a foreign language?

Whatever happens, and this is just a chance wartime encounter, I must cease being a German if I ever was one. I have passed into limbo, into statelessness and now I must choose what to become. I can probably stay here and take out British papers. The Fentimans and the others I have met through them would help me. Or I could go to the United States, to Cousin Willy and his family. Or I could go to Palestine where they talk more and more of establishing a Jewish state 'when the war is over'.

Yet I feel myself a European. That has not gone and I do not wish to be forced back upon religion. Sometimes I go to the synagogue here but nothing moves in me, more than it ever did. The singing is nice but I do not hear God speaking to me and if he exists then he cannot be the God of the Jewish people who should hide Himself in shame. It is true the Jews have always suffered throughout history and some, the religious and the Zionists would say this is no worse than the Diaspora but it is clear from what is happening in Poland, what has already happened in Germany that it is much worse, that it is different in kind from anything else. Even the pogroms of Russia were spontaneous manifestations of the hatred the oppressed turn on each other when the oppressors are too high to reach. This is calculated, with a basis in philosophy and politics, with its lists of those who are going away 'to work', and never coming back.

However the English still do not understand because they are not trained to think. They do not study philosophy at school as we did. It is not a British subject. They prefer not to think, to pretend to themselves that they are muddling through. Thinking is not good. The intellectual is despised. It is of course part of their strength in this war. Because they do not think, they cannot be defeated, cannot visualize defeat. Even when they are beaten back as they are in North Africa they believe it is only for today. They criticize their leaders. Churchill is unpopular because it goes badly at the moment but they still discuss it all in their House of Commons and put it to the vote in the middle of this war. Everyone is sustained by illusions but especially the British. Their illusion is that if you don't admit something it is not there. This I remember is called 'solipsism'. No English person except perhaps one or two in their universities would even know what I mean.

If Germany is gone for me for ever then German must go too, at least as an everyday language, a mother tongue that has to be cut out like the little mermaid's in the

135

Hans Christian Andersen story. (That word too 'mermaid' I had pleasure to look up.) Whether I go to America or stay here I must perfect my English. Fortunately I am in an English house not a German one, which would make everything more difficult. And my evening class in English literature is a help because everyone else in it is British and I have learned to discuss the poets in English. Now we are following the English novel. Mrs Fentiman is very happy when I tell her that I am studying English. She says she will lend me books to read other than Dickens and Galsworthy which I already know.

This afternoon I bought this child's exercise book. The paper of course, very poor. It is like their wartime bread, grey and coarse but without any flavour. I shall write in it every day I can when I am not too tired after all the cleaning and queueing and cooking, and then perhaps helping in the centre or taking the tea to the underground train shelter where the poor are sleeping above the rails as if on one long tombstone, side by side in their stink. In a little I shall put out my torch I am using to write this to save the electricity and open the curtains to look up at the sky. Tonight there is no moon so perhaps there will be no warning and we shall not have to go down into the basement. The broken nights are very bad for the doctor. If there is no raid I shall see the city falling away from my hilltop attic under the starshine, quite dark but peaceful with the scars hidden by night.

My Darling Harry,

How are you, where are you my dearest one? I don't think you can be in this country or you'd telephone me. I have so much to tell you that can't be properly put in a letter. Now that the raids have quietened down and not so many ambulance drivers are needed some of us have been asked to volunteer for special duties. We aren't supposed to discuss them and we have to sign the official secrets act. If I tell you that my ability to do the *Times* crossword in five minutes flat is very useful you will understand. It means being on regular part-time duty but also on stand-by for emergencies. The work is very exacting while you're doing it. You can really only stand a couple of hours at full stretch although we work six-hour shifts or sometimes more if something exciting is going on. I long to tell you all about it.

This letter is really to ask if there's any chance of your getting leave soon. If not Betty Charlwood has invited me down for a weekend and I think I might go if I can scrounge some petrol as the weekends are very boring here in the blackout without you. Last time I popped down her brother Gerry had one of his shipmates with him, a rather tragic Pole, a count, Betty said. I thought I might invite him to come and see us, have dinner when you're next home as I'm sure you'd find him interesting to talk to.

I saw our little one at half term. She's shooting up but still a rather strange child and doesn't seem to mix much with the others which is rather worrying. I think she still sees the evacuee boy from the village which is quite remarkable but not, I hope, sinister. I asked her about him and she was evasive, said something about his going into the navy. I didn't know whether to give her a pep talk but she seems so young, although I suppose all children grow up faster in wartime.

Everything is pretty grim at the moment, isn't it? I need you to explain to me what's happening and why we seem to be in such a mess even with the Americans in on our side. Most of the time I try not to think about it all, just live from day to day hoping each one will bring me news that you're coming home and that we can be together again if only for a few hours.

I can't remember if I told you in my last that the whole of Billy Borke's place has been requisitioned for an evacuated school and they are living in the boot cupboard or the maid's bedroom, I forget which, trying not to bump into the little horrors on the backstairs. She says the floors will never be the same again. They were allowed to shut up the drawing-room completely because of the plaster work. It must be galling to know the head and his wife are sleeping in your bed in the master bedroom while you're up in the attic.

Here we just get shabbier and shabbier. The terrible Mary Gore dropped in yesterday and I could see she was looking for dust and pictures askew as if I had nothing better to spend my time on, and I know she gets his batman to help her out. A regular little handyman about the place! She had the gall to ask if I'd made any jam this winter and gave me her foul receipt for marrow and ginger. Yuck! I find the beetroot and cabbage worthies v. boring. I know I shouldn't and they do do marvellous work but I always feel they're looking down on the rest of us, at least the Gore Blimey does. And she never smiles.

Must dash and get into uniform for my stint of duty. I shouldn't boast and wouldn't, except to you, but I did do rather well in the aptitude tests, for this special thing. Do let me know if you can when you're coming. We're expected to join in the station dances from time to time, and I'd hate to be out when you do come home. Of course I shan't go to Betty's if you get leave.

Masses and masses of love and jammy kisses from your devoted and lonesome wifey.

xx Daffy down-in-the-mouth Dilly xx

Sea Shanty
——————— *1942*

This * * * * town's a * * * * cuss,
No * * * * trams no * * * * bus,
And no one cares for * * * * us,
    In * * * *   * * * *

The * * * * roads are * * * * bad,
The * * * * folk are * * * * mad,
They make the brightest* * * * sad,
    In * * * *   * * * *

Everything is * * * * dear,
A * * * * bob for * * * * beer,
And is it good? No * * * * fear!

In * * * * * * * *

The * * * * flicks are * * * * cold,
The * * * * seats are * * * * sold,
You can't get in for * * * * gold,
    In * * * * * * * *

The * * * * dances make you smile,
The * * * * band is * * * * vile,
It only cramps your * * * * style,
    In * * * * * * * *

No * * * * sports, no * * * * games,
No * * * * fun, the * * * * dames
Won't even give their * * * * names,
    In * * * * * * * *

Best bloody place is bloody bed
With ice upon your bloody head,
You might as well be bloody dead,
    In bloody * * * *

           58 Maryland Street
               E 15
            Tues. 5.30

Dear Hilly,

    I thought I should write and tell you although this isn't my usual day for writing that Cousin Bet has bad news of Cyril. It seems he is a prisoner of war in Burma. She is very relieved to know he is alright as she hadnt heard from him for such a long time. The last she heard they thought they were going to North Africa or India but apparantly they were diverted to Singapore to help out there and were captured when it fell. Daddy says Cyril will have a hard time of it with the Japs who dont really believe in prisoners. They think you should die fighting. Also they have a different standard of living to us and can get by on a bit of rice. I shant mention any of this to Cousin Bet as she has had enough to worry about lately and is just pleased to know he is alive. Apparently we can send parcels through the Red Cross though they take a long time to get there. Daddy says the climate in Burma will be against them as it is very humid. I remember my brother Siddy writing this when he was in India in the 1914–18 war. Did I tell you they have taken Bet on at the dairy, not doing the same job as Cyril but working at the depot. She says the money is a great help as the children grow out of their clothes so fast. She has bought some extra coupons off of me as we dont use all ours. I said she was welcome to them but she wanted to pay me a pound for twenty. With the bit extra I bought 2 vests, blue wool for a cardigan, 2 new chicks a shilling each and still had 2/6 for the Russian Red Cross. I must say we have never been so well off with mine and Daddys money. I got a rise of ½d an hour which brings me up to £3 a week.

Well dear how are you going on. Daddy and I are going on nicely now the weather is getting better and it isnt so foggy for him going out nights. I hope you arent working too hard and you will be coming home soon, all being well. Things have been quite quiet recently and I don't bother to go down the shelter always when Daddy is out. His platoon has been moved to AA duty which doesnt suit him as they have lost the Duke of Cumberland as their headquarters and are not so independant. He says it means that they think Hitler has called off the invasion. Im sorry for the poor folk in other towns who are getting it now but I suppose we must expect it because we are giving Germany such a pasting. I was stood behind a young woman in a queue for tinned fruit yesterday dinner-time and she told me she was away working on munitions in Bath when she was bombed out and had to come home. She found the house had been bombed here too and the people who lived downstairs were gone. A lot of her things were missing. It is terrible that people can do such things in wartime. She seemed a nice enough young woman although a bit painted up for my taste and her hair peroxided but then everyones the same these days. She said her husband was in North Africa and her boy was evacuated so she had no one to come home for. Theyve directed her to another factory in

East Anglia so shes off there next week. I told her to take warm clothes because theres always a wind there from the North Sea. I told her you are working there 'down on the farm'. Should you have the time you might drop a line to Cousin Bet but most probably you are too busy. The young woman you are sharing with sounds very nice. I hope we shall meet her some time. Daddy and I had a good laugh at your story of the bull.

Well dear I must say cheerioh and run up the top to put this in the post before Daddy gets back wanting his tea. We are having stuffed hearts today and although I say it they are smelling a treat. This is all for now with all our love to you from your loving Mummy and Daddy xxx

x x x

He has been a good boy lately.

We set off early this morning for the valley where the scouts had reported a sighting of Group 3. I had found it very hard to sleep last night and imagined I could hear firing away to the north but I think it was only thunder and the flashes were lightning. Sometimes it seems wrong to be peacefully pursuing one's own interests while everyone else is at war but perhaps what we are doing here will lead to greater knowledge and understanding even of human nature and thus be beneficial in the end. It is hard to remember the excellent work done by German ethologists and pre-war visits to Berlin University and not be disturbed by what is happening.

The dew was very heavy on the tall grasses and although we were following a trail we were soon soaked to the skin. A fresh breeze chilled our bodies through our damp shirts but as we knew how hot it would be later the sensation was rather pleasant than otherwise. We began to see traces of chimp activity, broken branches and empty nests which we examined to try to gauge how recently they had been occupied. We then continued along the path through a grove of palm oil trees whose splayed bushes rattled in the morning wind.

All of a sudden I was aware of dark shapes ahead grouped in and around a pair of fig trees. We immediately withdrew and I focused my binoculars on the little gathering. If this was Group 3 they were not, as far as I knew, used to human contact. We had seen them only once before and believed they had come from further east. The group consists of an adult male, obviously the dominant member, another younger adult male, a juvenile aged about six, an older female with an infant about two years old and a young pregnant female. They were all feeding on the fig trees.

The juvenile stays fairly close to the pregnant female and is therefore perhaps an earlier offspring. From time to time he or the female wanders away in search of some different food but he always keeps an eye on her and if the distance threatens to grow too great between them he shortens it. After a while she approaches the older female and her offspring and reaches out a paw to touch it gently. The mother makes no move to push her away and indeed seems rather to approve the gesture which is a mixture of admiration for and interest in her young. It is as though in anthropomorphic terms the pregnant female were saying, 'Is this what it will be like?'

Meanwhile the leader, a fine mature specimen, is half-dozing against the trunk of a tree munching on a handful of hard nuts. His eyes seem to be closed but he gives the impression that he would be instantly and fully awake if danger loomed. The chimpanzee of course has no natural predators although they themselves prey on the young of other species. We were very surprised by this when we first observed it, since it has been generally supposed that the chimpanzee is, like the gorilla, exclusively vegetarian. In fact they seem to be like humans, omnivorous, meat forming an occasional part of their diet, and clearly a great delicacy, young monkeys and baboons being the chief items, rather like roast sucking pig, lamb or veal with us.

Like with humans, too, their chief enemies seem to be

old age and sickness. When a member of a group falls ill the others will try to support it with food for a time, but there usually comes a day when the group is seen without the sickly member and we know that it has probably died. In the forest of course the bodies are soon disposed of by an assortment of scavengers.

It is hard to explain this apparently altruistic behaviour of chimpanzees towards sickly members of the group, in evolutionary terms. What could be its genetic survival function? The strongest bond is clearly between mother and offspring. There is little between mating pairs since all adult males will mate successively with a female in pink, whether in their own group or a visitor. Group bonding is loose and impermanent yet seems to serve a purpose, although what this can be in view of the lack of large predators is hard to tell. Nor does it always apply since couples will sometimes go off by themselves and young adult males will travel alone until they find a suitable group.

This, which we have numbered Group 3, continued feeding peacefully but I sensed a certain wariness about them as though they might be aware of our presence or perhaps had suffered some unsettling incident in the recent past which had made them a little on edge. The juvenile male seemed particularly uneasy. At last the young adult came a little too near to the leader who opened his eyes fully and stared hard and motionlessly at the intruder. The young male stood his ground for a moment and then backed away rather like someone leaving a royal presence. Then he ran noisily to the nearest tree, swung himself into the lower branches and vented his frustration by screaming and shaking the leaves wildly. The others looked up at him and then went back to feeding.

Eventually he climbed down, in both senses of that expression, and moved surreptitiously towards the pregnant female and her young escort. The two males began a rough and tumble which ended when the younger one ran screaming to the female for protection. The adult male then approached her gently, putting out a paw, and

143

all three joined in a grooming session. If they are to stay in this area we shall have to give them all names as we have done with groups 1 and 2 in order to keep a proper record of their movements, relationships and social interactions.

Song of the Millenium

They put a thousand in the air and sent them off to
bomb.
We steered our way by the radio grid and most of us
came home.

We burned a city in revenge and laid its centre low
Then turned and climbed the flaming sky to make our
run for home.

The bomber's life is short and hard at twenty ops or so
We drink and gag and chase the girls and pray we'll get
back home.

We once were teachers, students, clerks with all the
world to roam
But now we're only bomber boys who may not make it
home.

That battered kite low in the sky limping on broken
wing
Carries seven weary flying men; two dead but coming
home.

We do not ask for grace or gongs as our wheels brush
the foam
Only to top the chalky walls that bar our way to home.

The rear gunner's so shot to bits they'll hose his turret
down
To wash away the blood and brains of what we carried
home.

They'll find enough to box and lower into the English loam
We'll know as the padre does his stuff he'd be glad we
brought him home.

Though the next millenium he sees must wait til
Kingdom Come
Those of us left will be up next week a thousand miles
from home.

Through flak and fighters, fingers crossed, to collide
with friend or foe
A thousand aery battleships, and some won't make it
home.

Oh the bomber's life is short but sweet as any down
below
So here's to beer and grateful girls tomorrow when we
get home.

Alan Purbright

Dear Ole Buddy,

This is the first chance I've had to set down and give you the jazz from somewhere overseas though I'm not allowed to tell you exactly where we is stationed. However I will tell you it's as flat as a Midwest prairieland, going on for miles to the sea, and the freezing wind and rain never seem to stop. Apart from that everything round here is jess fine and I'm sure glad I joined the army to see the world though did I tell you in fact I is in the air force brother. Forgive all these touches of jazzspeak. Us coloured boys talk cool cat when we're together so that the big ofay flying man caint dig our meaning. Cos of course they don't allow us near the machines except to take them apart and put them together again when our masters have busted them all up and to wipe they arses (I mean the machines, figuratively speaking) when they messed themselves and fill them up with gas and oil. Whitey don't believe niggers are smart enough to make flyers or maybe they afraid if they teach us to fly and put us at the controls we never come down to earth again.

Meanwhile back at the camp we got our own band going in which your ole buddy is blowing a mean horn again, and this way we get to travel around this countryside a little, playing for the locals as well as at other US service stations and for the Limey troops as well. Also we get passes to go out into town and they even lay on transport to get us there. Now this has been a big surprise to me, more than mebbe it would be to you cos you been north and I ain't, but in this country ain't no bar. We is mixing with white folk all the time, socializing in the English pubs, being invited to their houses to take tea, riding in the same buses, sitting anywheres, and in the movies too. First time I went to a moviehouse, me and some of the other cats on our first trip into town, we looking for the white and coloured signs everywhere and when we don't see them we don't know what to do. We think mebbe we ain't allowed in nowheres. We still arguing outside and we see there's two lines but white folks in both but they got a sign in front with 2s. 6d. and 1s. and 1s. 9d. on them which we have learned from the booklet they give us on the way over is English money. So we pretty flush and I say: Last one in line's chicken, and I join on the end of the 2s. 6d. because that is the shorter and suddenly we's all going forward and there's this old white guy in a kinda commissionaire's uniform smiling like Uncle Sam and saying, 'Come on in boys, plenty of seats', and there we is up in the balcony like young gods.

That was just the beginning. Comes the end of the first month and our sergeant calls us all to in the mess hall for a piece of news. We is going into town to the American Red Cross dance which is organized by the local Limey ladies. But Sarge, says some cat, what's the good of a dance with no chicks. We can't dance together. Chicks will be provided, says the sergeant, and you will behave yourselves and any man who steps out of line will find himself in the pen.

Sarge, says another one, we gonna step it with white chicks? There sure as hell ain't no other round here, says our sergeant. Well you know old buddy our mommas told us never to mess with no white chicks cos they sure as hell mean trouble, but an order's an order so come Saturday night you could of lit your Lucky Strike off our shoes and our faces and our hair, and cut your fingers on the creases in our pants. We oiled our bodies with anything we could lay hands on in the camp. In our hut (did I tell you we all sleep in wooden huts in a field just like white folks' summer camps back home only it raining all the time) some smart cat snuck a bottle of corn oil from the cookhouse and we just glisten except for one fool say it make him look too dark and he rather leave those scaly salt marks on him skin.

I so nervous time we get to the hall where the dance is I glad I'se not trying to blow my horn, my mouth is that dry. I feel sick too right to my stomach. We get out of the truck and smooth our hair and set our caps straight and head up the steps into this hall. Soon as we get to the door I can hear a band beating it up and then we inside and is all white folk. A lady is selling tickets and we all dig in our pocket books and she smile and we smile back. That way, she say, and we go forward through the swing doors with the noise of the band busting out. I knowed first thing it was a British band and they all airmen in uniform playing nice and easy but nothing jumping, you know what I mean, but jess fine for dancing close. The music stop and somebody jump to the mike while we still standing there looking about nervously and announce a Paul Jones. Our hands is grabbed and we is galloping round the hall to the music with all the white chicks holding hands going round the other way in the middle, and then the music stop and we all stop and I step forward to this chick expecting her to slap my face but she all break out in a smile and hold out her arms and I think in a minute you gonna wake up man.

So that's how it all started. I swallow and feel like my Adam's apple just been replaced by a baseball and away we drift and she's a good mover not so kinda liquid as our chicks but smooth and quick to follow. I think we better make some talk before the Paul Jones begin again and I ask her can I have the next dance when this is over cos she the first girl I danced with in Britain and she smile and say yes. I say 'girl' but she a mature woman I can see that straight away, just nice and ripe and that's all the better. In the next dance we talk some more and she says her man is away in Africa somewhere, and that seems strange and like life is pulling some sort of a fast one on us all. Her name's Milly and she's working on parachutes. I like the way she's told me the truth about her ole man straight away when some chicks would have pretended to be free. So here I am already dating a white married chick, but ain't nothing wrong about it, jess friendly like.

Course people stare when they see we walking out together but only a quick look and away quite polite. And indeed these people like us coloured cos our mammies brought us up to be respectful whereas some of the ofay American troops are a mite loud and pushy for them. That's what the ladies at the Red X sez anyways. These people had a hard time ole buddy and they desperate and grateful for anything we give them, and the little children go begging in the street for candy and gum and pennies. The chicks look pretty low man, with no stockings and very short skirts showing they bare legs. We take them tinned stuff from the PX, corned beef and butter, bananas, grapefruit, anything. You know what gets them most is the wrapping paper. They really love it because everything here is wrapped in newsprint or brown paper and even that you have to take with you to the shops. The food is mostly terrible, especially the coffee. The beer is warm and like goat's piss and water. They drink it by the gallon to get some sort of kick out of it. How I longs for good liquor and a plate of collard greens, red beans and rice, Southern fried chicken, good Creole eating. The only good food is fried fish and French fries, called by the British chips. That is something like home cooking. You stands in line to buy it in a little shop where they is frying all the time, and for a few cents you can get as much as you can eat in a piece of newsprint.

Everything here is pretty run down and dirty and it all looks worse in the rain. Us coloured feel the cold here badly. The government is always giving us shit about why this country is so grimy as if we is so dumb we couldn't work it out ourselfs. But I'm glad I'm here and I wouldn't have missed the trip for anything cos I know now it's the first time I been treated like a man not a black boy. These people is so poor they make we seem rich but they is still free and we ain't. No way.

I almost forgot to tell you. For Independence Day they let some of our great white flyers join in a raid on Holland, their first since we got here. . . .

Darling,

How is it all going? I hope it isn't too bad at home and your mother is better than you feared. Did your brother get compassionate leave and is he there now? I long to know everything. Your bed looks very small and white somehow without you in it. I've just finished the milking. Bessie seems rather low and was obviously a bit tender to the touch. We're hoping it isn't mastitis. Mr Jeavons says he'll go over for the vet tomorrow if she's still sore. He's grumbled a lot about your absence. I can't say he misses you but he's worrying about whether you'll be back in time for harvest. Typical!

I miss you horribly, but I'm really more worried about the cause of you going and hoping desperately that all will be well for you. Meanwhile we keep as busy as ever and Mrs Jeavons came up with a splendid shepherd's pie for supper. I have to confess I more or less ate your share. Afterwards she looked at the dish and said, 'I thought with Gwen away there might be some left for tomorrow.' So I said rather sharply I thought that since I was doing the work of two I needed to eat for two. That isn't meant to be a complaint, darling, but rather to make you smile and to let you know that life goes on in the same way in your absence but very emptily.

Does your brother look like you? You said he is in the navy on a destroyer. Are you very close? As an only I find it hard sometimes to imagine what it's like to have a brother or sister and I'm not sure I should like it very much. We have always been just the three of us. In fact until I met you I'd never really loved anyone except my parents. Sylvie, I've told you, was just a friend, someone to talk to and go around with.

I've been reading *A Dusty Answer* as instructed. It's very moving but does everything always have to be so sad? I don't really understand why she goes to bed with Roddy, except that she always thought he was the one she was in love with. See how dangerous it is when onlies get involved with families. You'll have to keep me away from your brother, especially if he looks like you. But seriously to go back to the sadness, I don't feel like that at all. I feel liberated, as if I want to dance and sing and tell the world, starting with the Jeavons. Do you think they suspect? No it would never cross their minds, any more than it would my parents'. What about you? Does your brother know? Oh so many questions and you're not here to answer them or to. . . . But suddenly I'm shy of writing it even in a letter to you.

You don't know how good it feels not to have to pretend any more, not to have to go to grotty dances with spotty boys and wonder why you don't enjoy the obligatory grope in the back seat of the one and nines. If it hadn't been for the war and you I might never have found out there could be anything else. You're my Welsh witch who has opened my eyes when all the so-called handsome princes failed. Shall we go and live in Wales when the war is over and have a farm or a school or a teashop? Now I can hear you saying: Don't look too far ahead. Enjoy the moment.

But darling I want it to go on, and on. I want to see us stretching ahead for miles, aeons. There's so much I have to read and find out about. Until now I've just done what was put in front of me to pass my exams. In our world, I mean at home, going to college and being a teacher is the highest aspiration. We're not really en-couraged to think too much or too far. I know Daddy thinks a lot about history and politics but it's almost like a secret vice. And anyway it's somehow alright for men to think but not for women. Mummy actually believes you should vote the same way as your husband and you certainly shouldn't have different views of things. There's so much that can't be even mentioned let alone discussed. When I said to you that I just didn't know it was possible for people of the same sex to really love each other beyond the school crush stage, that was literally true. I thought it was something you went through and then came out of into real sex. *Nightwood* looks exciting but strange. I think I shall go on to that next and hear your voice reading it to me as we cling together in one bed. Come back to me as soon as you can and if not write to me. I've never had a letter from you. That's something to look forward to.

Fonthill School
3 July 1942

Dear Lennie,

I am sorry but we are not allowed to receive letters from or write to people that our parents do not know, and I am therefore returning this.

Yours sincerely,
Ailsa Pearmain

Dear Mr Gardiner,

Thank you very much for offering to publish *Song of the Millenium* in your *In Times Like These* issue of *Poetry Vanguard*. Will it be exclusively work from people in the Forces? I enclose a brief biographical note as requested. There really isn't a lot to say in any case since I came straight into the RAF from school. I don't know how other people find it but there doesn't seem to be much time for writing in this job. I look forward to receiving my three free copies of the magazine. Perhaps you should send them to my home address in case I have moved on by then. . . .

Largs Aug. 42

Dear Harry,

I suppose that in retrospect it will be said that we have learned a great deal from this fiasco but all I can see at the moment is the cost. Some Jubilee that turned out! What I can't understand is why when the first dummy Yukon was such a disaster anyone should have thought the thing could succeed. True the second was a bit better but somebody with an ounce of nous ought to have seen that only made a fifty per cent probability of success, unless it was believed we should get progressively better, always a dangerous assumption because of unforeseeables. It must have been a political decision, I suspect, pressure from both sides, the Yanks and the Russkies to do something, instead of piddling around in N. Africa. Obviously the Russians would like some of the heat taken off them which is perfectly understandable with the Jerry summer campaign pounding away, but I would have thought the Yanks had their hands full in the Solomons with the Japs, and wouldn't be thinking seriously of a second front in Europe yet.

I can't help feeling like a guinea pig though we came out of it better than the wretched Canadians. I feel so steamed up about it all I'd love to be able to get down to see you and talk it all out but Scotland's a bloody long way and I'm tied down here trying to sort things out. I hope your wound isn't a Blighty one that will let you off the hook and leave us all to get on without you. I expect you're hamming it up a bit to be fussed over by the nurses. What bad luck for that American Ranger to be the first Yank killed in Europe.

At least you and Lovat's lot managed to achieve your objectives to some extent and God knows everything would have been a damn sight worse if you hadn't kept that battery busy, though having said that I almost wonder if things could have been *much* worse. Really Montgomery was lucky to be on his way to Africa before it happened. How strange fate is. Gott would never have done for there to pull things together. He was too tired, war weary. He must have been praying for something like that crash to take him out of it all but not so finally of course. The whole war could be changed just because a man died before he could take up his command. Not that I think it will necessarily be so. We can but hope.

Anyway it should have shown our masters what folly it

would be to launch a second front modelled on that little jaunt. The troops would never get off the beaches even if the LCs could get them there. I'm sure you'd agree even though your lot made it up the cliffs. As soon as that flare lit everything up like day I knew we were sitting ducks, all strung out behind that antiquated steamboat that was meant to be the HQ.

In the long term I suppose we may have done some good by drawing some of Jerry's troops away from the eastern front or from reinforcing Rommel but on the other hand we've surely alerted him to the idea that one day there will be a real landing on the French coast not just this kind of hit-and-run affair and caused him to strengthen his defences. The word has it that Montgomery wanted the whole thing called off after the first postponement because he was afraid it had been compromised. Certainly it looked as if Jerry knew we were coming. As for the tanks I wonder whose brilliant idea that was? Once again it looks to me like an attempt to make the whole thing seem bigger than it was to impress somebody or other, and I don't mean the enemy.

First reports indicate a fifty per cent loss in killed or wounded. The RAF are admitting to over a hundred planes shot down and the navy lost a destroyer as well as the LCs. Of course Joe Public isn't being told this, only that we're hitting back. I suppose the psychological effect on morale has to be put on the plus side, but I feel sickened by the general rejoicing and can't help thinking of Peter who'd only been with us a day. The men, what's left of them, don't seem at all cast down and are looking forward to the next go but it will be a long time before we can rebuild enough to make anything except very small in-and-out jobs feasible.

There's apparently a fuss going on about the prisoners who got put down while they were tied up. It's hard to see what else can be done with prisoners on a raid, at least til you get them into the boat and if you can't spare men to look after them. I saw one of them being taken off when we got back to Seaford. He looked pretty windy. I thought the RN rather let us down for once with their

covering fire. It might as well have been peashooters.
Incidentally have you ever seen anything like what Jerry
threw at us? That makes me think he must have known.
We might just as well have sent the planes in the night
before but I suppose they were worrying about civilian
casualties. All in all I'm glad it's over and it's been a
great help to write this bellyaching letter to you and get
it off my chest.

I suppose you'll be going back to the divine Daphne
for a bit of home cooking. Do give her my love. I don't
imagine they'll let you lie around for long so gather ye
rosebuds as the poet says. . . .

. . . and about bleeding time too. You are a man now
since you joined the navy so you will understand that
sometimes this life leads you to cuss and swear a bit.
This has been a right shambles for months. We all got
very down when Tobruk went and it built up a feeling
that Rommel couldnt be beat. Now this new bloke has
come to sort things out. He started right off at GHQ
combing out those whod been on the mike there in cushy
numbers, mainly the old soldiers. Hes also sorted out the
men from the boys or old boys and we now have a new
CO. As part of all this I suppose, Ive got a third stripe
and moved into the sergeants mess. Theres some in there
dont care much for us WSO boys being given promotion
but theyll have to lump it.

The new AC is a little wiry bloke. They call Rommel
the Desert Fox but this ones a bit foxy too, little tash and
sharpish features. We was due a visit from him yesterday
and all lined up on parade. He made a thorough job of it
and I got spoken to. Perhaps he could see I was new
made up. Asked me very quietly how long and said it
was a good time for it and there was a lot to be done. So
we shall see if things go any better.

I had a note from your mother which took a long time
to get here so I dont know when this will reach you if it
ever does. She wrote that the house was very badly
knocked about including most of our stuff and she was

living in a hostel near her work. When this lots over well have to start again looking for a place and everything. Somehow I cant see meself going back on the buses. But then I cant see no end to it at the moment neither. Its funny, being out here so long you lose all sense of time and place. Its partly the desert. Were in a front line position with the minefields and sandhills all round but not much else. Were dug in very nicely waiting for Jerry to attack. The moon here is very big, more like a harvest moon back home only every night. The RAF is doing its job better too. Perhaps the new AC had geed them up a bit. The planes go over us towards the enemy all night and we put down a heavy barrage ourselves also. You get the feeling its any minute now.

In some ways Id rather it was like this than when we go down the coast for a rest. Its hard keeping everybody at it and up to the mark when the need seems to be gone and yet its got to be done or blokes get flabby and then the whole caboodle goes down the drain as it has been doing. The NCOs have been told to pull it all together which is what weve been about these last couple of weeks.

Now son I want to say Im proud of you joining up to be a sailor. Do your best and nobody can do more and keep your head down. Youve got an education there as well as a job for life if you want it. When you first wrote me you wanted to sign on and would I give permission I was in two minds for a bit because as you know Ive never thought much of the old soldiers in this outfit but thinking it over I see the navy is different. Theres a lot more to learn like navigation, and you can work your way up better if youre starting from a boy. Who knows where you might end up. Youve had a good beginning at the high school and done well to get all your exams as you did. Just keep that up and youll be alright and do better than your Dad ever done or your mother either.

It seems funny her living away. Were all separated now on our different roads and no home to go back to. I suppose it will all work out in the end and well get together again somewhere when this lots over. I ought to tell you to watch out for the girls in every port. Always keep yourself clean and if you go with a woman as you will in time though theres no need to rush at your age make sure to give yourself a good going over with soap and water after. You know what I mean. Drop me a line from time to time to let me know how youre going on also your mother of course though shes not much of a hand at writing herself. Did you know your great grandfather on my mothers side was a sailor, merchant that would be in those days. There was an old photograph of him up the rigging my mother kept at the bottom of the trunk. I wonder what became of it. Perhaps if you have time and have your picture taken you could send me a snap. You must look a bit different from when I saw you last just before you was evacuated still in short trousers. Your old Dad has got some brown knees now I can tell you.

Well son its time to do the rounds before lights out. The guns are coming on very strong tonight and I reckon Jerry will try his push before long. This will be our first test to see how were coming along under the new bloke. I dont think hes one for heroics but rather a steady sort which suits me fine. This has been quite a long letter for me. I hope I get one back from you some time.

All the best,
Your Dad

Witham, Sat.

Dear Gracie,

I am in the club. Can you fix something up for me. Ill be down London next weekend and come round your house to see whats what. Its a Yank. Its early days but I missed this time and Im always regular as clockwork. Hes a nice boy. I havent toled him nothing nor no one else.

Milly

Dear Lennie,

I'm very, very sorry I had to write to you like I did from
school and send back your letter unopened. It was because you put your name and address on the envelope.
Our old toad of a head intercepted it and called me into
her study. She sat there looking like a witch with the
letter in her hand. I almost. . . . myself with fright as I
couldn't see what it was. Then she asked me who
Midshipman L. Kirby, Royal Navy, might be and if my
parents knew him and had given permission for us to
write to each other. It was absolutely ghastly. I couldn't
lie in case she asked Mummy. I said you were the
brother of a friend, which wasn't true either I know, but
no one could check on it. Now I'm on holiday at my
grandmother's at the address above and it's all right to
write to me here. Please, please do, even if you only send
the last one back again. I hope you weren't too cross.
The head made me show my letter to you to my form
mistress so I couldn't even explain properly. If you send
a letter here after I've gone back to school I've arranged
for Nanny to send it on to me in another envelope so that
no one will suspect it.

I keep thinking that you might be in Southampton
very close by and wondering what excuse I can make to
get Nanny to take me there. She's very keen on the war,
too, as she has a brother in the army and we have a big
map on the nursery wall and stick flags in it to show
what's happening. It's all pretty awful at the moment
isn't it, but I think we are holding our own, especially in
Russia.

Did I tell you my father has been wounded and that's
why I'm here because he has to be kept quiet at home
and needs all my mother's attention when she isn't on
duty. He was in a big job somewhere. He doesn't say
where but I think it was Dieppe. He was shot in the foot.
It isn't serious but he's still on crutches and gets rather
cross.

I wonder if you can get to the cinema very often. Last

157

week Nanny and I went to see Sabu in *The Jungle Book*. I think he is beautiful. I wanted to see *Reap the Wild Wind* but it's an 'A' and Nanny said it wasn't suitable. It has a giant squid at the end. Have you seen it? I wanted to see it because it is about the sea.

I go back to school next week. I shall send this to your last address and hope it reaches you.

Best wishes
Yours sincerely,
Ailsa

Near Alexandria 5 Nov. 1942

Dear Hilly,

I ought to be in bed though I'm utterly whacked, we all are, I'm too wound up to sleep yet. Sometimes it seems as if we haven't slept since we got here and in the last few days there hasn't been time to take all our clothes off, only our uniforms which we hang up ready to fling on if we're suddenly called. I don't think our Sister-in-charge lies down at all but she's one of the old guard and as tough as nails. They've never had nurses out here before. The army has always looked after its own. It makes you feel very Nightingalish, especially as the boys are so glad to see you and grateful for anything you can do for them.

We can hear the battle going on even though it's thirty miles away and the dust and smoke is tremendous. It's been going on for ten days and we seem to have won in the end and now be chasing Rommel along the coast. The wounded all say it's been very hard and confused and they're often glad to be out of it and as one said, 'Sleep in a bed with sheets on'. I feel so sorry for them as apart from whatever wounds they've got and some of them are heartbreaking, they're completely exhausted as well. But they don't complain.

They're also a very mixed lot. Masses of Aussies and New Zealanders and some Indian troops as well. I was speaking to one of them yesterday who'd been brought in with a head wound and been in a coma ever since. We're supposed to keep talking to them even when they don't respond because it sometimes helps to bring them round. He suddenly said, 'You're from London too', and opened his eyes. He said he came from Upton Park. I could have cried but Sister bustled up just in time and said, 'Well done nurse. Now, young man, no going back to sleep', and shoved a thermometer in his mouth!

Home seems such a long way away so how must it seem to them. Some of the veterans have been out in Africa three years with no home leave, just letters to look forward to and they take ages to get here. I'm so glad I volunteered to come out here rather than being stuck at home with all the old starchiness. Even though Sister is a bit of a harridan things are very different in a field hospital. They have to be.

We're right in the desert and there really are miles of sand, some hard and some very soft where the trucks all sink and then everyone has to pile out and help to push. Needless to say it's very hot, at least by day, or rather it was when we first arrived, it's cooler now, and surprisingly cold at night with very clear skies and bright moon and starlight. It's still terribly romantic even though there's a battle going on, and we're promised a trip to Alexandria when this lot's over and a dance at the officers' club. Perhaps its wrong to be thinking of such things with people being killed or disabled for life but somehow it makes it all the more important to live while you can. If we get a long weekend we can use the tennis courts in Cairo as honorary RAMC while putting up in a hotel terribly cheaply. Do you remember that last game you and I had in the park when the war hadn't even begun? I often think of how we were then and it seems like two different people, as if I was looking at them from a great distance and I don't just mean because I'm out here; two girls playing together in that summer evening with the smell of cut grass and the shadows of the trees growing longer over the bowling green. Now it's full of cabbages and potatoes.

I think I must be falling asleep to ramble on in this way so I'll say goodnight. It's much quieter now. I hope you're still enjoying digging for Victory. Perhaps you'll marry a farmer and I'll be carried off by an Arab Sheik! Write to me when you've time.

Lots of love,
Sylvie

Damn me when I went aft there was Harry crouching by the funnel so hung about with weapons he looked like a walking armoury. 'Hallo,' I said. 'I thought you were still at home licking your wounds.' 'Oh,' he said, 'it wasn't as bad as it looked and anyway I couldn't miss this.' 'I thought you were always popping on to enemy beaches,' I said. 'Yes,' he said, 'but this time we're here to stay for the first time. It isn't just in-and-out.' 'I hope you're right,' I said.

We were about three miles off Algiers and suddenly all the lights in the town went out, search lights came on and some shore batteries opened up. Fortunately the stuff bounced into the sea a few hundred yards away. 'Clearly they have not seen the American flag we are flying,' Karol said in his funny stiff way. They'd made us run one up in the belief that the French wouldn't fire at an American ship but no one told the French they weren't supposed to even if they could see it on a cloudy, moonless night!

All of a sudden I saw Harry's lot get up and change sides to starboard, I presumed for easier disembarkation. I was back on the bridge by now. A brilliant searchlight sprang up and trained on us and a couple of batteries opened fire again, one big shell landing on the port side of the funnel where Harry's lot had been and causing terrible carnage among the Americans who had taken their places.

Then all hell broke loose. We were listing badly and losing way. Our lads wanted to take down the Stars and Stripes and run up the White Ensign and hit back at the French gunners. Boxes of ammo on the deck began to burn and two chaps on Harry's lot had to cut the lashings on some crates of mortar bombs that were on fire and heave the lot into the drink. Even so our skipper wanted to attempt another run into the boom across the harbour, but in the end decided we hadn't sufficient knots so we had to put out to sea again and beach further west about five miles from the city, land what was left of the chaps and their gear and then get off again as best we could and back to Gib for repairs.

The news here is that they're having quite a sticky time of it, especially the Americans who are all green troops but there's also a great sense of elation. Next stop Italy, has my money on it. Nobody is very enthralled by the politicking that's gone on with the Vichy French, which seems to have been a mucky business all round but I suppose it was devil and deep blue sea. It wouldn't have looked good to start our comeback by killing a lot of Frenchies. It does make you wonder what you'd have done in their place and of course they're especially agin the senior service because of our bombing and shelling their ships in Oran in 1940. Now the fight is on again from both sides to see who gets the French fleet in Toulon, us or Hitler.

You'll have gathered from all this that I'm post officer at the moment and so can chatter on in this way. It's reckoned that Hitler will take over what's left of France because of the help we've had from some of the people in Algeria. The Arabs of course are pretty chuffed because they don't care for the French anyway and would like them all to go home. They've taken the chance to line their pockets, except that they don't have any but you can get an awful lot under a burnous. While they're patching our old girl together we take a run across with the supply ship to keep an eye on what's going on. It's a bit odd to see the officials who a few days ago were presumably strutting about passing on German orders now doing the same for us. The Yanks don't notice these things as much as we do and in the long term it's probably as well we provided the transport and they provided most of the troops.

Fancy seeing old Harry. I wonder what they were up to. If you're in touch with Daph don't mention it. I'm sure no one is supposed to know they were there. They were dressed up like American Rangers. We have a nasty feeling we shan't be allowed to hang around here for long, but will be sent off again on convoy escort or U-boat patrol probably the Arctic run again so we are soaking up the sun while we can and enjoying all the benefits of the Rock's night life when the *Luftwaffe* let us. Karol sends his love. . . .

Hugs and kisses,
Your bro, Gerry

Reading the reports in the newspapers I can feel the cold. The English don't know what it is like even though London is further north than Stalingrad. Their mother sea keeps them warm and wet even in winter. In Hamburg we were warmed a little also by the sea but Berlin is bitter with the wind from the east, and at Stalingrad men will freeze to death at night in their cold metal tanks. Should I feel pity for their young blond heads crowned with icicles? I should feel pity for everyone but I can't. Not even for the English who have housed me and fed me and who are grey and shabby with rationing and this war that consumes everything, all the necessities of life: food, warmth, clothes, houses. They endure because now I understand many of them, most did not have much before and therefore had less to lose. They are used to this life of enduring, of making do. They take a kind of pride in it.

The Germans will fall in Stalingrad. I see it as clearly as if it had already happened. The Russians encircle them and the cold cuts into their bones. Almost last month they had taken the city but the Russians refused to give up. They know that in their hearts the Germans despise them as they do us, that they and we are not fully human to the master race and there can be no compromise with them.

What must it be like to have a country to love with the very movement of your blood? We love something we have never seen, that is an idea, a memory rather than a place. The Russians fought house by house for every brick and stone of the city, with guns and grenades hand to hand as we should have fought when they came to the door with their bloody list. Now they will die by their thousands in the cruel wind. But if I feel no pity I feel no exaltation either. I think of Milton whom we are studying in class. Sometimes one wants to cry, 'Avenge O Lord thy slaughtered saints', and at other times, 'Nothing is here for tears'. I do not understand how the English have produced their poetry and their Empire and left their people so poor.

Now at last they have the Americans to help them, with their production of technology, which is almost Germanic except that it has a kind of vulgar luxuriance no continental could contrive. Sometimes when I meet other refugees and we talk about these things I feel I am very different from the rest of them too, as I am different from everyone else around me. I only wonder that everyone does not feel it. Most of them are happy for the war to be over so that they can go on to somewhere else. I feel I might stay here, that I don't want to see the Promised Land in case it turns out to be just another country I can not belong to.

Perhaps that is why when I meet a man at the Polish club that I think I will fancy and take into my arms, at the crucial moment I hold back. In my bed alone as I will be in a little, I think of making love and long for it but when there is the flesh and blood man the desire dies. This I do not understand and have not experienced before. Possibly it is the diet or the spirit's diet of loss. Soon it will be Christmas again, my fourth here. The Fentimans will give me cards and little presents and make a celebration not for the God of the Christians but for hope, for a turning towards the light, for a new year.

The winter has saved Russia once more and this time Hitler will find it harder to mount his summer campaign. Surely in Germany some will see it and understand that now is the time to stop before they all die in the desert or on the snow plain. Perhaps if they stop now I shall see Anna-Lise again. Perhaps Fräulein Blumberg will come back from the dead to teach English literature and I will tell her all I have learned about Milton. . . .

Hi there,

I don't know whether you've come back to Gib or have gone to find a new ship after your compassionate leave. I hope your mother is feeling better. I've only once played in Wales, in Cardiff at a factory. It was kind of you to come to our little impromptu and take me out to dine and dance. Your poor ship looked so battered I'm surprised you got her back to port at all. The other officers all seemed very nice. I expect you will miss them. It must be rather like us. You become almost like a family in the troupe. Sometimes I get very fed up with Fred's jokes and Jean Passmore's knitting but we've all stuck together though at the moment it looks as if we might be broken up as Fred has gone down with dysentery, after being shot through his trousers, fortunately the baggy clown's outfit, by a Jerry plane that came down and beat up our portable stage just as he was in the middle of his routine. The band was so surprised the horn player fell off the platform. The audience must have thought it was all part of the act because they roared with laughter. They liked it so much in fact that when the show was over they all went outside the wire and joined the queue for the next performance. We had to do three shows on the trot and even then they didn't want us to stop. If only more performers at home knew how they feel. We had to tell them we couldn't lay on a Stuka (that's what someone said it was) every time.

I think since we've lost Fred we shall be asked to join in with other parties and that will be the end of the Beltones which is sad. Some people are going on to West Africa, the White Man's Grave! Apparently it's all yellow fever and mosquitoes as big as bumble bees but they're desperate for female artists and in some places they haven't seen a white woman for years. Others are going to Tunisia to entertain the new forces there and some are following Monty's push westwards. Our trip

out here ¸from Gib was hair-raising. The plane had no
seats, just little aluminium trays like rows of bedpans and
no heating. We were blue with cold by the time we got to
Cairo. Perhaps that was what did for Fred rather than the
bullet through his bags. . . .

Soukrai POW Camp
Thailand
Jan. 1943

Lovely B. & B. with all home comforts. Tell it to the
Marines. Your letter received through Red X. Happy New
Year.

Love to all,
Cyril

From the unpublished memoirs of
Major, later Brigadier, Harry Pearmain, DSO, MC

We were in fact fighting two interrelated wars whose
origins, purposes and effects were very different. One, the
war in the east, may be said to have begun in the fifteenth
century when the first Europeans set sail to discover what
to them had become, after the fall of the Empire, unknown
lands that were, however, perfectly well known to their
own inhabitants and to the empires of the east; the other
was an internal European war in which ideology had been
made the hypothetical underpinning of a bid for territory
and dominance. The European war acted on events in the
east initially by a process of psychological contamination to
reverse centuries of colonialization, and ultimately con-
verted the military struggle to an economic one.

It is an interesting question how far Britain's imperial
supremacy in the late eighteenth and nineteenth centuries
contributed to keeping the majority of her own people as an
industrial peasantry or proletariat. In many ways the gov-
erning classes of Britain regarded her lower orders in much
the same terms as they did the conquered peoples of other
lands. Far from being Napoleon's (attributed) 'nation of

shopkeepers' we were actually Disraeli's two nations. The free yeomen who formed a wide social band in Elizabethan times had become factory hands and agricultural labourers while the other nations of Europe were developing their bourgeoisie. In freeing the Russian serfs the Bolshevik revolution adopted a model devised by a German intellectual based on British conditions. It was therefore oddly appropriate that Russia and Britain should become close allies, before America was forced into the war by Japan seeking to remove white domination in Asia while at the same time contesting who should be ultimate Asian boss of the liberated area with China, in a war that was in many ways a mirror of the struggle between Russia and Germany.

Hitler's ideological basis for invading Russia was that all that was best in the country was of German origin and that only in Russia could the Aryans find the room they needed to develop as a world power. This new Germany would then be able to compete with Britain and the Americanized (Hitler's own terms) mulatto state of France. The suppression of both France and Russia were his expressed aims, together with the destruction of the Jews whom he saw as engaged in a bid for world domination by a conspiracy which was both capitalist, in that it controlled finance, and Marxist. His politics were essentially paranoiac in tone. His early successes, in their swiftness and their completeness, seemed to be confirmation of his theories, both to himself and the German people, soldiers and civilians alike. Even Rommel did not question the concept of the 'New Germany', only the means of attaining it when they seemed to be going wrong as they began to do in late 1942.

At this stage many Germans started to think seriously of ending the war. They had not realized that their leader and those close to him were following not a rational political theory in which there was room for manoeuvre and compromise but a rigid paranoid fantasy which had to play itself out. It was Britain's insistence on being involved in the war in the first place when Hitler would have preferred to have her as an ally along with Italy, and her belief that if she could hold on she must win in the end that disrupted his original scheme. If it is true to say that had Hitler not opened up the Russian front he would have defeated the British so it is almost certainly equally true that if he had not had to fight the British as well, he would have achieved his true aim of conquering Russia, following up his conquest with a massive policy of genocide and Germanization. Stalin himself saw that the maintenance of pressure in the west was essential if Russia was to survive. He was less able to see that the defeat of the Axis forces in Africa was the first essential component of this, along with the double attrition of the war at sea and in the air.

Hitler however realized the great importance of the North African campaign. The Dieppe raid showed how difficult it was to invade a continent where the victor was in complete command. The invasion of Great Britain would probably have been easier but even so Hitler did not dare attempt it without air and sea control. The continent could not have been invaded from the south if Germany had still held North Africa. Without the turning of the tide by the British at El Alamein the war would at the very least have gone on much longer since the American troops were inexperienced, except for those who were otherwise engaged in the Pacific War. The battle for North Africa was their training ground for the invasion of Europe but without the experience and determination of the British Desert Forces it would have been a costly and lengthy affair whose outcome was by no means a foregone conclusion.

Victory in North Africa enabled the Allies to invade Europe through the soft underbelly of Sicily and southern Italy, that is directly attacking an enemy homeland and effectively depriving Hitler of one of his allies since many Italians were rationally sick of war. It suited British propaganda to present the Italians in wartime as feeble and unwilling soldiers but this was far from universally the case. Many of the crack Italian brigades fought bravely on various fronts but they were not fanatics and they refused to go beyond the point where reason told them nothing was to be gained. They preferred to sue for peace rather than see centuries of civilization destroyed by guns and bombs to no purpose. The destruction along the Garigliano and of Monte Cassino itself must have convinced them that they had made the rational choice. Going to fight in Abyssinia was their reward to Mussolini for making the trains run on time. When it seemed that the whole railway system might be under threat they withdrew their support. Those whose ships were bombed to bits in Taranto harbour went quietly home to pick olives. For them the war was over.

Chaplain *Dearly beloved brethren I humbly pray and beseech you as many as are here present to accompany me with a glorious thirst and some ready cash into the bar of the Service Institute, saying after me:*

Almighty and most merciful Records we have heard and obeyed thy commands like lost sheep; we have followed too much the vices and desires of our own hearts and there is no wealth in us. But thou, O Records, have mercy upon us miserable first offenders, restore thou them that are penniless according to thy promise declared unto us in King's Regulations and Air Council Instructions. And grant, O most merciful Records that we may hereafter live a goodly, riotous and inebriate life for the glory of thy most perfect filing system — Airmen!

Housewives!
Better Pot-Luck with Churchill today
Than Humble Pie under Hitler tomorrow
Don't Waste Food!

Who is the chap who hits the high spot,
The greatest comedian now of the lot,
The definite radio star number one,
The life of the party, the bundle of fun?
Lord Haw Haw, the humbug of Hamburg,
The chap with the tonsils and tone.
His homburg he raises in Hamburg,
The comic of Eau de Cologne.

168

IV *Overlords*

And she was sure now that she would never see him again. Well maybe it was best that way since it had to end sometime. The camp seemed almost deserted when the bus dropped her off outside. They'd been confined to barracks for the last four days but it was just like him to get through the wire to meet her in the copse behind her billet. He'd laughed and said at least he didn't have to black up. And she'd laughed back and said he must keep his mouth shut then. She loved his teeth that were so much stronger than her own that would probably go soon and then she would be an old woman, and she loved his smooth brownness, her drop of chocolate sauce as she teased him, and the hard buttocks below the dipping waist that she dared to press down into her.

She had heard the planes themselves climbing away, and almost she had thought, the trucks going off into the dawn but perhaps it hadn't been them just other traffic the roads were full of going south, droning by hour after hour so that anyone had to know something was coming. She'd held on to him and hoped he'd be alright and he'd laughed and said he wasn't a fighting man and he was probably safer than she was. They had both known it was the end and he hadn't asked her to write. She'd given him the best time she could because he was going away and anyway she liked it with him and always had. If she could have she'd have told him he was beautiful.

She had never told him about their little slip-up, never would now. That was best too. They'd always had to make love outdoors, lying down together on the ground or standing up against a tree with the branches whispering above, and beyond them stars or the reaches of moon-washed cloud he wasn't allowed to fly into. He said he didn't mind but she knew he did. He said doing it standing up was new, the English way and she said it was because of the weather always being so wet, and the houses so crowded you couldn't get any privacy. But she'd felt closer to him with her back against rough bark than she'd ever felt in the double bed back home. They'd danced so fine together and sometimes she'd gone to where he was playing his trumpet, at least she thought it was a trumpet, his horn he'd called it – when he took the solo it was as if he was playing just to her, and often in the middle of the morning after, that dead time just before tea break and Workers' Playtime, it would all come back to her with such strength she'd stop in the middle of packing the folds of silk smooth as the skin on his back, and just stare until Winnie nudged her awake because the forelady was on her rounds.

And you knew it was on at last because the very air was alive, jumping as if with static. Even before she had taken her coat off she could feel it and couldn't wait to sit down at the set and put on the headphones.

'What's up?' she'd asked and Maisie Horton-Smith had put a finger on her lips and raised her eyebrows as she handed over. But she knew of course. They'd recognized the verse from Verlaine the first time it had gone out four days ago. Tonight's had been a further confirmation if she'd needed it, if she hadn't seen the troops on the move and felt the curious vacuum when they were gone and there was nothing to do but wait. Harry was on the sea somewhere if he hadn't already landed. It was all 'ifs'. She must concentrate. 'The isle is full of noises,' came to her from some open-air performance in the dark, beside a lake with only the shore lit, magic and mosquitoes in the garden of Worcester College centuries ago.

They had heard the message and were calling in their reports of readiness or of things done already, of blown lines and power failures that would harass and delay reinforcements. It made her feel part of it, as if she too were cycling through the summer night between the high hedges towards what? Her imagination failed to supply a goal. She moved the needle delicately on the dial fingering the wavelength for a voice through the whine and stutter of atmospherics and then suddenly there was a clear staccato of morse she could read now after all these months, as easily as an aural Braille. It was one of their regulars, Jeanne d'Arc reporting in. Automatically her hand translated out the letters for decoding, ripped them from the pad and took them across to the stooped young major with the pebble glasses.

'Put it into clear Pearmain. It's no use to me like that.'

'Yes sir.'

Some of them were friendlier of course and it was first names but he always felt his authority was so fragile it needed all the formal supports. Perhaps he was afraid they would, one day or night, rise up from their keys in some wild bacchanal, whirl about the desks, pin him to the wall and tear off his specs and crush them underfoot before wrenching at his clothes. She wanted to giggle wildly at the thought but instead bent herself to the day's codebook and began to transliterate the details of actions hundreds of miles away. If they had come here would she have been as brave as this pseudonymous Frenchwoman whose words were forming under her hand? She hoped so. But if they had come, there would have been no one and nowhere left to pick up the message. Suddenly it was very important that this woman she didn't know except as a stutter of morse should come through like her coded letters, changed of course, weren't we all, but out into the clear at last from the dark. She hoped the name wasn't an omen, only a banner lifted for others to look up to. Or perhaps it was a wry little joke. It was after all the English who had burned her namesake.

. . . and had been afraid that he would be afraid the first time.

'Why do they call you a Snotty?' the foreign lieutenant had asked.

'I don't know sir,' Lennie had answered.

'Because they're too young, midshipmen, to wipe their own noses,' the Number One had put in. 'It's a bit rough wishing you on us like this at the last minute without your ever seeing green water.'

'Sorry sir.'

'Well I don't suppose you're responsible for the decisions of the Admiralty.'

'No sir.'

'Try not to get underfoot once we're underway.'

'Yes sir.'

'And keep your head down. This is just a trip round the pier. After the vast expense of training you we don't want you getting your head shot off before you've learned to be of use.'

'No sir.'

'He can come with me and be of use taking messages,' the foreign lieutenant had said, and turning to the boy. 'If we are damaged it is up to us to put it right, to make sure that bad doesn't become worse.'

'I hope you at least know port from starboard and fore from aft,' Number One had said.

'Yes sir.' And now he was really at sea, even though it was only the channel. It stretched around the ship on all sides, pitching it gently when they moved, stomach churning when they were hove to as now. He was glad he wasn't in one of the little boats that filled the spaces between cruisers, battleships, destroyers, grey blurring silhouettes in the evening like those in the recognition manuals.

'We can expect dive bombers,' the lieutenant said, 'unless the weather keeps them away. Perhaps they will think that nothing can happen while the wind blows. Certainly we cannot launch landing craft in this sea. They would all be washed over. We shall wait I think until the wind drops. They will be uncomfortable tonight in the transports. But perhaps worst of all for you will be our own barrage. It will be very noisy when the guns start. Ah here is the steward with the Kye.'

'Kye sir?' the boy had asked.

'Cocoa to you sir,' the steward had said, handing him the brown soup steaming into the night air, and winked.

And he'd never seen anything like it as they flew over the Kent coast. He was bloody glad he wasn't below there to the west, pitching about on the sea. They stared down through the dark, comforted together in their metal box with the magic wings that lifted them above the thousands of craft crammed, as they knew they must be, with men.

'I bet they're pissing themselves, poor buggers.' They were packed tight too with extra men for the job, another pilot in case he bought it or went off his rocker, another navigator so that every reading was double-checked and three jokers with stop-watches to make sure they let the stuff go dead on time.

'There's our convoy.'

It was mad. How could anything so bizarre succeed? A fleet of eighteen small ships towing balloons was to impersonate an armada. With their help of course, stooging along at 3,000 feet at exactly 200 m.p.h., forward for 32 seconds.

'About turn!' Back for thirty seconds while the bomb-aimer and an erk flung the shining bundles of window out into the night, to part and stream their glistening tinfoil down towards the sea, jamming and confusing the enemy radar into seeing a phantom fleet. They had to keep it up for four hours before the second flight took over, and they had to be good because the madmen of 617, the suicide squadron, were flying it with them. Not that you could see anyone else, only the pathetic small ships and beyond, the French coast of the Pas-de-Calais. He wished he'd seen it in peacetime, Paris in the spring. 'To the City I Have Never Seen' he began to rhyme in his head.

'You're drifting Skipper.'

Perhaps he was going bonkers. Not many managed a second tour. It got to you in the end; must do. You went on hoping against hope, crossing fingers, carrying all kinds of lucky talismen above the clouds. This one was a piece of cake compared to what they went through these days. The Berlin trip had been the worst, with crates flaming down all round once the fighters got in among the bomber stream. How much luck did you have? Was it like an hour-glass, a trickling heap of sand that flattened and dwindled through the inverted cone of itself until the last few dry grains were flowing out, only nobody could turn you over, start you off again once your luck had run out.

Upend me. Let your lips. . . .

'Drifting Skip. Time to turn.'

And took the telegram from the postman, knowing that nothing good ever came to hand this way and signed for it seeing the OHMS and the Admiralty heading and Gwen's name, and went back slowly into their cottage wondering what she should do with it: take it with her to the field where Gwen was haymaking with Mr Jeavons and the boy, or prop it against the mantelpiece above the unlit range to make its own point, a biscuit-coloured square in the gloom when Gwen came through the door out of the afternoon sunlight for her tea, before going back to the fields for the long evening, getting as much cut as they could in case the weather turned again. If she hadn't been here, hadn't popped back for a couple of aspirin and to change her towel before the blood soaked through her dungarees in full view of everybody, she wouldn't have been the one to take it. The boy would have had to come up again on his bike or they might have missed it for days, getting up and going off early and coming back late as they did every day now, and would do until harvest was in and then it would be potatoes.

Hilary climbed the steep stairs to their bedroom. The sagging brass bed looked cool and tempting. In winter when the weather shut down early on work they could come up on Sunday afternoon and snuggle under the maroon eiderdown, gradually stripping each other's clothes off with a leisurely passion that warmed the cold, slightly damp bedclothes until they were down to their opened shirts and unhooked bras and could lay their smooth warm bodies face to face against each other. Well even if they got Sunday off this week there would be none of that in her state.

She mustn't be long mooning about here. She undid the safety pins and pressed the pad against her to soak up the flow before taking it away, gingerly folding it in half and wrapping it in a half-sheet of newspaper, her nose twitching slightly at the unmistakable acidic smell of stale menstrual blood. Hilary pinned the fresh pad in place. Gwen had shown her how to make towels that could be thrown away out of gauze and cotton wool. 'I think it's quite disgusting using the same ones again and again,' she'd said.

In time the folded pieces of old sheet grew hard with washing and rubbed sore places on your thighs and they were always stained even if you boiled them for ages. 'Who'd be a woman,' Gwen always said, resenting the monthly pain and mess. It was partly why they had jumped at the empty cottage, even though the walls ran with damp in winter and there was only a bucket in the outdoor privy with its thatched roof that turned it into a dwarf's house.

'You'll be cold out there. We can't spare no coal,' Mrs Jeavons had objected, not wanting to lose the money for their board.

'We can gather wood,' Gwen had answered firmly, knowing that the Jeavons were a little afraid of her because she wasn't afraid of them, and because of her dark hair and pale skin that made her seem like a gypsy. In the cottage they would be able to hang up their washed pants to dry on the elastic stretched between the mantelpiece and the range; they would be able to take all their clothes off and bath in front of the fire; they would be able to cry out loud into each other's mouths.

When she went downstairs again, conscious of the comfort and safety of the new pad and hoping it didn't show too square a lump in the bottom of her slacks, the telegram still posed its question squarely. She remembered her mother stretching out her hand with the unopened envelope that contained the news of her sister's death. 'You open it Wilf. I can't,' and her father's neat fingers taking his small folding penknife from his pocket and slitting the top as if to tear it wasn't respectful. Gwen wouldn't want them all watching while she read the words. Hilary closed the door and mounted her bicycle, the pad as she began to pedal rubbing gently between the seat and her swollen sensitive lower lips with a sensation that was both pleasure and pain.

And it was bleeding good to be marching through Rome and then to sit outside a caff drinking wine. The beer was like gnat's piss. Jerry must have brought his own with him. But the red wine was bright as blood. He held the glass up to the light and looked at the rest of the section through it, all of them brown and laughing a bit cock-eyed. It went to your head quick in this heat and the sunshine poured into your eyes until you were dazzled and the old buildings, with the giant figures like gods of the squares in their dry fountains, loomed larger and larger and larger as if they could top right up to the sky and all fall down.

The Eyties seemed pleased to see them, glad it was all over.

Rome had been declared an open city and he could see why. You couldn't let off a mortar here without reducing a chunk of history to dust, something that couldn't never be replaced. The girls had called out and thrown flowers and tried to kiss them as they'd come through that morning. They didn't understand except the words 'Tommie', and 'Inglese'. Now they could try out the bits they'd picked up as they fought their way north: *vino* and *pane* and *ragazza*.

Sitting there he knew, suddenly and for sure that he'd come through now, that he hadn't got all this way just to stop one at the last. A bell began to ring from the church on the other side of the square and people mounted the steps with heads bent, first a lot of women in dusty black and scarves over their hair, next children and at the back, men of all ages, hands clasped behind them, talking in subdued voices to each other and crossing themselves, he could see dimly, as they went inside through the high carved door where a candle seemed to be glittering in the black mouth.

The sun had gone and already the brightness though not the heat was fading. He'd noticed you didn't get the long-drawn-out evenings here like at home, even though it was Europe not Africa.

'What are we gonna do about grub?' Slogger was asking.

'Find somewhere with a bistecca. I can't take no more of that spaghetti with all that oil and garlic. Gives me the runs.'

'You know what the bistecca is don't you?'

'Horse.'

'Me and Bloater had one in Naples, I said I was sure was pork. And when I asked, the girl said yes, it was: beefsteak of pig. We had a Yankee jewboy with us nearly spewed the lot up when he heard.'

'Shouldn't eat pork without an "R" in the month.'

'That's oysters stupid.'

'I feel terrible.'

'You know the MO told you not to drink with them pills.'

'Shut your face!'

'Alright, alright. That's enough argy-bargy.' The wine was making them fractious. He'd have to get them moving or they'd end up on a charge. 'On your feet. We'll go and look for some proper chow.'

The streets between the high old buildings were full of people sauntering over the cobbles. Lights were coming on in the shops. Bats fluttered, patches of deeper black on the sky. The warm air brushed their faces, bare arms and legs with soft wings. It was a different way of life out here. Oh Africa had been different too of course but that was A-rabs. You expected it, and down in the south of Italy that was more like Tunisia in a way, though without the desert. But this was a city, big and old like London. He couldn't say it to any of the others. He knew they wouldn't see it his way because they were always romancing about home but he sensed an ease, an openness, the way the people came out on the streets to stroll up and down, not going nowhere, just talking, men together, boys together, women with their children, young girls. When they met they shook hands and the voices rose in welcome. The air was full of greetings. All his life, he reckoned, he'd been too buttoned up.

Later as the woman pulled off her dress and he undid his shirt, he thought briefly of Millie. She wouldn't have been faithful: she wasn't the type. He felt the woman's nervousness filling the little room. Perhaps it was a fit-up to roll him.

'What's behind the curtain?'

'*No capisco.*'

He got off the bed. Three steps took him across the room. He lifted the curtain with one hand, the other on his knife. The woman stepped forward with a little cry. A child, he couldn't tell whether boy or girl, with dark sweaty curls round a sallow face, lay heavily asleep in a packing case. It was her turn to be afraid now. He let the curtain drop, feeling cheated. The sight had taken him off the boil. But he couldn't be angry with her. Perhaps the father was dead or had given her a kid and buggered off; maybe even a Jerry. He thought of the women in the south and their terror of the Moroccan troops who had run wild, raping and looting. Another sergeant had explained in the mess that it was their fear of a black baby. No one would marry them then. They would end up as nuns. All's fair in love and war, he thought. The woman was looking at him. Her dress had fallen back over her pale body. He sensed her mixture of relief and disappointment. Anger ran through him again. He wasn't such a bad bloke. He'd seen a bloody sight worse.

He stepped forward and gently touched her face. 'Come on.
I won't hurt you.'

And he couldn't get the words out of his head:

> Our King went forth to Normandie
> With grace and might of chivalrie.
> The Lord for him did marvellouslie,
> Wherefore England may shout and cry,
> Deo gratias.

They had sung it at school: boys' and mens' voices as the sun
bannered through the chapel windows of the hall on Edward's
Day. Now it wouldn't go away. Hardly surprising when you
looked out at the fleet at anchorage in Southampton Water.
But it ran on still though it was dark now and there was
nothing to be seen but the blacked-out ship and figures
stumbling against the cloudy sky.

They'd eaten well. He'd downed a whole tin of self-heating
soup. The troop cooks had dished up all the compo rations in
one huge meal! The condemned men ate a hearty breakfast,
Welshy Jones of No. 3 Troop had joked. That was after they'd
sailed, when they'd been told where they were going. He'd
mustered them on deck and explained the whole plan briefly,
and their part of it more carefully. The paras should already
be there but nobody knew in what shape or if they'd been able
to secure the bridges. That was their job if they hadn't been
taken or the Boche hadn't blown them. They'd listened
quietly as he'd spoken, looking from man to man, especially
the new faces they'd had to bring in to get No. 3 up to strength
after Italy. They had been training hard for five months.
There were enough of the old hands seeded among them for
him to feel confident if they got a good landing. That other
Harry must have just stepped ashore dryshod or rode his
horse up the beach.

The wind was fresher now. He ought to get his head down if
he could. Really the craft was pitching most alarmingly. A
figure pushed past him. He saw it silhouetted above the rail
for a moment and then the blob of a head vanished and he
heard the unmistakable sound of someone being violently sick.

The captain had lent him his sea cabin. He would be better up there in the fresh air than packed below with the troop. They had orders to wake him at first light. That's if he could sleep.

When he opened the door of the little hutch again, the rail was lined with green-faced men. The cooks offered breakfast to anyone who could stomach it. Before them lay the flat bit of French coast that was their landing. They were getting closer all the time. Now he could make out the spouts of water round the pitching boats ahead. The enemy were awake too. The landscape was just like all the photographs from the Great War, broken buildings along the front from the naval bombardment, a tank or two spewing flame, a desolate beach.

Suddenly the air burst overhead. They were coming under fire as they ran into beach. He crouched behind a ramp as shrapnel smacked into the water around them.

'Look at those two mad buggers.'

In the stern of the nearest boat two men were sitting shouting instructions to the enemy gunners and cheering each time a shot missed. He recognized two of the old hands with charmed lives.

They were very close in now. No. 6 boat suddenly began to sink as its mortar ammo exploded. He hadn't time to look properly but the casualties would be heavy. He felt their craft ground. The ramps went down. Men were streaming up from below. He led the way over and found himself up to the armpits in the sea. They had hit a false beach. They were struggling forward, some men encumbered with bicycles as well as their other kit. A photographer snapped them as they ploughed on.

He felt the sea falling away and pushed ahead faster. The shells were dropping behind and in front but the waterline was safe. He risked a look back. The others were coming out of the sea, water streaming from their sodden clothes. He waved them up the beach towards the sand dunes, dodging the wire and the shell holes. Men were crouching in the sand hills unwilling to go further. He shouted at his lot.

'Come on lads,' and ran towards the battered row of houses between the dunes and the road.

'Check them out, Jones and Withers. Everybody all right? We make for the forming-up point, those bushes. Let's go.'

There were clumps of reeds but that was the only cover. They were crossing a marsh. A man to his left sank to his waist in slime. Shorty Williams pulled him free.

'Christ, what's that?'

'That mate, that's a moaning minnie. Come on.'

He saw Lieutenant Sanders go down and two men pick him up and carry him on towards the bushes, and staggered on himself, his wet clothes dragging at him, holding him back, his breath coming hard and shallow through the pain in his chest. They were ashore. Thank God, they had done marvellously.

And if he should step down on to dry land and keep walking east into the rising sun over there he would come to Poland if he wasn't shot on the way and didn't step on one of the mines that Hitler would have sown the soil of Europe with until it was just a huge field of dragons' teeth that would erupt in warriors of beaten metal and flame to scythe you down. Sporadic bursts of fire and long bead strings of tracer etched the paling night sky. At any moment they would be heading back into the channel towards England to pick up a new convoy. He had heard Polish voices at embarkation, and after his months of immersion in English they had sounded almost foreign, certainly unreal, disembodied echoes from the past. He wondered what the soldiers who had voiced them expected, hoped for. They had perhaps kept their identities intact while he, through his own choice, had lost his. Sometimes now he even thought in English, surprising himself. They would hope, in driving east across Europe, to strengthen them as they neared Poland. They were taking half-empty water-bottles back to the well, to be refilled with cool fresh water they could drink from again and again and be renewed. But when, if ever, they reached it they would find the well overgrown with poison bushes, the brick round filled with carcases and rubble, the water fouled, undrinkable, their thirst forever unslaked. Was it only his own pessimism that made him sure it would be so?

For them the first step ashore had been the first on the way home. He wondered whether he would even have taken the chance if he had been offered it, if they hadn't had to lie off the coast, joining first in the barrage and then brooding over the LCs as they had run in to drop men in the sea, where they sank and drowned under the weight of equipment or on to the land to be spattered over the beach or lie cowering under a broken wall.

At least the expected dive-bombers hadn't come. The sky was a washed-out ink now. He was aware of a figure climbing the bridge ladder: Number One coming to take over.

'How's it going?'

'It's hard to say. I think most of the first ones are off the beach but there are so many arriving all the time they are hindering each other.'

'No sign of the *Luftwaffe*?'

'Not at all.'

'We can be grateful then. Some aren't so lucky. That sub we had, Peter Evans, went down with his new ship. It's just come through. Torpedoed in the Atlantic by a U-boat. No survivors.'

He saw the boy's face under water as his body turned over, sinking, outlined in bubbles, the hair on end like seaweed, turning, turning, his hands plucking at the empty ocean as he went down and down.

'He was so young.'

'Could happen to any of us. Under way in half an hour. I'll take over the watch now. You get your head down for a bit. Ask someone to rouse the snotty. He can start learning how to take a ship out.'

And feel the child clinging close to her as she climbs. She is still nervous for it. The memory of her first-born has faded a little but not the image of the wasted body she carried lifelessly about for days until the smell of decay warned her to leave it, that it was no longer hers. Sometimes when she looks at the new one, that other small figure with the distorted arm and the lolling neck is superimposed on it, bringing her dread.

They all feel more afraid since the Boss went away. Even Karka who sometimes boldly challenged him is apprehensive, starting at strange sounds, his fur standing up all over his body while he screams and beats the air with a branch. The rain pours down over them all.

The smooth apes had come with their firesticks; one pink one and a handful of brown. Rua and the others had run away into the thickest sodden vegetation but the Boss had stood his ground, screaming defiance. They had heard sharp cracks that were the firesticks breaking open in lightning and the sound of a crash and the smooth apes calling to each other.

After a while it had gone silent and they crept back. There was nothing except crushed foliage and the smell of meat as when they take a young monkeyface to eat. They had lingered, feeding around the clearing on a giant wild grape tree until the smell of fire had reached them, not a forest fire but one that came with the smooth apes. She wanted to go and see if the Boss was with them but when she tried to leave, Karka stood in her way threatening, and, heavy as she was, she had given in to him and let him lead them away, a long travel towards the rising sun where they had never been before.

It is soon after that she feels that she must make a birth nest. Houmi senses her restlessness and tries to stay even closer to her than usual but she pushes him away, grumbling gently. For a while he sits at the bottom of the tree she has chosen, hugging himself until Tondi and the young Mala wander past on their way to a fig grove and Mala runs up and teases him into play. He feels safe with Mala. She is full of tricks, pulling at his fur, dragging on his hands to make him tickle her or join in a game of chase, swinging among the vines. She is still too young to interest Karka so Houmi isn't disturbed in his play with her.

Alone in the nest high up, Rua begins to feel pain. She grunts a little, straining down on her thighs which are wet and slimy. She is splitting open like a ripe pod to let the large round nut of the baby's head drop into the leafy bed at the bottom of the nest. She takes the child up and begins to clean and groom it. She bites through the umbilical cord and waits for the afterbirth to finish the process. The baby wails, opens its eyes when she cleans them, twines its fingers in her hair, and begins to seek for a nipple to pull on with its mouth. She hugs it to her, murmuring quietly as heavy drops start to patter again on the leaves that surround them, hiding them from the world and the cold probings of the rain.

*

And asked me to marry him if he returns and I said I would think about it because he was going away and if he went away sad he would not have so much the chance to survive. There is something wrong with that sentence but I can't go back. I find I can't correct my mistakes any more. They are there like the colour of my eyes, part of me, and in any case no one will ever see this. I suddenly thought yesterday, after I had closed my book for the night, that all over the world in strange circumstances there must be people writing down what is happening to them to try to make sense of it and for it to survive perhaps if they don't. For thousands of years there was only the memory for most people, passed down in stories like the Talmud, of kings and prophets and migrations. It was the task of priests to keep the holy word, the word holy. Now everyone can write and we are all keepers of history.

He asked me to write to him but his English isn't so good and I dare not write in German. In any case what would I say? It is one thing to lie in someone's arms and enjoy the bodies together but quite another to write that lie: I love you. You must believe as you say it, even if you are deceiving yourself. You cannot say it not believing, in cold blood, and to write it would be worse. Therefore there is nothing I can say to him, write to him, since we have nothing in common but being displaced here. He cannot discuss the English poets with me. He doesn't like to listen to music. He likes only to drink with his friends at the club and to talk of old times and places. He gets angry with me when I say they will never come again. How can they when the whole world is gone that he describes?

The nights are quiet now, usually without warnings. Most people no longer go to the shelters all night but the city grows shabbier and more broken because there is no one to mend anything, except that people have put back the glass in their windows. We need light to come in and to be able to see out. Today I am very restless otherwise I should be downstairs preparing the tea instead of writing and waiting although I don't know what I expect; the Second Front I suppose, that everyone has talked of for so long. The British and Americans will land somewhere in France and begin to push Hitler back towards Germany. He will fight and fight and perhaps it will be the World War I all over again and it will go on and on until everyone is exhausted. I cannot imagine how it will be because for me there is only this room at the top of the house and tonight my class in the English drama:

'I am but mad Nor Nor West. When the wind is southerly I know a hawk from a handsaw.'

Whose ghost am I?

And wondered what the shit they were doing there. 'We ain't infantry Sergeant. We's aar-force. Engineers.'

'You're soldiers, soldier. You had combat training.'

'Hell that was months ago.'

'Well brush up your memory.'

Shit this was Whitey's war. 'Hey Sarge what's this I'm carrying?'

'It's a bazooka. Now shut up.'

'Where we all going Sergeant?'

'Omaha.'

'Omaha! Some jazz.'

'I got my horn here Sergeant. Shall I play reveille or Last Post?'

And it was so exciting she thought she might burst. They had all gone into the common room to listen to the news, some of them groaning as ever that it was boring and the little ones pushing and giggling. She'd heard the first announcement at one o'clock. She'd been alone in the room then, the rest were on their way to lunch, corned beef hash today and she'd switched on the set which they weren't supposed to do but very quietly so that she could only just hear it with her ear against the cloth.

'Under the command of General Eisenhower, Allied Naval Forces, supported by strong Air Forces began landing Allied Armies this morning on the northern coast of France.' She'd let out a hoorray in the emptiness that beat against the linenfold panelling and then run all the way to the dining-room to fling open the door where they were all, staff and girls, busy with their hash and boiled potatoes and tinned watery carrots and cried, 'We've landed, we've landed!'

There had been a moment's hush in the clatter of voices and knives and forks on china, and then someone had laughed and the head had stood up at the staff table and said loudly, 'Ailsa Pearmain why are you late for lunch? You will learn the whole of *The Charge of the Light Brigade* and recite it to me before supper. Now go to your table and sit down in a quiet and composed fashion.'

She had known it was no use to argue. She knew most of *The Charge* already and had it off pat by the time she presented herself. 'You must learn to take things more calmly and not to react in such an impulsive way.'

'But my father's there. . . .'

'So are a great many other fathers, I'm sure.'

Had the old bat picked it because it was long or because it was appropriate, she wondered as she volleyed and thundered with the cavalry? Now they were grouped in front of the set. The words she had heard earlier dropped into the room again but followed by the first sighting of the invasion fleet. The news ended but the voice went on, leading to the modulated sentences of John Snagge. 'War Report! Night by night at this time this programme will bring you news of the war from correspondents and fighting men. . . .'

The head was standing up, turning down the volume control. She mustn't switch off now!

'The staff and I have decided that fifth- and sixth-form girls may stay to listen to this programme after the news each evening if they wish. We realize that several of you have fathers and brothers at the front.'

'And lovers,' Caroline Ducie muttered under her breath as the younger ones left, but she wasn't listening. She was running up on the beach under fire, the landing craft picking its way through the staked-out mines. The craft shuddered to an explosion. She was going down the ramp behind the Bren carrier, wading up to the armpits until the last reassuring words, '. . . the Germans weren't really putting up a great deal of resistance.'

When the set was switched off at the end she found she was trembling and even her bitten nails had dug deep half-moon weals in her palms where she had clutched her hands so tight.

'I'm sure my father's out there.'

'It isn't your father you're worrying about it's your sailor boy.'

Later that night in bed she thought of them both. In a foolish moment when she had been reading Lennie's last letter in their study she had let Caroline Ducie snatch it from her. Now the others ragged her about him mercilessly. She was only safe in her own bed, looking over at the lighter navy square on black that was the window and saying in her head:

> Well here's luck my dear and you've got it never fear,
> But for me the war is poor fun.

And thought, looking down at him, that he would never make it home, that Fred was dying, he was so shrunk under the bedclothes he hardly seemed to make any hump at all.

'Wouldn't you like to be flown back? I'm sure it could be arranged.'

'What for? I'm fine here my darling girl. Lots of pretty nurses. Besides winter's coming on and I never liked touring in an English winter.'

'I've been recalled. The Second Front's started and they want us to follow the boys into Europe.'

For a moment tears showed like glitter in his eyes then he said, 'You'll end up singing and dancing at the Folies Bergères. Don't worry about me. I'll be fine, and thanks for, you know, keeping in touch. I know you always came to see me when you were in Cairo.'

Outside the hospital a hot smoky dusk was already falling, scented with burned camel dung and petrol fumes. Red, blue and green lights were coming on above the shops, cinemas and dance halls. Trams clanged past, festooned with clinging boys. Shrouded figures drew back into doorways. The shop windows of confectioners were stuffed with almond and cream cakes. She could spend the evening at the Gezira Club, drinking and laughing under the flowering jacarandas. It might be her last chance before the bleak darkness of Europe swallowed her down again. Would she ever come back here when it was all over to lounge with an ice in the afternoon at Groppi's or dine at Shepherd's under the desert moon? An invitation was waiting for her when she reached her hotel, and flowers. She was a star now. As she brushed her hair she hoped that she would be able to catch the BBC news at the Gezira, even if it meant making her escort wait for his dinner. She wondered briefly when Peter would answer her last letter. She must remember to leave a forwarding address so that his reply could follow her to France.

And leaned against the breach to roll a fag with the long snout of the barrel funnelling up into the night sky above his head. Jerry wouldn't come now. He'd be much too busy, he hoped. Getting off the beaches would be the problem. If the blokes got stuck there then the sand of Normandy mixed with blood and rain could turn into the mud of Flanders once more.

Still this time they was more mobile, more like a glorified commando do, coming in from the sea in little boats and out of the air by parachute and glider. In his day you'd walked down the gangplank off the troopship, setting your first foot on foreign soil, and then marched to rear HQ and then up the line, singing like a piecan as you went, until you reached the trenches and dropped into them in inches of water and dead men's boots.

They'd have tanks too ashore as smartly as they could. That was something we'd learned from Jerry. These days you were mechanized or you was nothing. He licked the edge of his fag paper, rolled the thin flattened cylinder up and pinched the dangling shreds of tobacco off one end.

'You want a light, Goss, before I blow it out?'

'Thanks, Sarge.'

'Don't come the old soldier with me.'

'Can I have a light, Sarge?'

'Boys shouldn't smoke. And anyway you never light three from the same match.'

'Why's that, Sarge?'

'One to know you're there; two to pinpoint the spot; three to fire. Except that nowadays they'd probably mow you down with a machine gun.'

'What do you reckon it's like over there?'

'Bloody hell, mate. Bloody hell.'

v *Elegies*

She has never heard a sound like it before and she pauses in the afternoon house to listen. A moment ago she was out the front whitening the doorstep. She doesn't do it so often now she's out to work til four every day but from time to time its dinginess strikes her and she gets out the hearthstone and rag and the old enamel bowl with clean cold water and goes down on her knees to those ancient gods of hearth and home who have hidden themselves in disgust since no one has time any more to whiten their altar stones and clean their brass. She's glad she managed to get the store curtains down and washed. They're so fragile now she didn't dare boil them in the copper. She stood out last Saturday in the yard, up to her elbows in the galvanized bath on its wooden trestle, and rubbed the tops which were black with the winter's smoke and soot, gently against the glass knuckles of the scrubbing board, and the dirt had run out of them like gravy. If it all ended tomorrow at least she would have the curtains clean.

The shorter ones for the half-windows that she had crocheted herself were standing up better than the finer bought net. Well soon they might all be able to buy new and chuck the old away. She should sweep the passage but first she will just go and give those peelings to the chickens. It is as she thinks this and closes the front door on the whitened step that she hears the sound. It is mechanical, in the sky, but not like any aeroplane she has become used to. Suddenly it stops. 'That's alright then,' she thinks. 'It's gone over.' It stuttered like clockwork, quite different from the pulsing drone they have learned to recognize. It put her in mind of the Zeppelin in the last war when she was a girl. She is aware of a screaming sound, a high-pitched hurtle and stands quite still with the hearthstone and rag in her hand, drawing her last breath in sharply.

The shockwave throws her against the stairs as they burst upwards in a shoal of splinters. The terraced railway cottages which have stood for a hundred years collapse in on themselves and each other, all falling down. The chickens fly for the first time, together with their shed, upwards in a shower of blood and feathers. The chimney stacks topple into the living-rooms. The little mirrors in the overmantel craze and blow out in a thousand chandelier fragments that still hold a complete image in each splinter. The furniture is all jumbled in a giant ragbag except for Hilary's bed which sails through the gap where the back wall of the house stood to land upright, and with the pillows still neatly at the head, on the top of the Anderson shelter. The cat on his way home several gardens away, cowers in a coal bunker as the dust and debris rain down then turns and flees, cutting his paw on broken glass and leaving bloody prints.

He hardly recognized the street, it was such a ghost of itself with holes punched out where houses had been and wooden sleepers propping up the walls on either side. Some instinct had warned him to park his kitbag at Charing Cross station before he set out, not knowing what he would find, not knowing even whether she'd got his letter saying he was coming home on leave. She'd told him the house had been hit but he hadn't really taken in that it was gone completely. Now he stood and looked at the gap and the neighbouring houses shored and boarded up.

'Is that you Mr Kirby?'

He had heard the door opening across the street but hadn't turned until the woman spoke. She shocked him as everything had shocked him since they had disembarked, the other blokes all full of what they would do, not realizing that nothing had stood still while they had been away, that they and everything they had left behind were different. He had been very quiet, suspecting but even so not prepared for the reality.

The woman was in her forties. He didn't remember her but then he'd never taken much notice of the neighbours. On the buses his hours had been irregular, building up no pattern that people could rely on and they hadn't drunk in the local once the boy had come. The woman was pasty-faced, her hair in curlers under a dusty turban, her short skirt showing white legs with slippers that had once been trimmed with pink fluff below them, now rubbed bald and grimy.

'Would you like to come in for a cup of tea?'

Perhaps she would have some news of Millie. 'Thanks very much.' He followed her into the small front garden. 'Didn't there used to be railings?' He could see the square metal cicatrices where they had been sawn off and the empty gate sockets.

'They took them for the war effort. I suppose they'll give us new ones soon, now we're winning.' She led him down the dark passage smelling of greens and boiled cloth to the living-room. 'Sit down. I was just having one before going on shift. It's nice to have a man about the place. Millie's still in the country working. I expect she wrote you.'

He remembered now the woman's name was Grace. She'd been Millie's mate, gone dancing with her when they were single and worked at the shirt factory.

'You still at Barhams?'

'Still there. It's all army stuff now of course: khaki and blue. Gets a bit dull. Still we mustn't complain, must we. Not these days. You might be wearing one of mine. Saccharin? There's no sugar I'm afraid. Have a piece of my hard bake.' She pushed a yellow wedge of cake towards him that when he bit on it was first coarse and dry and then broke into crumbs that threatened to choke him. 'I managed to get a packet of dried egg and knocked it up yesterday. Must have known I'd be getting a visitor. Try a bit of golden syrup on it, makes it go down better.'

She pushed a 2lb tin towards him and took the spoon out of her own tea to scoop up a gleaming oily dollop which she let run over the slice of cake on the chipped cream plate with its fluted rim. 'The last of my wedding service. When the bomb dropped on your place all the china got shook off the sideboard.' Her hand picked at a few dry crumbs on the ringed American cloth covering the table with its dark red sheen that smelled of petrol and tar. The fingers were stained with nicotine and the short nails rimmed black with occasional flecks of red varnish.

'You could go down and see her; Norfolk she is.'

'Yes. I've got the address somewhere. I wasn't thinking straight. Just felt I ought to come here and take a look.' He didn't know what he had expected: that she had been lying and the house was alright and she was living there with someone else? Boss Barham had always fancied her.

The woman was looking at him. 'You'd best let her know if

you're going. She lives in a hostel. You'd have to stay in a bed and breakfast.'

'We've got a fortnight's leave. Then I reckon they'll send us off to France to help them out there.' There was something about her that nagged at the back of his mind. Her husband hadn't come back with the others at Dunkirk but it wasn't that. Something else. She'd had a reputation. He'd never paid much attention to the gossip. It was women's business. 'You don't see much of her I suppose?'

'She comes up sometimes. Misses the smoke a bit. Your boy's been to see her. Going for an officer I gather.'

'He's doing well for himself. Better'n his father.'

'Oh I don't know. You haven't done so bad. You look well on it too.'

'That's the sun out there.' He thought suddenly of the Italian women leaning in their doorways, or linking arms to stroll under the hot stars. 'Well I'd best get going. Thanks for the tea and the cake.'

'My pleasure. Will you be seeing her d'you reckon?'

'I suppose so. If I can fix it all up.'

'Tell her I could use another parachute if one comes her way. Same as before. Where will you stay tonight? I could put you up for a bit if you've nowhere to go.'

'Oh, I'll find something. Thanks all the same. I'll tell Millie if I see her, about the parachute. So long then.'

He felt her eyes on his back as he went up the street. It was some time before he heard the door slam. The day was overcast and windy. The streets seemed half-deserted. Back there the sun would be shining. The lads would be sitting out under the vine leaves having a bevvy, unless they'd started to push north. He'd reckoned they'd been well out of a winter campaign in the mountains. Now he wasn't so sure.

'If that was the heel and toe of Italy where we landed, this must be her thigh, mustn't it, Sarge?'

'That's right.'

'See. He wouldn't believe me. And what comes after the thigh?'

'Venice.'

'Venice – Venus.'

'Where you'd pick up your next dose if you wasn't going home.'

Home. He didn't give a toss if he never saw it again. If he got through the last lot he wasn't coming back to Esmeralda Road and the buses. He'd sign on as a regular and see what come of that and if Millie didn't like it she could do the other. He didn't know if he would go and sort her out in Norfolk. First of all he was going to enjoy a bit of leave, pick up his kit, find somewhere to bivouac with other NCOs and then out for a jar and maybe a bint. He'd see about that.

France was different again now he was over his first funk and the army had stopped trying to make soldiers of them and let them go back to being engineers servicing the machines. The twenty-four hour pass had let him get to a Paris that still had an air of liberation about it. Even in England he was looked at on the street but not here. Once he came across a coloured guy in a soft hat talking fast to a white girl on a corner, in French like a native, and those words falling unintelligibly out of black lips seemed strangest of all.

He had walked and walked, taking it all in until his legs were aching and he was hot and thirsty. He turned into a little bar smelling of coffee and the raw French cigarettes and asked for a beer. The bartender poured himself a glass of straw-coloured liquid, clinked it on his and refused his money. He preferred it like this, on his ownsome, rubbernecking. He would steer clear of US ofay troops who always meant trouble. A coloured who ran into them on his own or tried to enter one of the pubs they'd taken over in England was liable to get his head kicked. The sons of bitches didn't even realize they were on the same side. He wondered where the woman was now. She'd been good to him. He hoped she wasn't grieving.

'That man got a heart like a rock cast in the sea. . . .' Suddenly he ached for some music. Perhaps it was too soon for the city to have that organized but he would try. 'Music? Jazz music?'

'*La musique*? Swing? *Oui*. Le Hot Club de France, Django Reinhardt.'

He was in a cave, a basement café like those he was used to back home. There was no whiskey so he drank brandy. The air was a curtain of wreathing smoke above the tables and between him and the little stage where there was a quintet thrashing out, smoking, but with strings only: a couple of guitars, a bass; a violin. Next time he would bring his horn and ask to join in. Their leader was a dark-skinned man with a cap of black shining hair and a little moustache, a white man. Or was he? He played with a dark passion, not as fast as the black cats who were the real stompers but cool.

'Do you mind if I sit here?'

'Go ahead.' The man was in his thirties neatly dressed in a pressed suit unlike most of the other watchers who were what he recognized as a version of the zoot suit with pegged pants, long hair moulded into waves, and baggy checked jackets. The girls were nondescript beside them though he could see they were trying. Their little white faces were slashed with red mouths, their skirts were short, as he'd become used to in England, but there it was 'utility' she'd told him, here it was protest.

'I have been watching you and I think you are a musician? Yes?'

'That's smart of you sir. Yes I am.'

'What is your instrument?'

'I blow the horn, most any horn.'

'Like Louis Armstrong.'

'Well, I ain't as good as Satch but then nobody is.'

'What do you think of our band?'

'It's very different. I never heard that combination before. Who's the leader?'

'That's Django.'

'I been trying to figure out his colour.'

The man laughed. 'He's a gypsy. Neither black nor white.'

'So he combines the two and makes something of his own.'

'That's right.'

'How did he make out in the war?'

'He went on playing. It was a strange thing. Swing was a kind of protest but the Germans let it go on. We had to pretend we were playing French creole music. You know of course the *St Louis Blues*. That became *La Tristesse de St Louis* because English was a forbidden language, and St Louis was a French king. Thus the music could continue.'

'And all these kids?'

'They are the zazous.'

'After Cab Calloway's scat singing?'

'Just so. This way they defied their elders who had betrayed France, and the Germans. They were doing nothing wrong. They were not Resistance. They were too young and there was no opportunity. Later on some of them joined. That one there whose hair is short. He has come back to swing with his *copains* now it is all over. Our young Fascists hated them and called them decadent. They wanted to enrol barbers to go and cut off their hair. Sometimes they made it difficult for us, *Les Petits Swings*. You are lucky that you come now. A little time ago when Paris was just liberated we were crazy at first. There were many ugly things. Now we are calmer. That is lucky for you and us. A Lucky Strike.' The man laughed without real humour.

He thought of the dance halls of servicemen and their girls he had played to. 'We've got a pretty good combo going in our outfit. We could maybe give you a show sometime.'

'We would be very happy. It would be true liberation for us to hear again the real American swing. Where can I contact you?'

Dawn was already greyly waiting as he stepped out of the double doors of smoke, heat and sound and began to walk through the washed-out streets of the city towards the metro. He found himself singing in his head an old number from years ago, jazzing it.

> How ya gonna keep them down on the farm
> After they seen Paree!

That would be a good one to do. He and the boys would work on that.

'Perhaps you'd like to read it out to the form. I gave it a B plus because it's a little uneven but nevertheless a very passable attempt at a modern ballad. One might say that you owe something to Tennyson but perhaps more to Sir Henry Newbolt?'

She stood up and swallowed, the exercise book wobbling in her hands. She hoped no one would laugh. Havers herself was smiling a little.

'*Arnhem, or the Charge that Failed.*'

They were all waiting. Her voice had sounded high and strange in her own ears.

> 'They floated neath the great white domes
> Of silk and wondered if their homes
> They'd see once more, then with a thud
> They landed in the slush and sticky mud!
>
> Their aim to cross the raging Rhine then
> And hold the bridgehead till the time when
> The main troops could force their way through too
> And relieve them as they planned to do!
>
> Again, again the enemy attack
> Again, again they pushed him back
> But men grow weak unless they eat and sleep
> And here a watch they must always keep!'

She could see it so clearly as her own words unrolled that the room and the others in it fell away. She no longer knew nor cared if they were laughing at her. She read on:

> 'The planes came dropping food supplies
> And then the Huns before their very eyes
> Took the precious pockets while they stood
> Powerless, for resistance was no good!
>
> The scattered groups of men held out
> In the vain hope that before their rout
> The main force would get through, and then from home
> This message came from across the foam!
>
> Hold on until your men may cross, in
> Safety to the other side, sacrificin'
> Yourselves is no good for we can't help
> You when for men you cry an' yelp!'

She felt the tears begin to blur the page, the lines of her own handwriting waver, her voice breaking.

> 'Retreat! then all had been fought in vain
> When you'd gone to the safe side again
> You'd remember all who'd perished there
> While you'd run away like a startled hare!

Retreat! when all those lyin' stiff, stark
An' cold, the butcher boy, the office clerk
An' all those you'd come to like and cherish
In those past eight days an' seen 'em perish!

Retreat! an' leave 'em lyin', their blood
Mingling with the oozing sticky mud
Their blood which they had so cheerfully given
To think in vain their bodies had been riven!'

She paused. She didn't want to read the last verse. Endings were always difficult and she didn't much like it. It was the rest she'd written it for but it had to be tied up somehow. It wasn't that she didn't believe what she'd said, every word of it, but the verse seemed bald, the rhythms bumpy, the first line, which was meant to clinch it all, somehow inconclusive. She swallowed the last of the tears and began:

'But we'd come back to avenge
Their deaths an' too we'd have our revenge
For all the wrongs they'd done us in the war
An' stop them from trying anything more!'

Deliberately she opened the drawing-room curtains again and felt the light stream out into the garden. She had closed them at first as a reflex and reached for the blackout to put up and then she had remembered that the only enemy aircraft that might be flying over were pilotless and couldn't see the light. If it was coming for her it would be sudden. She would see and hear nothing for ever. She would welcome it with light.

She realized she was very tired to be thinking like this, even though she had done nothing all day but try to chase the dust from surfaces that seemed to have been untouched for months. She hadn't been needed tonight. Jeanne d'Arc had survived and the French were taking care of their own now, out of hiding, dancing on the tables and searching for those who had betrayed them. What would she have done if. . . ? But it wouldn't happen now and she would never know the answer. There was a little naval gin left in the bottle that Betty had pressed on her when she had been down there last.

'Spoils of war darling. Do take it. I've simply lashings. Gerry likes to keep the stocks up for when he comes home. Can't stand a dry weekend. Do you know Noël Coward came aboard for a drink in their wardroom? They said he was just as you'd expect.'

She hadn't seen Karol, her count, this time. Gerry was recovering from a bout of fever and on special leave. The gin smelt scented and overrich. She could imagine it rolling down her cheeks in oily tears of self-pity if she wasn't careful. She felt ashamed and defiant. Why didn't they just give in? Why this new offensive? Somehow when the Eighth Army had crossed the Rubicon in Italy she'd thought, remembering her rather sketchy Roman history, that it would all be over by Christmas.

'Is it serious?' she'd asked Harry when he'd telephoned that he was in Southampton but didn't know if he would be home just yet.

'Nothing to really worry about. Might hold us up for a bit.'

She'd hung on to this when others grew grave and the nightly war reports told of loss and failure again. She had become like Ailsa, following every turn and twist but for quite different reasons. The child had shocked her when she had gone to see her at her mother's, in the far west, safely away from the buzzbombs. She was so tall and serious, hardly a child at all. In a couple of years, well four, no, less, the child would be coming out and she would be relegated to the role of duenna, eyeing other mothers and their daughters in rivalry, Ailsa the centre stage now.

That's if that world ever returned. Sometimes, often, it seemed impossible to imagine. Ascot and Queen Charlotte's Ball, and the Birthday Parade, peacetime soldiering. Harry could go back to his job at the staff college. But she would be in her late thirties, soon forty. The war had taken the best of her youth away from her, robbed her of that time when she'd stopped having babies and could have enjoyed herself at parties, with nights at the opera and theatre, smiling over her cigarette, flirting a little for fun where everyone knew the rules and Harry would have indulged her, smiling and smoking himself as he watched until it was time to go home.

She missed him so badly. The count had been just such a diversion, a frisson. She wondered how he felt about Warsaw? He might have relatives there, friends at least, being defeated,

202

dying. Why couldn't Harry come home? Perhaps he would suddenly just turn up, and see the light in the window. She didn't think she could take much longer of being alone with nothing to do, no purpose, if the war dragged on and they didn't want her any more at the Park. She was sick of the news. She switched on the wireless and turned the knob, searching for music. The set wailed and howled as she moved through the dial and then suddenly there it was, pouring oil over her jagged nerves, making her want to weep but soothing. 'How potent cheap music is,' she smiled to herself and the imagined watchers at the window.

> I never mention your name oh no,
> I never yearn for your kiss,
> I never turn all the lights down low
> To let the shadows reminisce. . . .

She took up a pillow from the sofa and holding its chintzy softness, smelling faintly of dust, it was time they were washed and the covers too, against her, she began to turn in the empty drawing-room.

> I never wait by the fire
> Expecting you to call my name,
> I never feel the slightest desire,
> To hold you in my arms again. . . .

Wheeling, gliding with her cushiony partner she was entranced, mesmerized. This was how they had danced aboard ship on their honeymoon. She had been so glad when Greece was retaken and the fighting with the Communists there was ended too, because she needed it to be as she remembered: hot and richly coloured and free. Now they could go back when it was really all over, and have another honeymoon, among the islands. Perhaps the dolphins were still curving their sleek backs out of the sea, and would leap for them again.

> I never mention your name, oh no,
> Except for ev'ry minute of ev'ry hour,
> Of ev'ry night and day.

They would get away, just the two of them, and it would all be as it had always been in memory. Why didn't he telephone?

*

She'd been afraid when she saw him standing there. She'd known it was him at once even without any warning. And yet he was different. She expected she was too. 'Allo,' he'd said. 'I got a bit of leaf so I come down to see you.'

They didn't fall on each other. 'Where are you staying?'

'At the Swan. I thought we could have a bit of supper and a talk.'

'Alright. I'll just let them know at the hostel.'

'Tell 'em you won't be back tonight.'

'Alright.' They'd gone on the bus together. 'My husband's down on leaf. We'll be staying in the town tonight.'

They'd found a caff where they could get liver and mashed, apple pie and cremola, and then they'd gone back to the Swan. She was glad it wasn't anywhere she'd ever been before, even for a drink, with someone else. The bar was nice, all old-fashioned though, needing a bit of doing up, as what didn't these days.

'So,' he'd said, 'we're off to Germany. I dunno what you want to do. I reckon on staying in the army. They've offered and I think I'll go for a regular. It'll mean postings abroad to start with and a pension when I come out so I could start a little business. It's up to you. No questions asked on either side if you want to give it a try, see if we can get together again.'

He knew; she knew he knew somehow. Or else he'd been up to something himself and this suited him. But who was she to pry? He was different, brown and tough, his blue eyes looking sharply out of the tanned creased skin around them as if staring into the sun across the huge flats of desert. It was like seeing his brother, the twin who'd gone away to Aussieland and made his fortune. If she hadn't known it was him she'd barely have recognized him and yet she did.

Changed inside he was too, she sensed straight off. Yet when she come to think of it he'd always been strong in his quiet way, only he'd never been quite able to put it over to her. She hoped he wouldn't get nasty with drink and lay one on her. She sensed he might now which he never would have done before.

'I'll have to think about it. A soldier's wife. Living in barracks abroad. I've never even been round Southend pier.'

'I'm a sergeant. You'd have your own house in married quarters. Plenty of money; well, enough. Time you saw a bit of the world.'

She thought: I have seen it. I've bin to America and Africa and back. And wanted to laugh. But instead she finished her gin and got out her purse. 'Let's have another. You get them.' She passed over a ten shilling note.

'Don't be daft. You don't have to pay. Put your purse away.'

'No, go on. I earn good money. And I've had your allowance all this time. I put most of that in the Post Office since Lennie went in the navy and I didn't have to pay for his clothes and his billet.'

He had took the note uncertainly and went up to the bar. She'd watched his back as he'd stood there ordering and looked away as he'd come back with the drinks.

'Cheers!'

'Cheers.'

'It'll be Christmas soon. What'll you do?'

'I reckon we'll be gone by then.'

They might meet somewhere in Germany and never know, share a table even, or another woman. She must be soft thinking like that.

'What'll you do?'

'Gracie said I could go up there. We only get a couple of days off.'

'Maybe the boy'll be home.'

'I think he's got a girlfriend. I don't see much of him. He says he has to study a lot.'

'I like your hair that colour.'

'Thanks.' She had touched it briefly. He'd come so sudden she hadn't had time to so much as wash it. Thank gawd she didn't wear her curlers to work as some of them did. There he'd been outside the gates and she'd known it was him straight off.

'You're a good-looking woman Millie. You always was. You don't need so much of that muck on your face.'

'It keeps me cheerful. Everyone wears it these days. It's called pancake.' The old Stan wouldn't have noticed or if he had he wouldn't have spoken up like that. 'Max Factor: it's American.'

'I'll get us another, though, as we're staying, we can go on drinking after time.'

She had never stayed in a pub, well hotel she supposed it was really, before. After that drink they'd gone through into reception and she'd handed over her identity card.

'Just the one night, sir?'

'At the moment, yes. If we like it we might come back.' He'd smiled and the old boy had smiled. She'd signed as 'Mrs' in case there was any doubt and he'd picked up the key and carried her bag for her up the steep narrow stairs. 'Here we are, number eight. This do you?' he'd asked when they were inside.

She'd felt shy of undressing in front of him and relieved when he went across the landing to the bathroom. She'd got undressed and into her nightie in a flash and was rolling down her nylons when he came back.

'That's nice.'

'Gracie made it. It's silk.'

'Parachute? She give me some message about you getting her another.'

'I'll just go across to the bathroom.' She slipped her coat over the nightdress. When she came back he was standing in his vest and pants looking out of the window.

'Not bad for an English moon. You should see the ones we used to get at night in the desert. Which side do you want?'

'I don't mind.' She felt shy of him. 'Ent you got no pyjamas?'

'Ent worn them for years. Wouldn't know how.'

She'd got into the bed furthest from the window. Her heart was thumping as if she'd never done it before. She didn't look as he got in, just felt the bed sag and then his warmth against the cold sheets.

He'd reached up and put out the light and she'd felt him turn towards her in the dark and his hands on the silk nightdress a little rough. 'Feels nice.'

And suddenly she wanted him. His smell was different and she could feel the hairs on his arms she'd noticed were blond from the sun, unlike that other dark smoothness. She'd clung to him, sliding under.

'Have you got anything? I don't want a baby.'

'Why not, we're married.'

'I'm too old to start that lark again.' She felt him hard against her. 'I thought you soldiers always carried something.'

'Alright.' He'd rolled off, switched on the light and gone to the battledress jacket hanging on the back of the chair. That too was hairy and baggy, not smooth, fitting cloth, defining the slim waist.

He'd got back into bed and switched off the light again. She

206

moved herself toward him and put out her hand to touch him under the sheet. She'd felt him hardening again, a quick fumble, her nightdress being lifted and then he was on her and she was raising herself to push against him, knowing she was moist and open. For a moment her back was against a tree and then she began to cry out as she'd learned to do, unashamed, and he did too.

He knew he was marking time but he didn't know how to begin again. Hilary had been given a fortnight's compassionate leave but he had sent her back after a week. They were no good to each other. Their combined grief was more than the power of two and since he didn't know what he wanted no one could help him get it. Now he came back to cousin Bet's on the underground in the evening and went in again for his day's work in the morning. He had no purpose. The Home Guard had been stood down: he wasn't wanted there. At work the others were quiet in his company, not knowing what to say. He had become an outcast by grief as if loss was a contagion that he might somehow pass on to the next.

It was good of Bet to have taken him in now that he had nothing. Of her, all that had been left to him in the rubble was her purse. He had it now: a leather oblong with central compartment and a flap like two ears. She had worn it shiny with her hand and his would close about it as if her touch had imparted something of herself to it that might rub off on him. They had found that, enough of her to bury that he wouldn't think about and a couple of books: the *Pears' Cyclopedia* and his last Home Guard training manual with instructions for dealing with the invasion that wouldn't now come. The cat had disappeared though they'd gone back day after day calling for it, to join the hordes of others that lived wild on the bomb sites.

'I'm a bit of an old silly at the moment. I don't seem to be able to follow what's going on.'

'That's alright Uncle Wilf. You take your time.' It wasn't fair to burden Bet. She must be worried sick about Cyril. She hadn't heard from him for eighteen months.

'What do you reckon Wilf? Could they push us right back?' They were sitting in the machine shop out of the bitter wind, warming their blackened hands first at the brazier and then round their enamel mugs of tea. It was the first time anyone had asked him a question since. They had allowed him his time of mourning, now they wanted him to take up his old place. 'It says here. . . .'

'Shitehawks. You don't want to pay no attention to 'em.' He could feel them listening. He laid a slim stained forefinger on the page of newsprint. 'The worst that could happen is if we get bogged down in trench warfare like the last lot, because of the weather. If the Yanks hold on Monty can send down reinforcements. Jerry hasn't got the resources. Not now, not with the beating he's had.'

'You reckon it's alright then.'

'You don't want to believe all you read in the capitalist press. I've told you blokes that often enough. They either bum it all up to make it more exciting and sell more papers or they play it all down for their own reasons. You have to look behind the words to sort out what's really going on. Now Jerry's got his back to the wall. He's making his last push. Once through this little lot and we can get back to crossing the Rhine.'

It had cost him an effort to explain it all, to carry them with him, to string so many words together again. Part of his mind must have been following events, taking it all in without his knowing. That night after tea, sitting in the armchair that had become his at Bet's, he turned to the section of coloured maps in the *Pears' Encyclopedia* and found the patched *Europe Political* with the green and brown *Physical* opposite that would give him the terrain.

He was glad he'd had a chance to convert to the Mossie. He'd begun to be afraid boxed up night after night in the Lanc, the four heavy engines pounding, the frame groaning off the ground with its weight of blockbusters, the load of the men he was responsible for, who relied on him to bring them home dead or alive. Now it was just the two of them skimming along high and fast, ahead of the labouring bomber stream, sometimes now flying by day with a brilliant mattress of opal cloud flowing far under the wings and the blinding limitless stratosphere above, the blue eggshell the world had hatched from in the beginning. He was almost a fighter boy at last, free as air.

The kite was frail as the models he'd made out of matchwood and glue. He no longer cared whether they slung bombs in the belly or marker flares. It only made a difference between day and night. In Stripes he had a steady navigator and bomb-aimer, seemingly unflappable. Together they could ride out the rest of the war above it all. If only the weather hadn't been so cold. The snow froze on the runways, making it hard to get off and back, but between was a still icy glitter as if they were flying through a frozen crystal. Sometimes it seemed as if they hardly moved but hung immobile in the chill sapphire heart of it, pricked by points of starlight.

Tonight it was Würzburg and a parcel of flares. Below somewhere there were soldiers, armies in the frozen mud, trying to sleep or on guard, hearing them drone above. The Master Bomber was ahead. They saw the first red go down and then he was calling them in to take their turn at reinforcing the marker glow so that the stream following them could all bomb on the red.

'Markers go home.'

He looked down at the city as they climbed steeply away from the incoming bomber stream. Among them would be night fighters waiting to pounce. Suddenly the bomb bays of the leading craft must have opened. He saw the phosphorous incendiaries burst into flame, a cloud of fire that sank towards the red markers below, joining in one fierce incandescence that would whirl a flaring dervish through the close streets whose skirts of fire would suck people and buildings under them.

'Time to turn, Skip.'

He banked sharply through the clouds, rosy with the burning city and then they were above, racing for home.

'Fighters about. I can hear one very close.'

They were unarmed but they could fly faster and higher. He poured on the gas. The sense of flight was exhilarating, if only he could pin it down in words.

'Bloody hell!' The burst had come from nowhere, out of the waning moon.

'What the fuck is it?'

'I don't know. Unless it's one of them new jets, 262s. Look out! He's coming in again.'

There was a blast of cannon that rocked the frail wooden craft. And then a strange silence, even the engines seemed muted, but there was a singing in his ears as of wind through high narrow defiles. It's the siren's song, he thought and almost laughed.

'Stripes, Stripes, are you okay?'

There was no answer. He twisted his head and knew that he was alone in the sky except for the Hun fighter. Should he bale out now? He didn't want to burn. Better to take his chance on a chute. But a terrible lethargy was creeping over him. It didn't seem worthwhile to struggle. The cannon shells thudded again into the frail hull.

He couldn't see the flame that began on the wingtip, turning the wooden cross to a blazing bonfire that spiralled down towards the pyre below with the two slumped figures silhouetted behind their perspex dome until that too burst into a melting curtain of fire and hid them from sight.

'What will you do when the war is over?' he asked the quartermaster sergeant.

The short thick fingers paused before putting the fresh Weight between smooth lips. 'Come back London, open restaurant, make some money, then I come back here. My nieces look after me when I'm old. After war Burma, India be independent, not British any more. Lotta confusion.'

He hadn't been able to tell Daphne where he was going until the last minute. Then she had said: 'Why you, Harry? Haven't you done enough? What do you know about Burma? Isn't that jungle fighting?'

He'd tried to shrug it off. 'One fight's much like another really. Anyway I hadn't a lot of choice.'

'I knew it really when I saw your red hat, although I tried to pretend it wasn't, couldn't be true.'

'We've had a good few days together. They wouldn't have sent me back for Christmas otherwise,' he'd said but she wasn't to be comforted.

'Other people sit out the whole war behind a desk.'

'You know I'd get bored.'

'And what about me?'

Now he wondered if he was right for the job, if he hadn't grown stale. It was a quite different world and a different sort of fighting, no matter what he'd said. There was no quarter, no honourable surrender by the Nips, which meant there could be none for them either. They came on again and again, calling in their high-pitched imitations. 'Johnny, Johnny Commando come down and get us,' as vociferous and persistent as the malarial mosquitoes that clouded the paddy fields. Already they'd seen every dirty trick in the pamphlet and more. It was a war of nerves, with the jungle as a second enemy which only retreated before a patch of water and mud or scrubby hill that had to be taken inch by bloody inch and then held against counterattack after attack so that when it eventually went quiet and you dared to creep out you found the dead entangled thick together. You learned a new kind of persistence and you were grateful to the comedian who could call out in reply to their taunting; 'Go home you yellow bastard. Your brother wants your boots.'

They are leaning on the rail in the sunlight that throws a galaxy of stars back from the calm surface of the ocean, when it happens. 'Two fish on the starboard side!' The water boils in opaque twin paths.

The klaxon blares. There's not time for evasive action. The torpedoes strike almost at once. She shudders and immediately begins to list. The second strikes the bow. There are screams as men are torn apart below and the stink of fire and oil. The klaxon sounds boat stations. They run together across the tilting deck.

'She's going down very fast.'

The port lifeboats swing uselessly above them as men fumble at the lashings.

'Jump for it and swim as far away as you can before she goes down.' He pushes the boy towards the starboard side. He sees the face turned back towards him as he runs towards the bridge and then the steepening angle pitches it over into the waiting sea.

How would she ever bring her tongue to call him anything but Dr Fentiman as he wished? She knew what it meant of course. He was lonely and he needed a housekeeper. She could be Frau or Mrs Fentiman if she wanted. It would make her a British citizen. But could she marry such an old man? She had offered to go when his wife had so suddenly died but he had begged her to stay and although she had seen at once what would happen she had agreed because she had nowhere else to go. Now it was coming to an end perhaps she should even consider going back to search among the ruins for her dead.

'Tilde, Tilde where are you?' He called her like a lost child, through the empty rooms of the house until he tracked her down in the pantry or the laundry where she was sorting the clean clothes for ironing.

'Is it true? How can it be? How could anyone do such things?' He was thrusting the newspaper at her, demanding like a child that she should reassure him, that she should say it couldn't be so, that the world wasn't that kind of place or man that kind of animal.

She didn't want to look at the grainy black and grey images he was forcing upon her in case she recognized a face, and the delicate balance she had made herself keep all these years tipped irrevocably and let her slide, hands clutching at emptiness, down, down into the deepest cellar. The page shook and blurred and then came inexorably into focus but she needn't have worried. The shapes no longer had any recognizable individuality. They were cadavres, livid pale skin stretched over bones that lay in heaps or were bent in half and propped upright against a wall as if sitting or erect as if strung from invisible puppet wires. Some had rags of hair or clothing. Their eyes were bony sockets brimming with night.

She had seen such figures and scenes before on the walls of art galleries or Christian churches. They were pictures of hell, of Doomsday, of the damned. The human imagination had conceived them and now brought them forth in dying flesh. They were more plant than animal, the sprouts from potato heads that had fermented whitely under mildewed sacking in the dark, the limbs tuberous, the skulls bulbs with wormholes for eyes.

In one photograph beretted British soldiers stood holding their rifles across their bodies as peak capped Germans took naked corpses by feet and hands to swing the bags of bones between them, up into a lorry while a small crowd of well-dressed and fed women and children looked on. The forms had no gender or age.

'How shall we ever know who they were?'

'There will be lists,' she said. 'They always kept lists.'

*

Adrift fifteen days now. It doesn't seem possible and yet every one has been twice as long and hard to endure as the one before. We have decided to keep this record between us, partly because it gives us a way of passing the time and therefore of reminding ourselves of how much has passed, which keeps us from going mad, and partly for a record, a log if we are not found until too late. I do the writing because Lieutenant Michalowski's hand is burned but we discuss together what we shall say and much of it he dictates to me.

We are now six on the raft which is very cramped. If we want to move our legs we have to ask the others first. We were eight at first but the two stokers were very badly burned and died of their injuries in the first few days. We buried them at sea, rolling them over the side. Some of the men said this would attract sharks to us but we had no alternative as they would have soon begun to decay. We said part of the burial service over them. The sharks did appear but I think they would have done so anyway as they can probably smell us since they can smell blood and wounds and several of us are wounded.

When the Japanese submarine's torpedoes struck I was ordered by Lieutenant Michalowski to abandon ship and since the lifeboats were not able to be lowered because of the steep angle I dived overboard on the starboard side, where the torpedoes had hit us, which was very low in the water. I swam away from the *Hausa* until I thought I was far enough to avoid being sucked down. Looking back as I trod water I saw her rear up on end, there was a dull explosion and then she slid stern first down into the sea. I have since learned that ships always go down by the stern but then it seemed to me somehow a brave sight. The *Hausa* was my first ship.

After he had ordered me to abandon ship, Lieutenant Michalowski ran back to the bridge where he found that the ship was indeed doomed and was going down so fast that many men must be trapped below, even though the captain had given the immediate order to abandon ship. The other officers and ratings were ordered to leave the bridge while the captain stayed behind as he was not prepared to leave while there were others still aboard. He was last seen still beside the bridge pipe.

Lieutenant Michalowski returned to the upper deck where he directed a party in freeing the liferafts and belts in the hope that they would float off as the ship went down. Some boats were able to be lowered on the starboard side but there was very little time between the torpedoes striking and the ship beginning to settle. He saw two boats push off under the command of other officers and was himself making for a third when the bow began to rise rolling everything towards the stern. He found himself in the water amongst a number of men and much debris and struck out towards one of the rafts which had floated off. He and the Bosun who was already on it began trying to pick up survivors as did those in the lifeboats but many men were injured and slipped away before they could be taken on board. I saw the raft and swam to it. Of the Japanese submarine we saw nothing. We were going to join the combined fleet at Okinawa.

Day Sixteen

Another man, Leading Seaman Askew, died in the night. We had not known he was so near to dying but when we woke in the morning he was gone. We buried him at sea like the others. The water boiled for a moment after we pushed him over and then he was gone.

Our ration is Bovril pemmican and biscuit, Horlicks tablets and 2 oz of water three times a day at sun-up, midday and sundown. At noon the temperature is 100° and we take it in turns to have the shade of the sail we have rigged. We do not know our position but in any case it would be useless to us since we cannot steer the raft but must drift with the currents. Had we been in the Atlantic we would all be dead by now with cold and constant soaking or else the raft would have been capsized or men washed over by the sea. But here we simply drift and although the nights are colder the sun soon, too soon, warms us in the morning. The raft is 10 feet long by 8 feet wide. We have to sit up with our feet in the middle. Last night we each had a square of chocolate. I sucked mine for as long as I could. It was very good but it makes you thirsty. We try to collect a little dew and lick it from where it condenses on hard surfaces like the wooden bits of the rail in the night but there does not seem to be as much as you would expect from the great heat. Perhaps this is because the nights are very clear. The stars seem to be falling towards the sea. During the day the glare from the water is very intense and we have to cover our eyes or we believe we would go blind. Today a seagull came and perched on the mast. We tried, that is the Bosun tried, to knock it down but it flew off.

Day Seventeen
One of the men, a cook, asked me what I was doing. I said I was keeping a log. He seemed to become angry at this and muttered things we could not understand. We are afraid that his reason is going. He was a fat man but he has lost weight very rapidly, more so than the others and is finding the lack of food and water very hard. It is strange to think that perhaps the war is over or at least part of it and we do not know. Nothing much happened today.

Day Eighteen
This morning we saw something in the distance. The cook said it was land and tried to paddle towards it with his hands. He became very angry with us when we refused to help because we were sure it was only a cloud, a patch of mist or a mirage. When the raft made no progress towards it but simply turned round with his attempts to paddle he broke down and cried a little, licking the tears off his fingers. He said they tasted of the sea and that if he could drink them he could drink sea water. Lieutenant Michalowski warned him that it would send him mad but as he is half-mad already I do not think he will listen. He said, 'You are waiting for me to die so that you can have my share of the water.' The others told him to be quiet.

Day Nineteen
The cook raving. We think he drank sea water in the night. The Bosun tried to tie him down but he was too weak himself.

Day Twenty
This morning after a very troubled night the cook suddenly fell upon the other rating Hardcastle and half-jumped, half-fell with him overboard. We leaned out to them as far as we

dared but the sharks must be following the raft and suddenly there were two dorsal fins coming towards us higher than the side of the raft and the two men disappeared. We were afraid that the sharks might attack the raft itself and so we held on to the ropes and sat with our backs to each other in the middle and our feet sticking out towards the sides so that we could draw them in quickly. After a while when nothing happened we judged it was safe again to sit in our old positions. We are now three but the Bosun is growing very weak and Lieutenant Michalowski's hand is much worse. I think by the smell it must be infected.

Day Twenty-one
We think the Bosun is dying. He seems to be in a coma. I tried to moisten his lips with some of his ration but his mouth was clenched shut. He has big open sores on his skin. We all have. His hair and Lieutenant Michalowski's has turned white. Perhaps this is the effect of the sun and the salt.

Day Twenty-two
The Bosun died today. He just stopped breathing. We buried him at sundown.

Day Twenty-three
There is room for us to lie down side by side now. It is very hard to talk because our voices are going from the dryness in our throats. Last night Lieutenant Michalowski told me that he will never go back to Poland because the Russians will take it. I did not understand all he was saying because sometimes he used Polish words but he said that the Warsaw rising was the end because it had been allowed to fail. He said that although his estate had been confiscated by the Germans he will not be given it back when the war is over. He said that division was the curse of Poland and that there were two armies and two governments and they would never agree. He seemed to be very cold and shivering so I put my arms around him to try to warm him. I do not want to be left alone. This morning he made me promise to go on with the log even if he dies and not to give up hope. He said the secret is to think of something you want very much to do or someone you want to see and to concentrate on that. He is

216

very brave because I know he is in pain. He made me drink the Bosun's ration of water although he only had one ration himself.

Day Twenty-four

Lieutenant Michalowski was gone this morning. I must have slept heavily because he left me a note and then must have gone over the side. The note is on the next blank page of the log. I will try to do what he made me promise. He left me his watch and wallet.

Day Twenty-five

It is very lonely. My fingers look a funny colour. The time goes very slowly. I sleep a lot.

Day Twenty-six

Today I saw a shark's dorsal fin rushing towards the boat, I mean the raft. I held on tight and it bumped the side once or twice. Then I felt it underneath trying to overturn the raft but it is too flat and heavy I think and in the end it went away.

Day Twenty-seven

I try repeating all the poetry, hymns, etc. that we learned at school. I talk to Ailsa about them. Nothing changes. The sky and sea are always the same. But I am changing. My hands are like bunches of twigs. There are things I can't write down.

Day Twenty-eight

I saw a plane. I stood up and waved. I don't know if it saw me. Perhaps I imagined it. It was a flying boat.

Day Twenty-nine

The plane came back. It dropped something in the water but I could not reach it. It means they did see me. Please God don't let me die yet. The shark came back for whatever the plane had dropped. The water twirled and it took the bundle down with it. I am afraid to go to sleep in case they miss me. There are some Very lights and a pistol on the raft. We used some of them the first two nights but then Lieutenant Michalowski said it was better to keep some in reserve. I shall fire one at midnight. I am glad the watch is still working.

Day Thirty

Nothing all day. Somehow this is worse than before I saw the plane. I can hardly write. My hands are like claws. The boy stood on the burning deck. Perhaps I didn't see it.

Day Thirton
This morning two planes came. One is circling above. One has gone away. I think. . . .

GOODBYE DEAR BOY. THANK YOU. LIVE AND BE HAPPY. KEEP THE WATCH. KM.

'You will be going home soon Miss Queen. We are so grateful for all your hard work and there are hundreds of our boys who must be too. Please accept our thanks on their behalf.'

It was an order though so charmingly dressed up, a dismissal. The officer seemed exhausted, depressed. Perhaps that was just working in the ruins of Hamburg where brick-dust still clung in the air and there was the sickly smell of the many dead who lay buried only under the rubble. As she had been driven through the countryside in a bouncing jeep, groups of grey beaten men shambling towards the city had stood by the roadside dully watching them pass, a defeated army making its way home.

Cigarettes were currency. She doled them out to the bands who played for them, half a night each because they were too weak with hunger to keep up a full performance. The wind players faded first, unable to blow on an empty stomach.

She had met the Passmores on their way home and been shocked at how they had aged. She had seen them billed as part of a concert party and stayed to watch the show for old time's sake. The audience of squaddies had whistled and catcalled; 'Get 'em off. Bring on the girls.' Afterwards in the shabby flaking dressing room, she hadn't known what to say. She needn't have worried; Jean was eager to tell her their plans.

'So we reckon we've got enough to buy a nice house on the south coast where we can put up one or two theatricals.'

'Won't you miss dancing?'

'My dear girl the old bones can't wait to give up. What happened to Fred?'

'I had to leave him in Cairo in hospital. He wasn't feeling too good.'

'Oh well. It comes to us all. That's why we're getting out while we've a bit of life left. I think we can say we've earned it.'

The Old Vic had come to the city bringing Shakespeare, and she watched them from a box in the Schauspielhaus with growing admiration and despair. Sybil Thorndike, Laurence Olivier, Ralph Richardson, these were the real professionals. Perhaps her talent had been 'for the duration of hostilities only'. The beautiful rococo theatre was packed, the troops attentive and silent until the time for applause. And yet it was her they had wanted in the desert and the camps; even here. She walked back through the broken city hardly hearing her escort as he begged to be allowed into her hotel room, her bed as she knew it would be. Sometimes, often, it was hard to tell where a street had been.

'Do let me come up for a nightcap old girl. I've managed to scrounge some gin.'

Would it matter if he did? What did matter anymore? She would go back to her mother's and start the rounds of the agencies.

'What did you do in the Great War Mummy?'

'I sang and danced.' Terpsichore in the train of Mars. 'I saw the world.'

'Where did you train my dear?'

'In the desert and a hangar at Swaffham.'

'You're looking awfully pretty tonight. Be kind to a fellow.'

It was then she decided. 'Oh piss off. I've got to pack.'

They are feeding quietly on milk pods when it happens. The two strange males suddenly appear at the edge of the clearing. Tondi and Karka have wandered away together. She is in pink and they have gone further up the valley. Rua is alone with Mala and Houmi and her baby. Houmi should be showing an interest in Tondi too but he is afraid of Karka and still prefers to stay near his sister.

The two strange males are big and strong. They are holding leafy branches which they begin to shake as they scream and hoot. The little group stops feeding and looks up at them. Then they charge. Rua tries to stand her ground. She screams back and threatens. The bigger one runs fiercely at her while the smaller makes for Houmi who screams in terror and runs off into the bush. Mala cowers away and presents herself submissively. The male pauses in his pursuit of Houmi to mount the young female in a token gesture.

Rua grins with fright and screams at the big male. Ignoring her he snatches up the baby bites into its neck and throws it aside. All the fight goes out of Rua. She cowers and whimpers and presents herself as he shakes his branch threateningly above her. She can hear Houmi crashing away through the leaves hooting and whimpering in fear. The other male returns with Mala and together they chivvy the two females towards another part of the forest.

From the unpublished memoirs of
Colonel later Brigadier Harry Pearmain, DSO, MC

> What can one say about a way of life so fundamentally different in its concepts, concepts that had history been ordered in another way might have been those of the major part of the world. As we advanced we released prisoners who had been in captivity for four years, often suffering extreme privation, especially in the forced marches and labour camps of the Burma–Thailand railway. Escape was largely impossible; to endure and survive was hard enough. For centuries the Japanese had lived by their own rules in a basically static society like the civilizations of the Maya and the Inca. They fought with great tenacity, not knowing the admission of defeat but rather the fanatic dedication of he who fights and runs away. Their rules of conduct taught that all was justifiable in defence of the Emperor, and the land of the Illustrious Ancestors. The morality of every action was judged in relation to this, not by the Geneva convention, liberal Judaeo-Christian humanism's attempt to regulate the economic disputes of an essentially homogeneous continent and its dependent (until then) colonies. Now in defeat they would be forced to live by the rules of the west, the last autonymous society to accept colonization and the impregnation of their culture by ours.

*

He had wanted to see for himself, and Hilary had said she would come with him since she had two days off. They had joined the one-and-ninepenny queue and waited for the house to come out.

'Bet's asked me if I want to stop on here now she knows Cyril isn't coming back.' It was the first time they had spoken of any of it as they sat in the Three Brewers before the pictures with their two sleeve glasses of IPA in front of them. It must have been brewed for the British in India, the soldiers out there, specially light for the hot climate, she thought as she let it trickle down her throat. 'Settling the dust,' her father called it. 'You must learn to drink pints. I can't keep going up for halves for you,' he had said at her initiation when she was sixteen but looked older, and Lil had laughed and said she'd stick to stout which was sweet and had a bit of flavour.

'I don't want you to feel you've got to look after me. What are you going to do? The lads will want their jobs back, especially on the land.'

'I've been accepted to go to university in October.'

'That's settled then. Where will you be?'

'Manchester. It's not all that far really. There's a coach and you can get me a priv. from time to time to come home.'

He nodded. 'I might put in for a transfer down the line, somewhere a bit closer to Bet's. We'll jog along alright the two of us. It'll be a bit of help to her with the children growing up, and if so be as she should want to marry again we can sort that one out when it comes along.'

'There'll be none of us left. I had a letter from Sylvie, you remember I used to go to school with, and she says she's staying out in Cairo for a bit, marrying a doctor.'

He nodded. 'I don't think I'm likely to get married,' Hilary said.

He nodded again. 'What happened to that girl you was sharing with. Welsh wasn't she?'

'She had to go home. Her mother was ill and her brother was in the navy posted missing. Their father was a steelworker who didn't live with them.'

'Was, was.' She was aware of her use of the past tense.

'I feel somehow as if all that's happened is our fault: your mother, my

brother, a punishment; as if you're not meant to be happy in that way. At least I'm not.'

'*I can't accept that,*' she had written back. '*I think that's just your old Nonconformist puritanism.*'

'It's a different old world,' he said as if she had asked him. 'War does that. It was a different world after the last one, the war to end wars, and it'll be different again after this. The Yanks and the Russians will divide it up between them for a start and we won't be nowhere.'

He was talking to her for the first time as if she were the boy they hadn't had. She realized he was glad she was going to university, although he wouldn't, couldn't say so. No one in the family had ever done such a thing before. 'Things will be different here too. They are already.'

He tilted the half-empty glass in a long swallow. 'Not enough. We haven't the discipline. All they want is rationing to be abolished and a new demob suit. We'd best get going. We don't want to miss nothing.'

They sat through the black and white 'B' feature and then a series of handwritten advertisements and a couple of trailers. At last there was the familiar cosy figure of a town crier in his three-cornered hat, ringing in the news to the pseudo-martial undertow of the music, and then the rapid hectoring upper-class tones of the commentator. She felt her father stiffen a little in the padded seat. Glancing sideways in the dark she could see his profile alert against the cinema's half-light. She understood that whatever it was he'd wanted to see was about to appear. She turned her attention to the screen.

The monstrous cloud mushroomed in front of him as it had in the newspaper pictures; once, twice. But there were other pictures now: of the dead, and the walking dead, men, women, children, scorched black and raw, dazed, ragged, wandering in the long flat ways between where the houses had been that were nothing but stumps jutting from smoking dust, a no man's land touched by a fiery finger from hell which had changed places with heaven and was now in the sky. He didn't see the technicolour dream that followed even though it was Roy Rogers and he usually enjoyed a good Western. The goodies whipped the baddies and rode off into the sunset and the love of a good woman. And then it all began at the first reel again;

unless somewhere the projectionist in his little box of tricks above the audience decided to smash the machine. But he didn't believe in that.

'My father's in Germany,' the girl said.

'So's mine,' Lennie answered.

'We're going out to join him soon, for Christmas.'

'We might be in Hamburg then. My mother's out there too. Our ship's doing some kind of flag-waving trip.'

'I knew it was you at once, even though I couldn't quite believe it, and you looked so thin and much older.'

'You look older too.'

'But not alas thin. My mother says it's puppy fat. She'll ask me all about you later.'

'What will you say?'

'I haven't decided. Perhaps I'll pretend I've never met you before tonight, and just hope she doesn't remember your name.'

'Why does it matter?'

'It just does. Now I can say you're a friend of Gerry's. She's known him for ever.'

'An ex-shipmate.'

'Do you want to talk about it?'

'Not yet. One day perhaps. Writing it all down helped.'

'My father's writing his memoirs. He says the army and navy are obsolete but nobody will admit it. He says war's obsolete too.'

'Perhaps we all are.'

The girl considered for a moment, but the room was full of foxtrotting couples turning to the local band's Joe Loss approximation, *Stringing Pearls*.

'Do you think we ought to dance?' the girl asked.

'We can try,' the boy said.

London, September 1986

Author's Note
Although I have consulted and used
the work and memoirs of many people
in the course of writing this book,
to all of whom I am deeply indebted,
without *The Almanac of the Second World War*
by Brigadier Peter Young, DSO, MC I could,
quite simply, not have written it.
The opinions and errors are, however, all mine.